ABRAKAPOW

BY
ISAIAH CAMPBELL

Illustrated by Dave Perillo

WITHDRAWN

Simon & Schuster Books for Young Readers
NEW YORK • LONDON • TORONTO • SYDNEY • NEW DELHI

SIMON & SCHUSTER BOOKS FOR YOUNG READERS
An imprint of Simon & Schuster Children's Publishing Division
1230 Avenue of the Americas, New York, New York 10020

For information about special discounts for bulk purchases, please contact
Simon & Schuster Special Sales at 1-866-506-1949 or business@simonandschuster.com.
The Simon & Schuster Speakers Bureau can bring authors to your live event. For more
information or to book an event, contact the Simon & Schuster Speakers Bureau at
1-866-248-3049 or visit our website at www.simonspeakers.com.
Jacket design by Chloë Foglia
Interior design by Hilary Zarycky
The text for this book is set in Garamond.
The illustrations for this book are rendered digitally.
Manufactured in the United States of America 1016 FFG
2 4 6 8 10 9 7 5 3 1

Library of Congress Cataloging-in-Publication Data:
Names: Campbell, Isaiah, author. Title: AbrakaPOW / Isaiah Campbell.
Description: New York : Simon & Schuster Books for Young Readers, [2016] |
Summary: "A New York City girl moves with her family to a Texas POW camp
her father runs during WWII, when, during a magic show she performs, Nazi
prisoners escape; she's the only one who can find and recapture them"—Provided by
publisher. Identifiers: LCCN 2015029762| ISBN 978-1-4814-2634-3 (hardcover) |
ISBN 978-1-4814-2635-0 (pbk.) | ISBN 978-1-4814-2636-7 (ebook) Subjects: LCSH:
World War, 1939-1945—Texas—Abilene—Juvenile fiction. | CYAC: World War, 1939-
1945—United States—Fiction. | Prisoners of war—Fiction. | Nazis—Fiction. | Moving,
Household—Fiction. | Magic tricks—Fiction. | Abilene (Tex.)—History—20th century—Fiction.
Classification: LCC PZ7.C15417 Ab 2016 | DDC [Fic]—dc23 LC record available at
http://lccn.loc.gov/2015029762

FIRST
EDITION

To my daughters, Zaya and Evangelina, who have all the qualities from the best magic tricks: They're beautiful, mesmerizing, and impossible to figure out

Chapter One

"Why, oh why, oh why did we move here?"
—Max's diary, Wednesday, March 8, 1944

Maxine Larousse climbed over the boxes in the moving truck, searching for the three boxes she had *specifically* labeled were only to be touched by her hands. Even as she looked, she knew she wouldn't find them. Her mother had selective illiteracy, and the GIs that were helping them move, well, they were GIs after all, far more interested in shooting at Nazis than ensuring an eleven-year-old's meticulously written instructions were followed to the letter.

"Hey, Buck! Lookie here, I got a magic wand!" one of the GIs yelled from just outside the truck.

Oh gosh, that's box number two, Max thought with a groan. She stumbled over the walls of cardboard as she rushed off the truck. The blond GI, who she remembered had said his name was Gil, waved her wand around in the air. "Somebody get me a sorcerer's hat so I can be Mickey Mouse!"

Max fought the horror in her throat and scrambled to snatch the wand from his hand. "Can't you read, you big gorilla?" she asked and pointed at the box from which the wand had come.

WARNING! AUTHORIZED PERSONS ONLY!

UNAUTHORIZED OPENERS WILL BE IN VIOLATION OF THE

MAGICIAN'S CODE!!!!

AND MAY BE CUT IN HALF!!!!

YOU HAVE BEEN WARNED!

Gil scrunched up his forehead as he read the label.

I probably should have made it shorter to account for limited attention spans, Max thought.

He grinned as he finished. "So you're a magician? That explains your weird-looking bunny."

She rolled her eyes. "It's a ferret."

"What is that, a long bunny?" he asked.

She ignored his question and carefully placed the wand back in the box.

Buck, the brown-haired GI, came over to try to peek inside. Max slammed the flaps shut.

"You should show us a trick real fast," Buck said.

"I'm trying," she said. "I'm making all these boxes disappear."

"Aw, come on, Squirt," Gil said and poked her in the ribs. "We've been doing all the work here. The least you could do is give us a magic show."

At what age do boys stop acting like chimpanzees? she wondered.

Mrs. Larousse came out of their new home carrying a

pitcher of lemonade on a tray with some glasses. "What's all this racket I hear?" she said with an air of charm she'd never used back in Brooklyn. The GIs instinctively straightened up, as though the wife of a major deserved a salute like her husband.

"They want me to put on a magic show," Max said.

Mrs. Larousse placed the tray in the truck's cargo area and poured lemonade into the glasses. She handed them to the boys. "And? Why don't you?"

"This isn't really the place."

Mrs. Larousse sat next to her tray, her legs dangling off the end of the truck, and straightened out her skirt under her apron. She gave Max the smile that was code for "do this or die" and took a sip from the glass Max had assumed was for her. "Oh, I don't know. This seems like a magical moment to me."

Max looked at their yard, with its brown grass and ant-hills and literally nothing else, and felt the breeze bringing the hot air of Abilene, Texas, wafting across her forehead. *This is magic? Then I've been doing it wrong.* She sighed and wondered if this was finally the time to become the second woman in history—after only the great Madame Adelaide Herrmann—to attempt the Bullet Catch Trick. She decided her mother didn't have the stomach for it and opened the box back up. She found a jar of coins and picked out a quarter.

"Here, take this and examine it closely." She handed it to Gil.

"You could at least pull it from my ear," he said. She didn't laugh. He looked at the front. "Okay, so it's got the standing liberty on the front, eagle on the back. Hey, it's 1925. That's the year I was born!"

"Good, good," Max said. She tried her best to channel her stage persona, The Amazing Max, even though there was literally nothing bedazzling about this venue. "Now, would you say you would recognize it if I showed it to you again?"

He nodded. "Yeah, it's pretty distinctive."

"So, if I had a group of, say, three quarters, could you pick out this exact one?" She took the quarter from his hand and held it up.

"Yup."

"What if there were four? How about then?"

He laughed. "Oh yeah, sweetie. You don't forget your birth year."

"Even if there were five?" she asked.

"Even if there were twenty-five, I could pick out that quarter."

"Okay, so you're pretty smart. In fact, I'll bet," she waved her hand over the quarter, and it vanished "even if there were no quarters, you could still pick out that quarter."

Gil and Buck both stared at her hand in silence. Then they looked at the ground. Then they walked around her to see if she was hiding the quarter behind her back. They made her move to check under her shoe. She even showed them both her hands to prove it was gone.

"Oh, wow, that's pretty good," Gil finally said.

"Sure, thanks," Max said. "But what do you say? Could you pick out that quarter even if there were no quarters?"

Gil shook his head. "No, of course not. There aren't any quarters to pick from."

"Check your back pocket," she said.

He slipped his hand into his pants pocket, and then he got the look on his face like a man who had just discovered oil in his backyard. He slowly brought his fingers out to reveal a quarter—liberty standing on the front, eagle on the back, and the year that was so familiar, because it was his birth year, emblazoned on the bottom.

"I knew you could pick it out," she said. And then she let THE AMAZING MAX go back to sleep. "Mom, seriously, why are you drinking my lemonade?" Her mother begrudgingly handed her the glass.

Gil and Buck started applauding. "Wow, that was amazing! How did you do it?"

She shrugged, swallowed her lemonade, and carried her box into the house. The trick was so simple she was pretty sure it wasn't covered by the magician's code, but she wouldn't give those oafs the satisfaction of an answer.

Besides, that would mean admitting that she had slipped

one of her 1925 quarters into Gil's back pocket thirty minutes earlier, just in case such an illusion proved necessary, and the fact that her hand had been close to his back pocket was a secret she would take to her grave. Other than that detail, though, the trick was a simple matter of palming the other quarter until they were looking on the ground, then slipping it into her own pocket so she could show her empty hands. Way, way too easy.

Max went into her room and set the box on her bed. She barely noticed the *rat-tat-tat* of Houdini trying to find a way out of his cage over in the corner. Which meant he wasn't really trying. That little white ferret had *earned* his name probably a thousand times.

Whoops, make that a thousand and one.

Max plucked Houdini off the floor just as he was scurrying to steal her freshly unpacked shoes. She nuzzled his nose and kissed his stinky head, then she let him go on the floor again and watched him drag the dress shoes that she hoped she'd never wear again under her bed.

"You know how I used to tell my friends that the saddest thing in the world was being almost twelve and still not being famous?" she asked him. He stopped in his shoe-stealing duties and looked at her. "Well, it turns out I was wrong. This place is the saddest thing in the world."

He licked his lips and pushed her shoe with his nose. She plopped down next to him and stared in his eyes. "Did you see what I did there, Houdini? I made you believe that I had friends." She took the shoe and tossed it on top of her dresser. "THE AMAZING MAX strikes again. Ta-da!"

Houdini was far less frustrated with the verbal trick she'd just pulled on him as he was with the fact that her shoe was now out of his reach. He shuffled over under her bed in search of some other item worthy of his thieving efforts.

She got up and plopped on top of her bed. "Oh well, whatever. I have you. And I'll probably make friends, right? I mean, boring west Texas friends who say 'y'all' and ride horses, but friends nonetheless."

She could hear Buck and Gil outside, mumbling some ignorant version of a magical spell. They must have found box number three. She groaned and got back up. "And maybe, if I'm really lucky, one of those friends could be a capable assistant and we'll put on the magic show of the century."

But probably not, she thought to herself, not even wanting to say that last part to Houdini. *Finding a kindred spirit here in cowboy land would be a magic trick even I wouldn't believe.*

She hurried out before the GI movers could violate the plainly written instructions and incur a well-deserved dismembering, regardless of how much she secretly would have loved to see that happen.

HOUDINI'S ★ GUIDE TO ★
Palming a Coin

What you will need

1 A Hand

and...

2. A Coin

HEY! GET YOUR OWN COIN!

GIVE IT BACK!

BING!

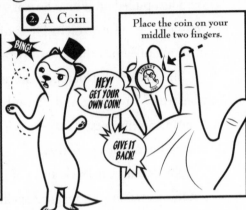

Place the coin on your middle two fingers.

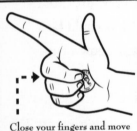

Close your fingers and move the coin to your palm.

YOU'RE GETTING GERMS ON IT!

Tighten your palm to hold the coin in place.

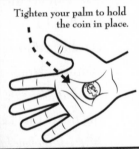

THAT DOES IT!

With practice you can hold the coin in any position.

GIVE ME MY COIN!

HEY! NO! WAIT!

AND WITH A FLIP OF THE WRIST...

Produce the coin at will!

TA-DA!

Chapter Two

Houdini wallowed on top of Max's dresser as she worked on the last three steps of the Floating Card Trick. He was miles away from interested in what she was doing, which meant she needed more practice. Ferrets, you see, are excellent barometers of showmanship.

She had just gotten the ace of spades to rise out of the deck, and Houdini had just started paying attention, when her mother called her to the kitchen.

"Max! I still need your help in here!"

Max had hoped that her vanishing act would go unnoticed. Sadly, she wasn't nearly the escape artist her ferret was. She dragged herself back into the kitchen, where her mother was surrounded by half-unpacked boxes.

"I thought you were going to the bathroom," Mrs. Larousse said. "Why'd you disappear on me?"

"I'm a magician, Mom. Disappearing is what I do," Max

said. "Anyway, I thought Dad was coming home soon. He's so much better at unpacking than I am. I might as well be a monkey the way I unpack your things. Breaking them, sitting on them, stacking them so they fall over. I'm such a burden."

Her mother rolled her eyes. "As grateful as I am for your sacrifice, your father isn't here, so you have to keep burdening me with your help."

Max sighed, rather loudly, and plopped down to start unwrapping teacups. Even when Major Larousse *was* there, he wasn't there. She could see in his eyes that he still heard the rumbles of tanks and felt the African sun beating down on his head, even though the battle was thousands of miles away. "When will he come home?"

"I don't know, sweetie. This is new for *all* of us."

Her mother had said those words at least a dozen times over the last few weeks: the entire time they were packing up in New York, the four-day trip driving across seven states to get to Texas, and at least three times since they'd pulled up to the little cardboard-colored house that looked like tornado bait. It helped Max to know that her mother, who had lived her entire life bouncing around the five boroughs of New York City, felt just as out of place in the land of cowboys as Max did. But Max knew there was even more to it than that.

Because it *was* new for everyone. New for her and her mother, whose big-city accents were now ambushed by the Abilene small-town drawl. And also new, in the worst sense, for Major Larousse, who had always enjoyed challenging Max to a nice game of hopscotch or hide-and-seek in Central Park before he had been sent off to jolly old Morocco. There he spent his time reminding GIs to hop and hide from bullets on the front lines. . . . That is, until he forgot to take his own advice and took a bullet in the hip. Now there was no time for games at all because he was stuck spending his days behind a desk, doing something she once thought he would never, ever do.

He was babysitting the Nazis. That's what Max had called it when her mother told her about the job. Of course, that wasn't the *official* name. Officially, he was in charge of the guards and prisoners at Camp Barkeley, a place for captured German soldiers that were being held by the American troops. They were prisoners of war, and her dad was a little like their warden. He was to sit in his office and make sure they were fed, had their bedtime, and had plenty to do during the day to keep them out of trouble.

But he wasn't supposed to be *punishing* the prisoners, so it wasn't exactly like a real prison in Max's opinion. He was *holding* the prisoners, which made no sense to her at all. These were the people that filled the newsreels with horror stories. They were bombing London, killing civilians, and shooting bullets into the hips of perfectly good fathers who had perfectly good daughters, perfectly happy back in their redbrick homes in Brooklyn. Letting the monsters work on farms and earn wages and go swimming and eat three good meals a day just seemed like a trick. And not a magic trick.

It was an hour and a half of unpacking all the knick-knacks and figurines they'd accumulated from both sides of the family, arranging them on the shelves, rearranging them, and then repacking the pieces that didn't quite "fit the décor," as her mother said. Finally, once she was satisfied with the display, she sealed the box back up and slid it over to Max. "Go ahead and put this away."

Max blinked. "Put it away?"

Her mother nodded. "Yes, we don't need the rest of these out."

"Then why do we have them?"

"In case we eventually need them. Or if your grandmother comes to visit."

Max tried to imagine the blitzkrieg they'd endure if her Grandma Schauder came and wasn't greeted by the Hummel figurines yodeling on the mantel. It sent a chill down her spine. "Where do you want me to put them, then?"

"Out in that storm cellar."

Another chill down her spine, only this one lingered. "Really? By myself?"

Her mother stifled a grin. "Are you afraid? The Amazing Max? Master of the Dark Arts? Madame Queen of the Ghostly? Scared of a creaky old storm cellar in the middle of the day?"

Max narrowed her eyes, picked up the box and Major Larousse's flashlight, and spun toward the back door so fast her ponytail whipped around and smacked her in the face.

"Oh, honey, I'm just teasing. I'll go with you if you want."

"Don't bother," Max said. "I'd rather die alone than bring a cantankerous old goat into the sacred Indian burial grounds and risk angering the ghosts."

"Was that referring to me? I lost track after 'alone.'"

Max let the slamming of the screen door act as her reply as she headed out to the door in the ground that served as the entrance to the creepiest place on earth.

The storm cellar.

Max had never seen a storm cellar before that day, and at first thought it sounded quite magical. Like a hidden room where a wizard might concoct thunder and hurricanes and then keep them in bottles on long, gnarled shelves in case of an emergency. Which, of course, she knew wasn't possible. There was no such thing as magic, at least not the wizarding kind. But there was the magic you could make yourself, and she would have loved to find a way to bottle a hurricane, even if only in an illusion.

Unfortunately, the entire vision of the kindly wizard and the tamed cyclones was itself an illusion. Instead, the storm cellar was a dark, dank, bug-filled hole in the ground, lined with cement, accessible only via the ricketiest staircase ever built, which was revealed by pulling on a cinder block that was dangling from a thick wire. The wire went through a pulley on top of a pole, and then attached at the other end to a heavy metal door. The door that was stuck in the ground.

The door she was now straining to open.

How do you get out of the cellar if the door is closed? she wondered as both her feet slowly lowered to the ground with the descent of the cinder block. She climbed on top of it. It took every last ounce of weight an eleven-year-old magician had on her body to open that darn door. Pushing it open from the inside, she imagined, would be impossible.

She shook her head. That scenario was the stuff of nightmares.

The cinder block touched the ground, and she stepped off. She peered through the open door, where the sunlight happily illuminated the first seven steps, but then lost the wrestling match with darkness and left the rest of the abyss as black as midnight.

Luckily Max had the flashlight. She turned it on and shone it down the staircase, which was a mess of warped boards that strained against the nails supposedly holding them onto a cracked beam on the right and the concrete wall on the left. She picked up the box of knickknacks, balanced the flashlight on top, and headed down into the cellar.

She made it down the first five steps with no problem, but

the sixth step was only fastened on one side, and so it moved under her foot. She tried to keep her balance and dropped down to the seventh step, teetered, then finally found her footing again on the eighth. Thankfully, the ever-important knickknacks were unscathed. Not thankfully, the flashlight slipped off the top of the box and bounced the rest of the way down, the clack of it hitting every step echoing off the concrete walls. The flashlight landed at the bottom, shining its beam back up at her face.

She squinted and inched the rest of the way down, trying very hard to not die while also not breaking any of the chubby-cheeked milkmaids stowed away in the box for the ride.

She stepped off the bottom stair and onto the concrete floor. Or, rather, into a puddle of very smelly water that was on the concrete floor. She yelped and tried to jump over the puddle, landing in a much deeper, much smellier one. She stretched her foot over to the flashlight and kicked it around so that it shone across the room and over to the far wall, where a wooden bench perfectly suited for a box of knickknacks was located.

She did her best to dance across the floor on all the dry patches, misjudging only occasionally. Once she was able to set her box down on the bench, she was a little surprised at how dry her left shoe was. Her right shoe was soaked through, but her left still had a dry spot right above the heel. Amazing.

She hurried over to grab the flashlight and decided to get better acquainted with the generally terrifying arena she was in. She was fully prepared for rattlesnakes or possums or some other vermin to jump out at her. Because she had a ferret, she was immune to surprise animal attacks.

She was glad to know she was the only thing alive down there. She did see what appeared to be a rat skeleton over in the corner, but it was unquestionably dead, as most skeletons are. She decided to leave it until she could sneak it into her room without her mother seeing. You never knew when you could use a skeleton in a magic show, and she'd rather have it and not need it.

It was when she turned her attention to the walls that she realized Major Larousse should probably put a lock on the cellar door. The house they were moving into had been vacant for a little over six months, and it appeared that someone had taken the liberty of stowing away down in the cellar during that time. They had also taken it upon themselves to decorate the walls with either chalk or white paint. If you could call what they did decoration.

There were the usual profanities strewn about. She was used to those. And there were the strange pictures of people doing strange things. She was, well, not *used* to those, but she wasn't shocked by them. When you've been raised around GIs, you learn to expect a new level of immaturity from people.

What she wasn't expecting, however, were the

incantations. Poorly spelled, granted, but she recognized them as lines from occultist rituals, dark spells, phrases used to summon the devil himself. They were scrawled across the concrete, framed by pentagrams, bull horns, and other odd symbols that she barely recognized. Which either meant that their cellar had been the location for some crazy pagan religious festival . . . or it meant something far more unsettling.

Somebody else out there was interested in magic. And, considering every last piece of that graffiti was almost an exact copy (sans the poor spelling) of *Secrets of Dark Magic: How to Weave the Occult into Your Magic Show* (a book her grandmother had made her burn when she'd found it on Max's shelf), she was fairly certain she was in for some steep competition.

Max cracked her knuckles and hurried back up the stairs.

Chapter Three

Max sat in the fluffy green chair outside her dad's office, a picnic basket filling the seat next to her. She was waiting for her mother, who had just run back home to get salt. They were going to have dinner with Major Larousse. He'd said he could come home for dinner, but Mrs. Larousse refused, because this would *not* be their first dinner together in the new house. The first dinner would *officially* take place after every box was unpacked, every shelf in the pantry was fully stocked, and every conversation regarding placement of furniture or location of plugs had been exhausted.

So they would eat an impromptu picnic in the major's office. Which was quite alright for Max. She didn't much enjoy eating dinner alone with her mother, since they'd done their fair share of that while Major Larousse was off in Morocco. Besides, sitting in that house was merely a reminder that her life was a half-baked, wispy version of itself, and that someone else out there was working on their own brand of magic. She'd much rather be biding her time in his office.

Except he was in a meeting. Which meant she was biding her time in the fluffy green chair in the hall.

At the far end of the hall, a man in a gray uniform swept the floor, head down, swinging the broom back and forth like a pendulum keeping time in a clock. The gray uniform was drab and unassuming, the activity dull and calming, and all of it together served as a screaming siren that this man was not a GI, but rather a far more sinister character. A Nazi prisoner.

Max tried to ignore the annoying shiver that crept up her spine. Her dad had threatened her life if she treated the prisoners as though they were freaks or outsiders. But they *were* freaks and outsiders, so this task was very difficult. No amount of smoke or mirrors could change the fact that she was less than fifteen feet away from a sworn enemy of the United States. And of all of humanity, really.

She shook her head, pulled out her deck of cards, and started working on the FLOATING CARD TRICK again, moving to the rhythm of the broom tapping the chairs. Without the judgmental glare of Houdini, maybe she could actually plow through the kinks in the routine.

She felt like she was really getting somewhere (probably not ferret-approval level, but at least good enough to mesmerize those GIs from earlier) when she noticed that the sound of sweeping had stopped.

She glanced down the hall to see where the Nazi had gone.

He stood in front of her. Watching her. His piercing blue eyes didn't blink. His mustache fluttered as he breathed, and it was the only movement he made. He stood there, holding the broom, looming over her like a colossus. Staring down at the deck of cards in her hands.

Her throat felt tight as she froze in his gaze.

Like a cobra breaking free from a trance, he moved toward her and she screamed.

He bent down and picked up the cards she hadn't realized she'd dropped and handed them to her. Then he spun around and began to sweep again. "Apologies, *fräulein*."

The door to the office flew open and Major Larousse rushed out. "Max, was that you? Is everything okay?" He rubbed his hip to alleviate the stiffness.

"Yeah," she said after a moment of collecting herself and making sure she hadn't peed on the fluffy green chair. "I'm just getting tired of waiting. Are you almost done?"

Major Larousse sighed and leaned down to whisper in her ear. "These boys are awfully long-winded. It's as if Hitler never let them talk before, so now they have to voice their opinions about everything."

Behind him, another man in a gray prison uniform came to the door. He was handsome enough that he could probably be a big star in the movies, but his accent was heavy enough to remind everyone that he'd much rather drop bombs on Hollywood than work there. "Major? Shall we resume? We are almost finished discussing the menu for dinner this week."

Major Larousse winked at her and straightened up. "Yes, Blaz, I'm coming. But I'm not budging on the meatloaf. You'll just have to get over your distaste for ketchup."

They went back into his office and closed the door.

Max glanced at the floor where the prisoner who was meeting with the major had stood. There was dirt scattered all around it. *That's weird, I didn't see that earlier.*

Before she could ponder this any further, the man with the broom hurried over and swept up the dirt. Then he turned and watched her again as she resumed practicing with the deck of cards. She counted to five and then looked him squarely in the eyes. He flinched and hurried back to the other end of the hallway. She felt a silent moment of victory, as though she'd just driven the Nazis out of Libya herself.

After a few more minutes, Mrs. Larousse finally returned carrying salt, pepper, and three more bottles of Coca-Cola.

"Are we staying with Dad for a while?" Max asked.

"I took one more look at those boxes and decided to wave the white flag. We'll attack them again in the morning." She took the cards from Max and put them back in their box. "Is your father still in his meeting?"

Max nodded. "The Kraut doesn't like meatloaf."

"Well, if he keeps me from my dinner, I won't like him." She stood, adjusted her skirt, and went over to rap solidly on the office door. After a moment, Major Larousse opened it.

"Yes, dear?"

"Major, I'm here to tell you that Sergeant and Private Larousse are famished."

Major Larousse glanced behind him. Blaz crossed his arms and shot him a stern look. Major Larousse returned the look like a tennis player returning a poorly delivered serve. Blaz's shoulders sank.

"Yes," Major Larousse said. "We mustn't let the hardworking American Magician and her mother starve for the sake of Finicky Fritz and his friends."

Blaz nodded, then averted his eyes as he passed Max and her mom on his way out the door and down the hall. Max glanced at the ground behind him, where a trail of dirt followed his footsteps. The man with the broom swept it up and shot her a reprimanding glare. She promptly returned it, though not as effectively as the major. The man fought a smirk and returned to his work.

"I have told you not to speak to them, haven't I?" Major Larousse said to her as she walked past him into his office.

"Yes, Daddy," she said. "I'm not to interact with the Nazis for fear that I'll mistreat them."

He chuckled and tousled her hair. "Exactly. No sawing them in half, my dear."

"Because then we'd be stuck with two Nazis."

Out of the corner of her eye, she noticed the sweeping man watching her out of the corner of his. Those shivers threatened to creep up her spine again. She forced them away with a magical curse. She'd learned a long time ago that her instincts were very susceptible to the mechanisms of illusions. So, even though there was no true magic to the curse, her body was unaware and hurried to follow her command lest she transform herself into a toad.

For an impromptu, we-haven't-a-thing-ready-to-cook-in-our-newly-inhabited-house picnic, Mrs. Larousse had really done a bang-up job. Turkey legs, ham salad sandwiches, deviled eggs, and pickled beets spread across Major Larousse's desk like a king's banquet, and there was a bottle of Coca-Cola with a straw for each of them to quench their inevitable thirst after such salty dishes.

While they worked to clean the gobbler meat off the bones, Major Larousse would periodically begin glancing through papers on his desk or making notes for himself on the yellow legal pad beside his telephone. Mrs. Larousse, every time, would kick him and give the subtle eye glance that parents believe children do not understand, reminding him that his offspring was in need of his attention. Finally, he let out a sigh. "Karly, I'm sorry, but there's just so much to do."

"You're right," she said. "Though I have a feeling you're also wrong."

The major turned to Max and cleared his throat. "Hey, kiddo, why don't you run over to the PX and see if they'll give you some licorice on my credit?"

"With the Gestapo running free out there?" her mother protested.

"I've got guards at every corner with rifles, and they all came out of Basic just itching to shoot at a Nazi," he said. "Trust me, she'll be fine. We need to talk."

Max groaned. Nothing boggled her mind more than the incessant need of adults to protect their children from hearing grown-up conversations. It wasn't as though she didn't already know what they were talking about. She'd read the letters from the colonel, explaining to the major that they'd just had to send a large group of Austrian "anti-Nazi" prisoners to other camps because they were being bullied by the German soldiers who were ardent Nazi loyalists, a group that called themselves "The Black Hand." She'd also seen his notebook, in which he outlined how the guards ought to deal with anyone attempting to escape. And she'd overheard him on the phone, explaining his view that if they treated the prisoners with civility and respect, he believed they'd return the favor.

She had a feeling that wasn't working as well as he'd hoped.

She stood up from her chair. "Fine. Where's the PX?"

"At the end of this road. If you get lost, just ask any GI

and they'll help you out." He winked at her, just like he used to, but it was more like looking at a photo of a wink than experiencing one in real life. "And stay away from the prisoners' hutment. I'm trying to make them feel safe around here."

As she walked out the door, she could hear her mother's reprimanding voice, "You need to focus on your family when we're eating."

"There's just so much to do here, Karly. These people need me."

"You have a daughter who needs you too. And she's been missing you for a very long time."

Max hurried to get away. Listening to them felt a little like a frog watching himself being dissected. Sick and wrong.

It was dusk when she stepped out of the building onto the patch of dirt called Camp Barkeley. She looked around for a bit, trying to see if there was anything about this particular base that was different from every other base she'd ever visited, since it was a prison camp, after all. It didn't take long for her to decide that, no, this was a plain Jane military camp, the only distinguishing feature being that this was in the desolate wasteland of west Texas, and thus it was dryer, dustier, and hotter than the other camps she'd visited.

Because the whole place felt so familiar to her, she didn't bother looking at the signs or asking for directions to the PX. She headed in the direction she assumed it would be and occupied her brainpower with unkinking the steps of that darn card trick. Why was it so difficult for her to perfect? She blamed Texas, an act she had already done a lot and would do many more times over the next few years.

But, as so often happens, it was when she was most sure of her directions that she got the most lost. She meandered along the dusty roads, turning down alleyways that seemed familiar, absentmindedly selecting directions at crossroads, and scuttling along sidewalks that gave no promise of taking her to her destination. And thus, thirty minutes later, when the last rays of the sun had vanished from the sky, she was still walking through the buildings, completely lost but doggedly determined to find her own way.

That is, she was determined all the way up until the moment she overheard a conversation taking place just around the corner ahead of her. A conversation entirely in German.

It was then that she noticed the buildings around here were all a little less inviting. A little more restrained. More hopeless and distraught.

She was roaming through the prisoners' hutment.

Oh dear, now the turkey leg was not agreeing with her. Her stomach cramped and she stopped walking.

"Was war für das Abendessen?" one of the prisoners around the corner said.

"Braten und Kartoffeln," the other man said.

Grandma Schauder, a German immigrant from the first World War, had taught her to speak German quite well. Unfortunately, Max's brain was refusing to translate anything other than her churning stomach, and thus she was forced to assume they were discussing how much they'd like to stumble upon an American girl as lost as an Eskimo in the desert. She froze.

"Ich bin froh, dass ich krank war."

"Ich wünschte, ich hätte vor dem Abendessen krank gewesen," the first man said. *"Stattdessen bin ich jetzt krank."* Both men laughed.

Max could feel her pulse beating in her neck. She slowly backed away from the corner and into the looming shadow she hoped would hide her until she found her way back to the free part of camp.

Unfortunately, someone was standing behind her.

"Lost, *fräulein?*" the man who had been sweeping the hallway asked. He was covered in the darkness, but his eyes still tore right through her. He was eating a banana, which somehow made him look even more sinister.

She opened her mouth to try to respond, but her stomach was cramping so much, she couldn't move past the pain to form any words.

He took a step closer to her.

She pushed the banana into his chest and ran back down the road as fast as she could.

When she ran through another unlit section, she collided with someone else. This time she screamed. Then she realized it was a good old American GI.

"Hey, it's the Amazing Molly!" the GI said. It took her a second in the dark to realize that it was Gil, all decked out in his guard gear. She glanced at the rifle hanging from his shoulder and finally began to grow calm.

"It's Max, actually," she said.

"You lost?" he asked with a maniacal grin.

"No, not at all. I was exploring." She adjusted her skirt around her waist. "But, since it *is* dark now, would you mind escorting me to the PX? I'm in need of some licorice. And perhaps another soda."

He gave her a mock salute and offered her his arm.

She blanched at first, but then remembered the banana-eating Nazi lurking in the shadows somewhere. She put her hand on the crook of his elbow and walked with him down the street in the only direction she hadn't tried all evening. He whistled "American Patrol" while they strolled, and she tried not to stare down every shadow along their path.

She didn't succeed very well.

Chapter Four

"We don't make friends for our own sakes, we make friends for our mothers'. I don't really know why our mothers make friends. Probably for our grandmothers. Yes, that has to be it. Friendship is a tool of motherhood to keep children occupied and out of their mothers' hair. Invented by Eve, I imagine."
—Max's diary, Thursday, March 9, 1944

Don't mess with your hair," Mrs. Larousse said on the sidewalk outside of the school. She fidgeted with the blue ribbon that held Max's ponytail in place. "And don't lose that." She tapped the letter of introduction pinned to Max's blouse.

"I've been to school before," Max said. "In Brooklyn, so I'm probably five times better at it than these cowboys."

Mrs. Larousse swatted Max on top of the head with her handbag. "Enough of that, missy. People around here already believe you think you're better than them. You don't need to prove them right."

"Well, they *are* right, I do think that."

"Of course you do. But you can't let them know." Mrs. Larousse licked a hanky to wipe a smudge of jam off Max's face. "And, please, try to fit in. Maybe wait a week before you start making things disappear out of your classmates lunch boxes."

"I think you underestimate how much people like magicians," Max said. Her mother was not amused, so Max sighed. "Fine, I promise I'll be boring and average and try to fit in."

Mrs. Larousse kissed her forehead. "At least for a week."

When the principal escorted Max to her classroom, she regretted agreeing to her mother's demands. Even just a week of "fitting in" with these boring children would set her back intellectually at least three years. She'd have to double her homework load to make up the deficit.

The teacher, a woman named Mrs. Conrad with a hooked nose and poorly applied lipstick, read Max's letter of introduction through Coke-bottle glasses and then showed her to a seat surrounded by three girls, all of whom had red ribbons in their hair, and all of whom crossed their legs exactly the same.

"This is Judy, Margaret, and Natalie. They're military as well. You'll get along just fine." That was the only introduction Mrs. Conrad gave her.

Max plopped into her seat, glanced at the six legs surrounding her, and tried her best to cross hers the same way. It wasn't comfortable at all.

The girl behind her leaned forward and offered her a stick of gum. "I'm Judy. My pop is over in France." She patted Max on her back. "Margeret's is in the Pacific somewhere. Natalie's got three cousins in the war, one in Africa and the others in Europe, and her dad is with mine in France."

Max accepted the gum and put it in her mouth. Since Wrigley's Spearmint was a military-only gum, you could get it only at the PX, which made her feel like she and Judy had a special connection. Perhaps this wasn't so bad after all.

"Thanks," she said.

"Who do you got out there?"

"My dad," Max said. "Though he's not 'out there.' He's in charge of the guards at Camp Barkeley."

"Oh, so he's here," Judy said. "That must be nice." Then she sat back with an air that implied it actually *wasn't* nice at all, and that perhaps if Max was a better American, the major would still be dodging bullets in the heat of the desert. It made the gum in Max's mouth taste flat. Which turned out to be a good thing, because Mrs. Conrad's hand was hovering in front of her face, beckoning the gum be expelled into her palm. Max let it roll off her tongue into custody.

"I don't know how they run schools back east—"

"Brooklyn," Max said.

Mrs. Conrad clicked her tongue. "Back east. But here, we don't chew gum in school."

Max glanced at the girls sitting next to her, both of their jaws subtly kneading the Wrigley's in their mouths. A lesser-skilled eleven-year-old may have felt it unfair that they were enjoying their contraband while she was singled out for the crime on her first day, but she was well-versed in the art of trickery. In fact, she admired the fact that they were using her as a diversion for a few brief moments of gummy goodness.

See, Mom? Everyone loves a good magician.

Mrs. Conrad resumed her post at the front of the room and ordained that the students be quiet. Max hadn't noticed any noise before this moment, but she most certainly noticed the silence that followed.

"We're starting late," Mrs. Conrad said with a tone that implied the horror she felt over this malfeasance. She glared at Max. "But I suppose it could not be helped."

Judy stifled a giggle. Mrs. Conrad's glare redirected momentarily.

"I will now call roll," she said, sliding her glasses down her nose and picking up the paper from her desk. As her voice droned along reading all the Browns and Davises on her list, Max started to feel the effects of her limited breakfast. Her eyes grew heavy, her muscles were losing control, and she knew it would be only moments before she'd be snoring in her seat. An act that would definitely destroy her first-day reputation. Unfortunately, she was far too sleepy to care.

Fortunately, that was when the list got interesting.

"Shoji Jingu," Mrs. Conrad barked across the room. Max perked up. *What sort of a name is that?*

"Here," a voice in the back answered. Max turned completely around to try and see who was the heir to the strangest surname in the world.

Mrs. Conrad clucked at her. "And we already know Maxine Larousse is here."

"It's pronounced 'La Roo,'" Max replied as she turned back around.

Mrs. Conrad clucked again and made a note, then she resumed her monotonous roll call.

"Were you trying to see Shoji?" Natalie whispered to Max.

"Just wondering what kind of name that is," Max said.

"Japanese," Natalie replied. "He's one of those *nisei*. Claims his daddy is fighting in Europe, too. But everyone knows you can't trust a Jap, so he's probably lying." She gently tugged on the edges of her eyes. "Oh, velly honolable father fighting against honolable Nazis please." She giggled at her own attempt at a Japanese accent.

Max couldn't argue with that logic, but she still really, really wanted to meet this Shoji character. She'd always heard the best illusions came from the Orient. Perhaps they could exchange knowledge. Perhaps it would start a move toward world peace.

Probably not, but at least she could expand her repertoire.

It didn't take more than thirty minutes for Max to realize that this school was at least two months behind her school in Brooklyn. This fact made the already boring task of listening to Mrs. Conrad lecture as tedious as sorting beads with her grandmother. She balanced a textbook on her leg in hopes it would keep her awake. It barely worked.

Max was fairly certain she was old enough to be a grandmother herself by the time they were dismissed for lunch. As they filed outside to eat, Judy linked arms with her and directed her over to a mesquite tree that offered marginal shade.

"It's time for the lunch exchange," she said.

Max felt a sense of foreboding as they joined Natalie and Margaret and sat on the ground next to the knobbed roots of the ugly tree. She tossed a glass bottle out of the way and tried to keep from getting dirty. She knew it was a worthless effort.

Judy took the lunch sack Max's mother had packed and unloaded its contents for the others to see. It was a ham salad sandwich, an orange, a bag of potato chips, and a bottle of Coca-Cola.

"Since you're the new girl, your lunch is up first," Judy said.

Natalie opened the ham salad sandwich and gagged. "Ew, it looks like throw-up."

"Don't you people have ham salad here?" Max asked. The little version of her mother who lived inside her head swatted her subconscious. "I mean, it's really good."

Margaret sniffed it. "It smells good. But it really does look like throw-up." She opened her lunch sack and pulled out a pickle. She broke it in half and set one part on Max's lunch sack. Then she took the sandwich.

Judy snatched the Coca-Cola and plopped a half-pint of milk in its place.

"Well, I love potato chips," Natalie said. She took the bag and gave a banana.

"Hold on, girls," Judy said. "Let's make sure our new friend feels like this has been a fair trading session." She raised her eyebrows at Max, like one might if they were coaxing first words out of a baby. "What do you say? Are you gonna be our new friend and share your lunch, or would you rather have it all back and go sit by yourself?"

Max took a moment to assess the nutritional value of a half pickle, banana, orange, and a half-pint of milk, hoping that her mental mother would make an exception to the "try to fit in" decree. That didn't work, unfortunately, so instead she channeled THE AMAZING MAX.

"Absolutely, this has been a most fair exchange of delicacies," she said. "And, as your new friend, I'd like to perhaps offer some entertainment. And a bit of a wager."

Judy smiled and batted her eyes. "I knew you'd fit right in. What's the wager?"

"First let's cover the stakes. If you win this wager, I will return to you every item you have given me, and I will only eat the orange for my lunch. On the other hand, if you lose, I keep what you gave me and you must give me back the items from my lunch."

Natalie shook her head. "No way. I'm starving."

"Let's hear her out," Judy said. "What's the challenge?"

THE AMAZING MAX grinned. With a flair, she retrieved the glass bottle she'd tossed earlier and set it upright in the center of their circle. Then she plucked some toothpicks out of her pocket. She set one of the toothpicks across the mouth of the bottle, making sure there was an equal amount hanging off both ends.

"The challenge," she said, "is to coax this toothpick to jump off the bottle."

Judy leaned in to examine the bottle. "So we just have to knock the toothpick off the bottle? What's the catch?"

"No, not *knock* the toothpick off. Coax it to jump off. There's a difference. The toothpick has to jump off on its own."

"You're crazy," Natalie said. "Toothpicks can't do anything on their own."

Judy scrunched up her forehead. "It doesn't seem very fair. You're asking us to do something impossible."

"Oh, never," MAX said. "I assure you, it can be done."

"No it can't," Natalie said.

MAX simply shrugged. "Not with that attitude it can't."

Judy sat up. "True. Okay, we'll agree." Margeret started to

whine in protest, but Judy covered her mouth with her hand. "But the only way we lose is if we can't do it but *you can.*"

Max fought the grin that wanted so badly to emerge on her lips. Only the best magicians could make their audience believe that they themselves had chosen the parameters of the illusion to which they would soon fall prey. And these girls had stepped into the trap of their own making faster than she'd expected.

"Sounds fantastic," Max said and then she stood up. "But don't start till I get back. I can't drink milk, so I'm going to get some water." She headed over to the water cooler, got a paper cup, and filled it. While she was walking back, she noticed another group of kids eating together all the way on the other side of the school yard. But while the girls under the mesquite tree were cookie-cutter versions of each other, the group sitting out by the fence was a grab bag of assorted novelties.

There was a Japanese boy, whom she assumed was Shoji. Then there was a kid who looked at least three years too old to be enrolled in their grade. Next to him was a girl, and she was so tiny that together they looked like an encyclopedia entry for "opposites." Rounding out the gang was a boy with an eye patch and a crooked smile. They all seemed to be having a great deal more fun than the girls under the mesquite tree. And they all had their own lunch. It really was a shame she hadn't been around for social-circle-recruitment day.

Plain-Old Max took a sip of water and forced herself to

return to her more professional persona. There was no time to fret over the condition of her lunchtime. THE AMAZING MAX had a fantastic illusion to execute. She returned to the girls under the tree.

She sat and watched as first Natalie, then Margaret, and finally Judy attempted to knock the toothpick off by blowing it, hitting the ground next to the bottle, or tossing a rock at it. And each time the toothpick would fall, she'd remind them that they had knocked it off, it hadn't jumped on its own, which would lead them to pound the ground in frustration. *This is plenty entertaining. At least for today,* she thought.

Finally Judy threw her hands in the air. "Okay, we give up."

"Told you it was impossible," Margaret said.

MAX nodded. "True, it is very nearly impossible." She moved over to the bottle and began to wave her hand over it. "But I'd assumed, since we're in the land of cowboys, you would have known the answer. How do cowboys make a cow jump over a fence?"

"With a cattle prod," Natalie said. "They zap their heinies, and the cows jump as high as the moon."

MAX nodded again and picked up a second toothpick. "Exactly. Now, with a magic incantation—*Zim-Zala-Bim*—I will electrify this toothpick and turn it into a cattle prod."

While Margeret scoffed and Judy rolled her eyes, MAX held the now-electrified toothpick between her thumb and finger and moved it to barely tap the reluctant one on the bottle. As soon as they touched, there was a loud *POP* and the rascally toothpick jumped six inches off the bottle and into the air.

Natalie yelped. Judy wrinkled up her forehead. Margaret's eyes got so wide, they almost expanded past the boundaries of her face. THE AMAZING MAX blew on the toothpick in her hand and dropped it in her cup of water like it was as hot as a coal from a grill.

"May I have my food back?" Plain-Old Max asked.

"How'd you do that?" Judy asked in return.

"A good magician never reveals her tricks."

Judy examined Max's eyes as she gave her back the Coca-Cola. "So you're a magician?"

"Looks like it." Max popped the cap off and took a sip of victory.

"Golly," Natalie said. "You're a witch?"

"No, a magician." Max snatched her bag of potato chips and crunched through four of them.

Margaret held out the ham salad sandwich. "Well, I guess you deserve this then."

Max waved it away. "No, you were right, it does look like throw-up. You can have it."

Judy laughed and put her arm around Max. "You're going to fit right in with us. I'm a performer too. An actress."

Max tried to hide her skepticism about such a foolish,

star-studded dream. She apparently didn't do it very well.

"Hey, don't believe me all you want," Judy said. "But I'm going to be the first girl from Abilene to ever stand in the spotlight. Mark my words."

Max didn't feel threatened by this statement, mainly because she would never consider herself to be a girl from Abilene, so Judy could hold that title at will.

"Anyway, I guess this trio just became a quartet," Judy said.

Max shot a look over at the ensemble by the fence, which still seemed to be having three times the fun of those under the mesquite tree. She sighed.

I'm doing this for you, Mother.

Chapter Five

Max had never been the sort to walk home with people, especially not birds-of-a-feather like Judy, Natalie, and Margaret. Yet that was the position in which she found herself after school, walking, arms linked with the Mesquite Tree Girls, attempting to find common ground with their giggling and gossiping as they escorted her back to her drab and dreary domicile.

"So do you do any vanishing tricks?" Natalie asked.

"Oh, sure," Max said. "What kind of magician doesn't have vanishing tricks?"

Margaret clapped her hands. "Oh, that's fun. What's the biggest thing you've made disappear?"

"Maybe, like, some birds?" Natalie asked.

Max thought about the question. "I guess probably a vase with flowers in it."

"Well, if you could make flowers from Frank Sinatra *appear* at my doorstep tomorrow, that'd be great," Judy said, and then the other two set off giggling. Judy was something of a comedienne, Max was realizing, and she had the show-biz sense to keep her best audience around her at all times. *She might even make a fine assistant.*

The Mesquite Tree Girls had collectively decided to go to Max's house after school so they could meet Houdini and also watch Max perform her finest tricks for their amuse-ment. Max had held her tongue from informing them that she was not a dancing bear and didn't even perform at birth-day parties without adequate payment, let alone put on a private show for three girls who really ought to be getting on to their homework. She decided that she'd instead use subtle mind-control over her mother and trust she would provide the necessary diversion.

When they turned the corner to head down her street, a strange gloom began to grow on Margaret's face. She still giggled at Judy's jokes, but she'd stopped skipping, and Max couldn't help but notice that every few steps elicited a pan-icked glance up the street from Margaret's eyes. Finally, just two houses away from Max's, Margaret stopped walking altogether. Her face grew pale.

"I have to go," she said abruptly.

"They have a restroom, Margy," Judy said.

Margaret didn't respond. She turned around and ran back up the street, leaving the rest of them to listen to her heels clack on the pavement until she disappeared around the corner.

"Well that's strange," Natalie said.

Judy shrugged. "More ferret for me, then."

They continued walking, but Max, always on the look-out for hidden mirrors and wires, examined the house that had inspired such a reaction from poor Margaret. It wasn't well kept, barely looked inhabited, and cast an overall unin-viting air that would even drive away an angel sent to guard its inhabitants.

Then, while she was looking, the blinds in the window moved.

Max suddenly sympathized with Margaret, just a little, and tried to hurry the pace of the others as they made their way to Max's house.

When they entered the Larousse's, Max was relieved to see her mother entertaining a guest in the front room. Even though this entire excursion with the Mesquite Tree Girls was to appease her mother, there was nothing more mortify-ing to Max than having an act of obedience noticed in front of her peers. Her parents believed their words of affirmation built up her confidence and improved her future behavior, but in reality all it did was establish to the general populace that their child was little more than a trained monkey danc-ing in a tutu on command.

Max hurried Judy and Natalie along to her room and then went through the seven-minute ritual of ferreting out the ferret from whatever cozy corner Houdini had chosen for his hourly nap. She finally found him curled up inside her left snow boot. The location of her *right* snow boot was a mystery Houdini was guarding with all his might. Which meant she'd find it later when he stole her hair brush.

"Oh my gosh, he's so cute!" Natalie squealed when Houdini yawned and licked his chops before collapsing back into Max's arm. He was not yet ready to leave behind the magical world of ferret sleep.

"Does he do tricks?" Judy asked.

"All the time," Max said and plopped him down on her bed. He immediately tunneled into the folds of her blanket. "But never on command. So he's probably the worst magician's pet ever."

Houdini lunged out from the far end of the blanket and attacked Natalie's foot, which she'd been bobbing enticingly off the edge of the bed. Natalie yelped a yelp of surprise and delight.

Judy picked him up and cradled him in her arm like an infant. He immediately climbed up to her shoulder, then slid down her back to the ground. He scurried over to Max's dresser and disappeared beneath it.

"So, how did you do it?" Judy asked. "The thing at school with the toothpick. Did you have a string we couldn't see or something?"

Max sighed on reflex. "A magician never tells her secret. It's the Magician's Code."

Judy rolled her eyes and plopped down to reach her hand under the dresser.

Max grimaced at the sense of foreboding she'd just gotten. "He's probably going to bite—"

"Ow!" Judy pulled her hand out and sucked on her thumb, where the tiny little indentations gave evidence that Houdini had, in fact, mistaken her hand for a free-range rabbit. He was certain that, one of these days, a rabbit would come to attack his beloved human and all of his practice would finally pay off.

"Yup, told you," Max said.

Judy narrowed her eyes in determination and crouched down to locate the adorable attacker so she could squeeze him and force him to cuddle.

"Are you going to do any tricks at school tomorrow?" Natalie asked, giggling at the prospect of seeing Houdini pulled from under the dresser, clawing at the ground like a forlorn soul being dragged to hell.

"I don't know," Max said. "Probably." She momentarily wondered if she should warn Judy that Houdini had already snuck around the room and was now about to attack her unattended ankles. She decided against it.

"What trick will you do?"

Before Max could answer, Houdini pounced on Judy's Achilles tendon. Judy released a hasty scream and rolled from her belly-down position into a curled ball. Houdini, now not entirely certain that this *wasn't* a rabbit, treated her heels to a flurry of nips and tugs before disappearing into a pile of clothes Max had left for him in the corner.

"Is he gone?" Judy asked over the wild and erratic laughter shared by both Natalie and Max.

"Temporarily," Max finally forced through her uncontrollable chortling.

Judy, clearly not nearly as amused as the others in the room, rolled over to stand. When she did, Houdini flew from his laundry den to pose another attack on her bobby socks. Judy was ready for him this time, and her hand flew and smacked him on the head. He rolled across the floor, shook the daze from his brain, and scurried back under the dresser.

Max was no longer laughing. "Please don't break my ferret," she said.

"He was trying to hurt me," Judy defended.

"He thought you were playing."

"I wasn't."

"Yes, you made that obvious."

They exchanged a tense glare that Max eventually won, and Judy fell onto the bed to stare up at the ceiling.

Natalie cleared her throat. "Anyway, as I was saying, what tricks are you going to do tomorrow?"

"Good magicians never tell the audience what they're going to do before they do it," Max flatly replied.

"Is that another of your dumb 'Magician's Code' things?" Judy sneered. The air in the room had been irreversibly tainted. She couldn't believe how quickly the adorable ferret had turned psychotic and these girls who were supposed to be her freinds didn't care. There would be no more civility from Judy that day.

"No, it's something Adelaide Herrmann always said."

Judy sat up and looked at her as though she were speaking a language from the least-explored regions of Africa. "Who?"

"Madame Adelaide Herrmann. She and her husband, Professor Alexander Herrmann, were the greatest magicians who ever lived."

Judy narrowed her eyes. "They sound German."

"They were," Max said. "I mean, sort of. Well, Alexander's family came from Germany. Adelaide's family was from Belgium, I think. But that doesn't really matter, 'cause they eventually lived in New York."

Judy stood and motioned for Natalie to follow. "I think we're going to leave."

"Okay," Max said. "Why?"

"Because now I know why your ferret is crazy." Judy bobbed her head as only those well versed in the art of disdaining can do. "It's 'cause you practice Nazi magic."

"Baloney," Max yelled. "There's no such thing."

"It's German, ain't it?" Judy yelled back. She actually

said "isn't," but Max's brain filtered the "ain't" in, as it better represented Judy's tone. "That's the same."

Max shook her head. "All Germans aren't Nazis, you cowboy idiot."

Judy stepped toward her. "I'd rather be a cowboy idiot than a Nazi-loving Yankee snob."

"Those insults don't even go together," Max growled.

Judy clenched her fists.

Houdini, now certain that the big-footed creature hovering over his human *was* a vile bunny, flew from under the dresser and latched on to Judy's ankle.

Judy screeched and kicked her foot in the air as she bounced in a circle. It took four kicks, all of which elicited barely repressed snickers from Max and Natalie, before Houdini flew off onto Max's bed. When Judy put her foot back on the floor, it was only to launch herself on the path out of the room and back home, safe from Nazi magic and demon-possessed ferrets.

Natalie watched her leave, seemed to debate her loyalties, and then followed. "I'm sorry," she called out as she hurried down the hallway.

Max sighed and checked Houdini for internal injuries. He licked her nose, doing the same. After they were both quite certain the other was still in fine health and only slightly distressed from those odd girls/bunnies, they collapsed on the bed and rested for the entirety of a ferret's attention span. Hence, when her mother came in a minute later to check on Max, Houdini was already off playing with his human's homework.

"Is everything okay in here?" Mrs. Larousse said.

Max was practicing rolling a silver dollar across her fingers. "Right as rain. I made friends today."

Her mother sat on the bed next to her. "Those girls that just left? The ones who called you a Nazi-lover?"

Max nodded. "Judy and Natalie. You missed Margaret, she did her escape routine down the block."

"I don't know if I'd classify them as friends."

Max smirked. "Things have changed since you were my age, Mom. We're in another world war. Civility is old-fashioned nowadays."

Mrs. Larousse pulled Max into a hug that knocked the silver dollar off her knuckles. Max didn't mind. She needed a little Motherly Magic.

"There's always tomorrow, sweetie."

Max blinked away a pesky tear that threatened to reveal the feelings behind the curtain. She sensed it was time for some conversational smoke to hide her emotional mirrors. "At least you made a friend, right?"

"Mrs. Morris?" Mrs. Larousse stifled a laugh. "Oh, no. She's our neighbor *and* the head of the Ladies Auxiliary. She was 'welcoming us to the neighborhood' and checking to see if I'd be attending their next meeting. In her own words, 'If men like my son can work morning-to-night patching up the wounded soldiers from this horrible war, the least we can do is bake some pies and pack some blankets.'"

"I don't think that's actually the least you can do. I can think of ten things that are less involved than that."

Mrs. Larousse tousled Max's hair. "Still, we must keep the neighbors happy. There's not enough of them to pick and choose, like back home—I mean, back in Brooklyn. Besides, I am the major's wife, and that apparently comes with certain expectations. So there's going to be a lot of pie baking in this house very soon. Are you up for peeling apples?"

Max had actually earned the moniker THE AMAZING MAX from her skills with a peeler long before she discovered a magic wand. Still, after she'd moved on to illusions, she'd tried to let her apple-skinning skills flounder on the wayside. But her mother was adamant that Maxine not forget her roots. And persuasion was the most powerful of the Motherly Magics. Max nodded against her will.

"Good. Then, since you still need to practice piano today, we'll start tomorrow," Mrs. Larousse said. "It'll give you something to focus on until those girls forget about your Nazi sympathizing." She winked at Max.

Max smiled. "I'm pretty sure Judy had pretzels with her lunch today. She's more of a Nazi sympathizer than I am."

Mrs. Larousse covered her mouth in mock horror. "She

was eating Hitler Twists? Oh sweet Mary." She stood to go back to the living room.

"Hey," Max called her back, suddenly realizing what had been slipped into the conversation covertly. "When did we decide I was going to practice piano today?"

"We didn't," her mother said with a smile. "Now, get your things."

Motherly Magic was terribly, terribly dangerous in evil hands.

HOUDINI

★ PRESENTS ★

The Jumping Toothpick

HERE'S WHAT YOU'LL NEED.

1. Two Toothpicks
2. A Soda Bottle

SODA

Step One: Set one toothpick across the top of a soda bottle.

PHEW! THAT WAS HARD.

SODA

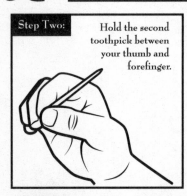

Step Two: Hold the second toothpick between your thumb and forefinger.

Step Three: Rest the nail of your index finger on the tip of the toothpick.

Step Four: When you touch the toothpicks together, flick the end of the toothpick you're holding with your nail.

I DON'T HAVE NAILS.

DO CLAWS WORK?

SODA

The other toothpick will leap off the bottle!

TA-DA!

SODA

Chapter Six

There were few tasks Max found as tedious and superfluous as practicing the piano. She was not talented at it, and the very fact that she could admit her lack of a gift was proof of just how bad she truly was at playing. Her fingers were deft and skilled at slight-of-hand and pickpocketing, but when set to the piano keys, they rivaled only an elephant's in lack of grace and rhythm.

This would have been worrisome but for the fact that Max wasn't particularly fond of music, either—at least not enough to view performance as anything approaching art or entertainment. They had a record player for those rare occasions when she felt particularly deprived, and other than that, she was content to make do with what she heard at the theater in *Looney Tunes* shorts. If she wanted a live concerto, she'd buy a player piano someday. Technology had made musicians obsolete, by her assessment.

Unfortunately, her mother did not share the same opinion.

She believed it was necessary, for the sake of developing a civilized intellect, that every young person learn to play an instrument, no matter what dire effects such knowledge would have on the general reputation of music in the future. Hence, Max had taken piano lessons since she was five. And she had hated every second of it.

When her mother sold their piano back in Brooklyn, Max had hoped she would finally find a reprieve from all the horrible piano practicing she was forced to do weekly. Sadly, this was not the case. Instead, Max was forced to sit in the rec hall on base and run through her scales and arpeggios on the upright piano that was used for everything from Sunday hymns to vaudevillian comic opera. All while GIs and the occasional prisoner sauntered through on their way to an assignment. And every single one of them paused to listen for at least three measures, which was humiliating enough. Then they realized there was no skill to be found in her playing and walked away, unanimously chuckling at her mistakes.

She made a mental note that the single most important trick she still had yet to learn was how to make herself disappear. Without a proper escape plan, she had to find hope somewhere else. At least she only had to endure this pain for thirty minutes, and surely she was almost done. She turned to look at the clock.

No, she'd only been practicing for five.

She crossed her arms and plopped them down on the keys. It was the most expressive she'd ever been on the instrument.

"Wow, Squirt, you're a magician *and* a musician?" the almost-giggling voice of Gil piped up from behind her, accompanied by an uninvited rib poke.

"If failing miserably at something is the same as being good at it, then yeah, I am," she said as she sat up straight to ward off any further poking. "I'm also really good at making friends, and I'm the perfect specimen of high fashion, by those standards." She felt slightly obligated to be civil since he'd helped her out of the Nazi shadows the other night.

He pushed her along the bench and sat next to her. "Don't be bashful. Play me something."

She sighed. "I've taken piano lessons for six years and couldn't play you anything even if I wanted to."

"You're lying," he said. "Surely you know something. 'Chopsticks'? 'When the Saints Go Marching In'?"

"Honestly, absolutely honestly, I'm terrible at this thing."

"Yeah, me too," he said. He put his fingers on the keys and, with grace and skill that would bring a music lover to tears, proceeded to run through the first few measures of Chopin's "Nocturne in E-flat Major." Even her music-indifferent ears could tell he was far from an amateur. "See what I mean?" he said when he was done. "Terrible."

"I ought to turn you into a toad," she said. "Now you've made the rest of my practice time even worse."

He patted her on the head. "Just giving you incentive to pay attention to your piano teacher a little better."

"Considering she's all the way back in Brooklyn, there's only so much I can do."

He feigned a heart attack. "No, no, no, this cannot be. Now you'll never realize your full potential."

She was poised to fire a snarky comeback when he grabbed her hands and moved them onto the keys. Suddenly she forgot every witty phrase she'd ever devised.

"I shall be your teacher," he said with bravado. "You will not be left in the wilderness of music without a guide."

As he began to count and move her fingers through the scales better than she'd ever seen her fingers move on their own, she couldn't fight off this single, embarrassing thought: *I never noticed how good-looking this obnoxious boy is.* She took a second to imagine him as her beautiful assistant and then allowed herself to enjoy these fleeting moments of pedagogy.

Suddenly Gil stopped playing. He stood up. "Dang it."

"What?"

"A gosh darn Kraut has been watching us through the window."

She looked in the direction he was glaring, but the view was empty of any peeping eyes. That did not keep Gil from running out the door, however. Somehow she had a feeling that Major Larousse had given the guards a lecture similar to the "no fraternizing with the Nazis" one he'd driven into her brain. Except in place of the word "Nazis," he'd said "my daughter." Which meant the Nazi from the window had just acquired powerful negotiation material from Gil's transgression.

Such is life. I may never find an assistant.

She couldn't bring herself to resume the scales on her own, particularly now that she'd experienced what it was like to actually play them well. Instead, she turned on the bench and examined the stage behind her. She imagined how she would set it up if she was performing a show. Where she'd put her table, and her curtain, and the not-yet-built boxes and apparatuses that made for a perfect presentation.

She could picture it vividly. The crowd in the chairs. The heat from the spotlight. She could almost feel the silk cape on her shoulders and the stiff collar on her neck.

And the applause. She could hear the roar of the applause echoing around the room. A standing ovation for The Amazing Max.

Her heart raced at the thought.

The door to the rec hall banged open, and she jumped out of her daydream.

A man came in, breathing heavily, with perspiration stains growing on his gray jumpsuit. He sat down in a chair and struggled to catch his breath. He looked at her from across the room for a moment, then looked away. His blue eyes, even in that brief glance, seemed to ask the same question she had in her head: Why do we keep running in to each other?

Max breathed another magical curse at herself to calm down and then walked over to him.

"Were you the one watching us through the window?" she asked.

He looked up at her, then dropped his gaze to the floor. "Apologies, *fräulein*," he said, exactly as he had in the hallway.

"Apology not accepted," she said. She leaned over to make eye contact with him. "Why were you watching us? Are you trying to get Gil in trouble?"

He raised an eyebrow and hid a slight grin in his mustache. "I wouldn't dream of it. I am merely a lover of music."

Now she hid a grin. "Then listening to me is a bad idea."

The door banged open again and the breathless form of Gil dashed in. He didn't waste a moment before he grabbed the prisoner by the jumpsuit and pulled him up to stand.

"What's going on, Felix?" Gil said, his mouth an inch from the man's nose. "Why are you spying on me?"

Felix dropped his head and stared at Gil's shoes. "Apologies. I meant no harm."

Gil glared at him, then shoved him so hard that he nearly tripped. Gil grabbed Felix's jumpsuit again and pulled him close. He spoke into Felix's ear. "You might have people fooled around here, but you don't fool me. I know you're nothing but a weasel. I heard what you did to those Austrian prisoners from before. And I'm not afraid to dig up enough evidence to make things worse for you."

Felix nodded. "Of course. Apologies."

Gil turned him and pushed him toward the door. "Now get out of here so this little girl can practice in peace."

Felix moved toward the doorway. He stopped at the exit and turned to look at Max. "Madame Herrmann would be happy that you are learning her ways. Just remember, *Anfangen ist leicht, beharren eine Kunst.*"

Gil rushed forward and pushed Felix out the door. Felix nodded and disappeared outside.

Gil turned back to Max. "I'm real sorry about that. I don't know what Nazi curse he just tried to put on you, but you're a good, God-fearing girl, so you don't have to worry."

She thanked him for his concern and went back to the piano.

She wished he *had* cursed her. But, thanks to Grandma Schauder, she knew he had done the opposite. What he'd said was, "To begin is easy. To persist is art."

And the fact that a Nazi was trying to encourage her in the art of magic was perhaps the most discouraging thing she'd ever heard in her life.

Chapter Seven

It was only her second day in school, but Max already felt as weathered and beaten as Major Larousse had looked when he'd first arrived back in the states from Casablanca. But there would be no Purple Heart awaiting her at her desk. Instead, when she sat in her seat, she discovered that an open pint of milk had been sitting there first.

She leaped and yelped, twisting around to examine the very large wet spot that now cohabited her skirt with her, as well as the trickles of milk that dripped down her legs and into her shoes.

Mrs. Conrad did not waste any time flying from her desk to Max's with a couple of towels and several stern words. As the sound of her clucking tongue filled the air, Max turned her gaze to whom she was sure was the culprit. The smug grin on Judy's face proved her accusation accurate.

"Be glad I started with the milk," Judy whispered and

pointed to the line of five thumbtacks on her desk that awaited their dispatch.

Max now realized she was not at all in the state the major was in when he arrived home months earlier. He had left the war behind. She was entering it. And, unfortunately for her, this was a war in which bloodshed would not be acceptable. Rather, this would be a war of pranks and humiliation.

Unfortunately for Judy, no one pranked and humiliated like a magician.

After wiping up the milk, Mrs. Conrad decided Max needed to visit the nurse. There was no good reason for Max to visit the nurse, but Mrs. Conrad greatly wished to punish Max. Yet, since everyone knows the adage about appropriate emotions to exhibit over spilled milk, she decided an unnecessary trip to the nurse would be the greatest inconvenience she could reasonably deal.

"Who will walk Miss Larousse down to the office?" Mrs. Conrad crowed to the room as she deposited the soggy towels into a bag next to her desk.

Judy turned and sent a silent message to the class. Nearly no one volunteered.

Nearly no one.

A single hand lifted in the air near the back. Max wondered who would dare be the lone dissenter in the room.

Then he stood and it all made sense.

Of course it would be the Jap, she thought with a groan.

"Who's that?" Mrs. Conrad asked, squinting through her glasses.

"It's me, Shoji," he replied. He didn't sound anything like Natalie's impersonation. Nothing like the Japs in the cartoons at all. Instead, with his drawl and the slight twang in his husky voice, he sounded more Texan than anyone else Max had met.

"Mr. Jingu, thank you," Mrs. Conrad said. She waved her hand toward the door as a disgruntled queen might wave away a putrid peasant.

Max struggled to motivate her feet in that direction. She leaned on Judy's desk as though suddenly burdened under the pain of humiliation.

"Miss Larousse," Mrs. Conrad hissed. "Please move along."

The *nisei* boy came to her side. "C'mon, milk-butt. Unless you'd rather stick around here and endure the Monster Society of Evil."

No matter what preconceptions she had toward Japanese boys in west Texas schools, Max couldn't help but appreciate the wit that went into so aptly renaming the Mesquite Tree Girls the "Monster Society of Evil." She shuffled her feet along as they walked out into the hallway.

And, of course, nobody noticed that there were now only four thumbtacks on Judy's desk.

They went into the hallway and Shoji turned right. Max stopped walking. Even after only one day at the school, she knew the nurse's office was to the left.

Shoji noticed her absence after a few steps. He returned and grabbed her arm. "Are you coming or what?"

"The nurse is that way," she said, pointing.

"Do you need the nurse?"

"No, but Mrs. Conrad said I should go."

"And we're going, aren't we?"

"But not to the nurse. The nurse is that way."

"We'll get there eventually," he replied. "Jeez, you're not very bright, are you?"

She bristled internally and pulled her arm out of his grip. "Bright enough to know how to stay out of trouble. I'm going to the nurse."

"Good Lord," he groaned. "You're stupid. You're already in trouble. You made enemies with the worst girl possible. I'm just trying to help you survive. But if you don't want that, if you want to be alone for the rest of the year and the rest of your life and some day die an old hag with a snaggle-tooth and a billion cats, that's totally fine."

Max felt the need to catch her breath from listening to him. "I think you're overreacting. I have milk on my butt. I'm not dying an old maid."

He huffed. "Just c'mon." He grabbed her arm again to drag her down the hallway, then yanked his hand away.

"OW!" he screamed and grabbed his thumb. A small bead of blood trickled down to his wristwatch.

"I really don't know how things work here in Texas, or how things are with you Japs," Max said, holding a thumbtack menacingly in the air between them. "But I promise you: Touch me again, and this goes in your eye."

He raised his hands up in surrender.

"Okay, okay. Sorry. I just thought that, since you're already at war with Judy and her idiots, you might as well become one of us. And the whole group is waiting outside to meet you."

She lowered the tack. "The whole group? You mean those kids that were with you at lunch yesterday?"

"Yeah, those guys. We're the *Gremlins*."

"Like in the Bugs Bunny cartoon?" she asked. It was a common myth in the military that there were little creatures, gremlins, sabotaging the equipment of pilots and bombers across the war front, on both sides of the war. Roald Dahl had written a book about them, which she'd read at the doctor's office the day before they moved. Rumor had it that Walt Disney was even going to make a movie out of it.

"Exactly like that. We're a group of misfits who've come together for the common good of destroying Judy through mischief."

Max grinned. "That's quite a mission."

Shoji winked. "I've been working on it for a while."

Max glanced down the hallway toward the nurse's office, where she imagined a thermometer and a blanket were waiting for her, as well as a phone call to her mother. Following Shoji would probably still demand a call to her mother, but at least she would escape the rest of Florence Nightingale's invasive habits. She returned the tack to her sleeve and followed Shoji down the hall and outside.

They made their way across the yard, dodging the eyes they could feel glancing their way from the classroom windows, and ducked behind the shed that housed the maintenance equipment. And also provided shelter for the Gremlins, apparently.

"It's about danged time," the boy with the eye patch said as soon as he saw them. He was leaning against the shed, picking something out of his fingernails.

"Shut up, Eric," Shoji said. "She wasn't the easiest to convince."

"How did you guys know to come out here?" Max asked.

The girl, who stood four inches shorter than Max, spoke up. "We didn't. This is where we always are. Shoji told us he'd bring you as soon as possible. Eric is just impatient, 'cause he's from Ohio." The girl grabbed Max's hand and pumped it up and down. "I'm Lola, by the way."

"Dolores," Eric said.

Lola grimaced. "Don't ever call me that." She shot Eric a glare. "Nobody calls me that."

"No, but that *is* who you are. You should have said, 'They *call* me Lola.' That would have been more accurate."

"So you don't come to class?" Max asked.

"One of us does, always. And we speak up for the group when Mrs. Conrad calls roll. That's why we sit in the back. I don't know if you've noticed, but Mrs. Conrad is as blind as a bat."

Max made a mental note to explore all the ways she could use this newfound knowledge to her advantage. "And nobody's tattled on you? Ever?"

"We have a bet going with the others on how long it'll be before she notices," Shoji said.

"Seems like even more reason to tattle," Max mused.

"Sure, except they wound up betting that we'd actually make it the whole year." Eric's grin drooped at the end, but it still seemed quite triumphant. "That was my doing. Talked them all into it, and none of them are the wiser."

Max was beginning to appreciate this little group more and more by the minute. They seemed hardy, cohesive, and just the sort that could be the perfect magician's stage crew. "Wasn't there another of you?" she asked.

"Carl," Lola said. "Big guy, yeah. He's at home. He wanted to wait to meet you until the rest of us weighed in."

"He doesn't do well with new things," Shoji said. "It makes him nervous."

"He's an imbecile," Eric interjected.

Lola punched his left arm. "Just 'cause he's not here doesn't mean you get to make fun of him."

"He's fifteen in fifth grade. What do *you* call that?" Eric rubbed his new sore spot. "Gosh, it's not right to hit somebody on their blind side."

Max pointed at his eye patch. "Is that . . . permanent?"

"Oh, no. I'll die someday and they'll take it off before they bury me. Nothing in this world is permanent."

"In case you haven't noticed, Eric is too smart for his own good," Shoji said. "Lola here keeps him, all of us, in line. She's our conscience."

"So he's the brains and she's the heart. What do you do?" Max asked.

"Gopher, mainly. I'm the legs to every scheme, which was why I got elected to go for you. And Carl's the muscle."

Max pondered these roles carefully. They certainly seemed to be all encompassing. "Okay, then what do you want with me? Sounds like you've got everything covered."

"That's what I said." Eric instinctively winced away from Lola's fists. Lola kicked him instead.

"If even half of the rumors the Monster Society is spreading about you are true, then it should be obvious what you bring," Shoji said. "You bring the magic."

I bring the magic. Max could already see that motto emblazoned on the bottom of a flyer for THE AMAZING MAX. *She Brings the Magic!!!!* It was like the Gremlins were *begging* to have a grand magician at the helm of their group.

"And you all have something against the Mesquite—er—the Monster Society of Evil?"

"One way or the other, yeah," Eric said. "We each got beef with them. The reasons aren't really your concern. Common enemy, that's what binds us."

"What sorts of things have you already done to them?" Max could only imagine, with such a unified force, that they had tormented and terrorized Judy and her minions worse than a tornado terrorizing a trailer home.

Shoji glanced at his compatriots. "Nothing. We actually haven't been able to agree on anything yet."

"Because you're all idiots," Eric said.

"Or because we all keep saying things like that," Lola muttered. "And by all, I mean exactly one of us."

Max nodded. This opportunity was only getting better and better. Her experience with the Mesquite Girls had turned her off the idea of seeking any friendship, and this ragtag group wasn't looking for another friend. Whether they knew it or not, they were looking for a leader. To have four people with such varied gifts and yet a common goal was a gold mine. Particularly because, if she played her cards right, she would not only have them following her in pranking activity, but she could also have them join with her in her own purposes. And a magician always plays the cards right. "Okay, I'll join your club."

"Great!" Shoji said. "Now let's get back to the classroom before Mrs. Conrad starts to think you have yellow fever or something." He went to grab her arm again, then thought better of it and scratched his head.

"So, when do I get to start skipping class?" Max asked as they walked inside.

"You sit in the front row, so probably never."

This cast a bit of a cloud over the whole club idea, but Max did her best to rise above. Eventually she would be making the rules for the club and then she could skip class all she wanted.

After all, she thought, *I bring the magic. There's nothing more important than that.*

Chapter Eight

"Where do you find ferret food in a desolate wasteland like this?"
—Max's diary, Monday, March 13, 1944

Elderly women are far more active than most people assume, if given the proper motivation. This was a fact Max discovered, thanks to Houdini, as Mrs. Morris screamed and attempted to strike the little ferret with her broom, all from the top of a barstool in her kitchen.

To be clear, the little escape artist hadn't meant to get himself into such a tight predicament. When he had popped open his cage earlier, it was merely because his human had forgotten to put her sock back in his hiding spot from which she'd retrieved it the night before. He'd had the purest of intentions.

But then, of course, after organizing the socks yet again, he discovered that the window to the room was cracked open, and he thought it would be best if he sniffed the air outside for any villainous rabbit vermin. While sniffing, he noticed how short a drop it was from the window down to the grass below. So, because he wasn't entirely sure of what a rabbit smelled like, he decided to perform a visual inspection of the grounds.

And, if this loud old lady didn't want a ferret in her house, why did she leave the back door open? And also, why was she enticing him by wiggling that broom on the floor? Surely she knew such activity was an invitation to any and all ferret-type creatures in the vicinity.

Max had actually been quite clueless as to the excursion her little friend had taken until she heard the sound that people make when they first spy a ferret in their house. The sound of screaming.

"Somebody help!" Mrs. Morris screamed. "There's a polecat in the house!"

Max charged across the yard and peeked through the window. "Houdini?" she said as she ran in through the kitchen door.

Houdini instantly feared that the old lady would swipe at his beloved human, too, so he bit the broom and held on for dear life.

Carl came in behind Max. "You got a ferret? I love ferrets." Houdini noted that this giant's hands smelled like sausage as he was grabbed and yanked off the broom. Houdini bit the giant as punishment, but the giant-boy laughed.

"You get that polecat out of here!" Mrs. Morris yelled.

Max apologized and she and Carl ran out the door, giggling all the way back to the meeting of the Gremlins down in the storm cellar.

Now, it is true that the dank air of the storm cellar was far from the most comfortable location for the Gremlins to have their first after-school convocation at Max's house, but after her previous experience with the Mesquite Tree Girls, she was wary of allowing any strangers to enter her bedroom. Besides, her mother had rules against boys touching the same bed as girls. At least, Max assumed she had that sort of a rule. It seemed like the kind of thing her mother would believe.

When Max and Carl returned to the midst of their group, they gleefully retold the tale of Mrs. Morris and the broom that attacked Houdini. Shoji and Lola laughed. Eric, however, was preoccupied.

"This place is creepy," Eric said. He was staring at the wall adorned with the occult drawings made by what Max could only assume were kindergarteners.

"Dark deeds require a dark place to conjure them," she said and kissed her ferret's head. She handed him to Carl, who had pulled out some string to play.

"I don't see why we can't just do my ideas," Eric said, shaking his head and turning away from the lopsided bull's head drawing. "I'm the brains, after all."

"Because dipping their hair in ink is the lamest prank anyone's ever pulled," Shoji said. "Max has some really good ones in mind already."

Lola and Carl sat on the steps playing with Houdini.

Max never planned any magic without Houdini around to offer his opinions. Besides, Lola's cousin had a pet ferret, so Max knew Houdini would be in safer hands than he'd been with Judy.

"Really?" Eric sneered. "Like what?"

"Show 'im," Shoji said.

Max retrieved a small plate from the bench mostly occupied by unwanted knickknacks. On the plate were two small candles. She held the plate between her and Eric.

"I will bet you fifty cents that I can eat a candle and you can't."

"See, that's stupid. And lame. And you guys think she's—"

Max lit a match and used it to light the candles. Then she blew them out and, while the smoke still rose into the darkness above them, she picked up the one closest to her and popped it into her mouth. After five seconds of chewing, she swallowed.

"All right, eat it or cough up fifty cents," she said.

"What? No way, I didn't agree. And . . . uh . . . how did you do that?"

"Oh, I see. So you're a welsher. Figures it'd be you."

Carl started laughing. "Yeah, he's a welsher. He ain't even given me back the nickel he borrowed for a magazine yet."

"I borrowed that today, you idiot," Eric snapped.

"What about the dime you borrowed from me?" Shoji asked.

Eric growled and snatched the other candle off the plate. He popped it in his mouth and began to chew. Or rather, he *attempted* to begin to chew. Unfortunately, the candle wax and charred wick were even less appetizing then they sounded. He stood for very nearly two minutes, his face contorting, his complexion fading, and his jaw straining as he mashed and scraped the waxy block in his mouth. Eventually he surrendered to the realization that there would be no masticating of this little tea-light, so he attempted to swallow. This activity took another thirty seconds, during which his complexion changed to a terrible pale-green color. Finally he ran to the corner to gag it out of his mouth.

All the while, the rest of the Gremlins fought unsuccessfully to contain their giggles. When he returned to the group, Max gave him a cup of water.

"Jeez, I spit it out as soon as I bit it," Carl said as Houdini crawled up his sleeve like Mickey climbing the arm of the giant at the top of the beanstalk. "And I'm the idiot."

"You pulled that on Carl?" Eric asked. "That's just wrong."

Max nearly blurted out a rather scathing commentary, which would have made the claim that the only thing worse than *calling* someone an "imbecile" was to actually treat them as though you genuinely *believed* they were mentally deficient, but then Houdini found his way to Carl's collar and proceeded to nibble on Carl's cheek. In the poor light, Houdini barely noticed the little lasso that Carl had made from the string and looped over his ear. The minute Houdini inched through the lasso, Carl yanked it and had the wily little ferret on a leash.

Carl pulled a band of cloth out of his pocket and put it around Houdini's neck. He adjusted it through a buckle at the end and then, as fast as lighting, he tied a tiny little bell to it, all while laughing off the barrage of bites Houdini was laying on Carl's giant bunny hand. Once he was sure the bell was secure, he released Houdini and the ferret scurried away into the dark, the little tinkling of his bell revealing his every step.

"There, now you won't lose him," Carl said. "I put those on all my rats. Keep a few on me at all times, just in case."

Max wondered why she'd never thought of that herself.

"Why *did* you draw all this junk on the walls?" Lola asked, having silently been reading the incantations scrawled around them for herself.

"I didn't. They were here when we moved in."

"That's kind of scary, don't you think?"

"Hobos are crazy," Shoji said. "But they're almost always harmless."

"What if it wasn't hobos, though?" Lola was the sort who asked the important questions. "What if it was pagan witches and they were using this place as their coven?"

"If they were pagans, they were amateur pagans," Max

said. "Trust me, these drawings are nothing more than some half-witted kid's way of showing that they have far too much time on their hands."

"Which is something we *don't* have," Eric said. "The longer we wait to put Judy and her buddies in their place, the less time we have to actually enjoy this school year. So we need to come up with some better pranks than this stupid candle-eating one." He sighed. "Or my pigtails in the ink one."

Houdini, clearly quite frustrated with the jingling passenger the giant bunny rabbit had put on his neck, inched over to Max's ankles and nibbled at her sock. She scooped him up and patted his naturally pungent ferret forehead.

"Oh, so just 'cause she fooled you, the candle thing is stupid now?" Shoji had had enough of Eric's nonsense. Max, on the other hand, knew Eric had a point.

"No," Max said. "Because every idea so far would be as sneaky as a ferret wearing a bell. They'll see us coming from a mile away."

As if to illustrate this dynamic, Houdini attempted to crawl onto her shoulder, realized that the little tinkler was still on board, and instead fell asleep. The giant bunny rabbits nodded their heads as they understood their natural predator's plight. This, at least, helped Houdini to have pleasant dreams.

"So what do we do?" Lola asked.

The room grew silent as they all attempted to find the perfect prank plan.

"We could get a bomb and attach it to their alarm clock," Shoji finally said.

"Wow, you really watch too many cartoons, don't you?" Eric sneered.

Shoji leaped at him and they fell to the ground, rolling around and smacking each other silly. After a few seconds, Carl went over and pulled them off each other by their collars. Max wondered if he had any bells he could put on *them*.

"Let me think about it," Max said. "I promise, I'll come up with something."

At the top of the stairs, someone knocked on the heavy door. "Lola, you down there?" a woman's voice yelled.

"Yeah, Mamaw! What you need?" Lola yelled back.

"Papaw needs some help with the feed."

Lola sighed dramatically. "I have to go, guys."

Carl stood, "Want some help? I can carry two bags at a time."

"What I want," Lola snapped back, loud enough that her grandmother could hear, "is for my grandfather to get over himself and hire one of those prisoners to help with the chores. Heck, even Judy's folks have one that tends their garden three days a week."

Max felt an inkling of inspiration coming into her mind. She was finally getting over her disdain for the practice of allowing the best-behaved Nazi prisoners to find jobs in the area to earn some money, which they could use in the camp or even save and take home with them. If they ever went home.

But she knew that others in the area hadn't yet embraced the concept of letting the animals out of the zoo. She would have assumed Judy was among that number.

She had no idea what exactly this fact was inspiring in her mind, but she was certain it would be brilliant. Or at least exciting. And probably the thing she needed to get the rest of the Gremlins to fall in line behind her lead.

She stroked Houdini's back. She'd take the collar off whenever Carl went home. You can't be hurt by that which you do not see happen.

Unless you were one of the Mesquite Tree Girls, of course.

HOUDINI

★ PRESENTS ★

The Edible Candle

HERE'S WHAT YOU'LL NEED.

1. A Small Candle
2. An Apple
3. Lemon Juice
4. An Almond Sliver

Step One: Ask an adult to carefully carve an apple to look like a candle

DELICIOUS.

Step Two:

Cover the apple candle in lemon juice to prevent yellowing.

Step Three:

Ask an adult to cut the almond sliver to look like a wick and place in the top of the apple.

AND NOW FOR THE SHOW!

Step Four:

Tell your audience that you learned to maintain a diet of wax from a monk in China.

Step Five:

Eat the apple candle. If you have two of them, offer the other to an unsuspecting audience member to see if they "like it."

Chapter Nine

Max generally made it a point to never become nervous. Or, if that goal proved impossible, she at least would never show how nervous she was to anyone.

As she rode in the car with her mother to meet Major Larousse in his office, even that ambition was severely threatened, for her mother had stated that they needed to have a "family discussion." Merely twenty minutes after the meeting of the Gremlins. A meeting which, she now realized, could have been easily overheard by the ever-listening ears of her mother. The cellar echoed quite a bit, after all, and her mother had been hanging laundry when they left its depths and entered the light of day. And she'd had that look, like a mighty eagle circling over its prey.

She knows we're up to something. And she's not happy at all.

Max tried to decipher what the punishment would be for conspiring to ruin the lives of pretty bullies, and she finally laid her best guess on a written apology and, perhaps, being forced to leave the Gremlins to their own devices. And, of course, the business end of the persnickety switch that had taught many a lesson to Max's backside. Usually from Grandma Schauder, but Max was fairly certain her mother had learned the fine art of swatting before they moved away.

When they arrived at the gate and the guard checked them in, Max decided to turn the tables on her mother and force her hand. "Is this about me and the Gremlins?"

Her mother laughed. "The who?"

"The Gremlins. The kids I was hanging out with in the storm cellar."

"No, it's not," Mrs. Larousse answered. "Though I am happy to see that you've moved on to an entirely new group of friends. That's very Manhattan of you."

Max breathed a sigh of relief. *You have no idea, Mother.* "Well, you can take the girl out of the city, I guess."

"But good luck trying to borrow her train fare?"

"Exactly. Though, I'm not so sure I'd classify them as 'friends.'"

Her mother grew silent after hearing this statement, a troubled look in her eyes speaking all the thoughts she didn't want her mouth to convey. Max could tell it was going to be a long evening.

They parked outside of Major Larousse's office and headed in. Mrs. Larousse paused at the door. "It's a nice day, why don't you wait here on the porch instead of in that horrible green chair?"

"Or I could just sit in his office," Max said.

"We need to talk before we talk to you," her mother said.

Max sighed. "Fine, I'll sit out here and die in the sun."

"That's my girl," Mrs. Larousse said and headed inside.

Max stood for a minute or so, watching the hustle and bustle of the camp maintaining its own busy exterior, and then she sat on the steps and began to draw on the concrete with a piece of chalk from her pocket. At first she doodled flowers and birds, then she decided to move on from the cliché and began to diagram different possible ways for the Gremlins to make Judy's life miserable, all without getting caught.

As she drew a bucket of water falling on a stick figure's head, a pair of drab boots walked up the sidewalk and stopped in front of her. She looked up into the blue eyes of Felix, carrying his broom and dustpan to begin cleaning the hallway again.

"Can I help you?" she asked.

"*Nein,*" he said. He stepped around her to go inside.

"Hold on," she said to his back as he opened the door. He stopped and closed it. "There's something that's been bothering me ever since the rec hall. How did you know that trick I was practicing was from Madame Herrmann?"

He turned and looked at the diagram she was drawing again. "And this? Is this from *Frau* Herrmann as well?"

She looked at the squiggly line she'd drawn for Judy's frustrated grimace. The whole diagram, nay the whole excursion, suddenly seemed even more juvenile than before. "No, of course not."

"Of course not," Felix said. "Perhaps you should apply your energies to the finer illusions and leave the"—he cleared his throat—"mischief to smaller minds."

"Okay, but why do you care?"

"Why would a chef care that a man capable of cooking fine French cuisine is instead making ham sandwiches in a diner? Why would an artist care if Picasso decided to paint signs until he died? Those of us who care about such things, care about such things."

Max pondered his words. "So, wait, are you a magician?"

Felix looked left and right, then sat down next to her on the steps. "I am Felix Roth, soldier of the Third Reich, now a prisoner of war. But before that, I was . . . a different man. I made things with these hands." He held his hands, calloused and cracked, before her. "Before I made war with these hands, I made marvelous things."

"Magical things?" she asked with a devilish grin, a grin he returned.

"For magical people?" he asked. "Perhaps."

"Where did you do this? In Berlin?"

Before he could answer, the door swung open and Major Larousse stepped onto the porch. Felix jumped up and cast his gaze to the ground.

"Why are you talking to my daughter?" Major Larousse asked.

"Apologies," Felix replied. He nodded to Max. "Apologies, *fräulein.*" He moved to walk inside the building. Major Larousse grabbed his arm to stop him.

"Felix, you're a good guy," he said. "Anybody else, I'd throw them in the clink right now. But I like you, okay? So, just don't let this happen again. Got it?"

"*Jawohl,*" Felix said. "*Vielen Dank,* Major Larousse."

"You're welcome. And we say 'Yes, sir' around here, okay?"

"*Jawohl,*" Felix said. "I mean, yes, sir."

Major Larousse patted him on the back and let him walk inside. He held out his hand to help Max up. "Alright, are you ready for our big family meeting?"

Max felt a lump find its way into her throat. Pesky things, they always picked the worst times. She followed the major down the hall and into his office, where her mother was seated in the most comfortable chair in the room, clearly rattled by the content of the upcoming conversation.

"Have a seat," Major Larousse said as he sat in the most menacing chair in the room. Which left the most diminutive chair for her. How fitting.

"Can I just apologize and get this whole thing over

with?" Max asked. Neither of them chuckled. This was not going to be pleasant.

"Your mother tells me that you're having trouble finding friends at school."

Max almost blurted out the newfound Gremlins as proof that they were wrong, but thought better of it. She'd already denied the quality of their friendship to her mother, and for good reason. Her relationship with the Gremlins was a coalition against a common enemy. And any such partnership forged in the fires of injustice would probably not suit the fickle tastes of her parents. Instead she nodded.

"Well, I can identify with that," Major Larousse said. He sat back in his chair and looked over into the dark shadows at the other end of the room. "Trust me, every day I realize that I'm not making any friends in this job. Between the prisoners who'd rather be back shooting at our soldiers, and the guards who'd rather be shooting at the Germans, I find very few friendly faces in this place."

Mrs. Larousse cleared her throat. He snapped his eyes back to his daughter. Apparently, he'd had his *own* lecture earlier reminding him of his long-neglected post as her patriarch.

"But I think we can change that. For both of us." He stood and came around his desk. "Maxine, what is your biggest dream?"

"To find a wizard's wand and finally make some real magic?"

He laughed. "Think smaller. And more realistic."

"To perfect the Floating Card Trick?"

"Bigger."

"To be the next Queen of Magic and travel around the world, performing in every major venue that Madame Herrmann did in her day?"

"Uh, smaller again."

Mrs. Larousse coughed. Major Larousse nodded.

"Right, right, okay, I'll just tell you." He took a deep breath. "Max, how would you like to do a magic show here, right in our rec hall?"

The skills of perceiving illusions had long been ingrained in Max's mind, so she quickly scanned both of her parents' faces to make sure this was not some high form of parental trickery before she allowed herself to respond. As far as she could tell, there was no hint of deception, which either meant that the major was an even better trickster than she was, or that he was serious.

And he's really bad at tricking people, which means . . .

Oh my gosh, he's serious!

She jumped out of her chair and attacked his neck with a hug so tight he might have been able to file for another purple heart, since it took place in the line of duty. He patted her, not how a father pats his daughter, but more like how one might pat a vagrant before they called the police. Still, she'd take it. Next she tackled her mother with the same gusto, thankfully not as unexpectedly, so her mother was prepared to fend off the onslaught of enthusiasm and protect herself from dying of her daughter's excitement.

"And this was entirely your father's idea," her mother croaked out from the vise of Max's arms. "Doesn't he know you so well?"

"Not *entirely* my idea," Major Larousse interjected. Mrs. Larousse shot him yet another look. He shrugged in desperation. "Credit where credit is due, Karly. The whole thing was sparked by a comment from that old boy you were talking to out on the porch."

"Felix?" Max was beginning to feel as though this German was somehow psychically connected to her. And she wasn't the sort to believe in such things. But it was awfully strange how interested in her life he seemed to be.

"Yes, Felix." Major Larousse caught the concerned look on Max's face. "He's not a bad guy, to be honest with you. Probably one of the nicer prisoners we've got."

"But still a Nazi," Mrs. Larousse said. "Let's not forget that." She seemed to be second-guessing this whole idea. Max shot the major a panicked look. To be this close and then have her dream snatched from under her just because her mother didn't like the person who sparked the idea would be unbearable.

"No, no, he's not like that," Major Larousse said, stammering, so unsure of his footing in this conversation anymore.

"In fact, he's been in the States before. Spent a good amount of time here before the war. He's commented on how fond he is of our country. I really don't think he has malicious feelings at all."

"Where did he live while he was here?" Max asked, hoping to add more ammunition to the weapon defending her magic show.

"I don't really know, to be honest. Not even sure how long he was here for, or why, or anything else. He's not the most talkative of the Nazis, that's for sure."

Max could hear the rhythm of Felix's broom out in the hallway, perhaps communicating far more about his character than words ever could.

"I should go tell him 'thank you,'" she said.

"I don't—" Major Larousse began, then he stopped himself. "You know what? Yes. This time only, I'll give you permission to speak to a prisoner. But only this one time, understand?"

Max's mother had the look of a person unsure whether to be adamant because her daughter was cavorting with the worst enemy the world had ever known, or to be joyful that, at last, her husband seemed to be trying again. She sighed and sat down.

Max hugged the major one more time—he again looked as comfortable as a koala climbing a cactus—and then she rushed out the door to express her gratitude to the Nazi.

Chapter Ten

Felix's back was turned to her when she entered the hallway, and for a brief moment she envisioned herself running up to him and attack-hugging him from behind. But then she remembered when the major had just returned from the war and she surprised him in the middle of the night. Major Larousse grabbed her by the arm and tossed her, head over heels, across the room. Thankfully she'd landed on their sofa, but it had knocked the wind out of her. This was when she'd learned that the war does not so easily leave its valiant soldiers behind.

And Felix was a Nazi. She'd hate to see what the war still living in *his* heart would do.

She approached him meekly and tapped on his shoulder.

"Yes, *fräulein*?" he said without turning.

"My father just told me that I'm going to put on a magic show in the rec hall for the prisoners."

He stopped sweeping. "That is wonderful news. Congratulations." He turned to look at her. "I'm certain you will do Frau Herrmann proud."

She blushed, which was not in her usual social repertoire. "He also told me that you had something to do with it."

"He is too kind, of course," Felix said and diverted his gaze.

"Well, thank you," she said.

He nodded. "*Bitte*." He turned back to resume sweeping.

"So you used to live in the States?" she asked.

The broom froze midsweep.

"Where did you learn this information?"

"My father told me."

"How did he find this out?"

"I don't know. I guess I assumed you told him, though he did say you weren't the talkative type." She began to back away from him.

"He is correct," Felix said. He turned back to her, his eyes piercing straight through hers and into her brain.

She coughed. "So, did you? Live in the States, I mean."

"I did." His words fell like a fog, densely filling the air between them and making the empty space seem impossible to cross. Yet, of course, Max was undeterred by the smoke and mirrors of his disposition.

"When? How long?"

He exhaled another plume of exasperation and leaned his broom against the wall. "What tricks will you be performing at the show?"

"I . . . don't really know yet. The usual, I suppose," she said.

"Have you performed for a large crowd before?"

"Yes." A lump, sensing at last that someone else in the room shared its suspicion regarding her skills as a magician (or anything else for that matter), rose in her throat. She swallowed to send it back into the depths.

"What sorts of crowds?" he asked.

"Well, just last year I performed for my cousin's bar mitzvah."

He chuckled, then leaned to whisper in her ear. "Performing for the Nazis will not be a bar mitzvah, *fräulein*."

The disparaging air in his tone, the way his words seemed to dismiss her as just another silly girl, the way he moved as though she stood on land he owned, all of these things acted as the magic spell her mind needed.

"I am aware of that," she said. "And, believe me, I'm going to blow the audience away."

He was not yet impressed. "I am sure that you will. Because I am sure that you already have in your possession the sort of apparatus you need for such a venture. Perhaps a vanishing box, a saw table, or a levitating chair. Just as Madame Herrmann would suggest." He stared into her eyes and let the pause grow to a silent roar. "You *do* have those, don't you?"

She wanted to spit in his eye, but she was sure her mother would protest, so instead she decided to let her words spit on his heart. "I'll check. When I leave this camp without shackles and go to my warm bed, where I don't have an armed guard watching my every move. When I'm able to go where I want, when I want, and do what I want even though I'm still a child, while you, a grown man, have more rules than a toddler in time out. When I'm doing that, I'll check, and then I'll let you know."

A hint of a smile stroked the edges of his mouth and he retrieved his broom to resume sweeping. *"Herzlichen Glückwunsch, fräulein."*

She wasn't finished. She was merely beginning. "So, Felix, when were you in the States?"

He swept for a full five seconds before he bothered to answer.

"I came to America in 1925. In 1929, I moved to New York City."

Max barely kept herself from dropping her jaw in amazement. It wasn't just that he'd lived in the United States for longer than she'd imagined. It was that he'd been to New York. *Her* New York. And, after having seen the Empire State Building, he still returned to Germany and joined the side of the war that hated every single one of the five boroughs. Such a decision could not be explained by logic, or by reason, or any other mental discipline. Instead, it could only be explained by the one medium that understood human nature explicitly. The movies.

"Did you get your heart broken or something?" she asked. After all, it was only a broken heart that could send someone off to fight for Hitler with the sound of Manhattan still echoing in his ears. Of this she was certain.

The broom slapped the floor out of rhythm and his shoulders tightened. "How did you hear about that?"

"I guessed. Was I right? Did you really run to shoot at red-blooded Americans just because of some girl?"

In one move, he dropped the broom, spun, and grabbed her shoulders. His face was flush and lined by the tears that had spilled down his cheeks. "Josephine was not some girl. She was—" he let go of her and closed his eyes, swallowing back whatever words were threatening to erupt.

"Oh, wow, I'm sorry," Max said. "I had no idea."

Felix rushed to pick up his broom and move out the door. "Sincerest apologies," he said as the door closed behind him.

Max felt a bit like he'd just said her line in a play.

Chapter Eleven

"Read this quote from Houdini (not the ferret) today: 'What the eyes see and the ears hear, the mind believes.' Which is why I think some people are idiots."
—Max's diary, Tuesday, March 14, 1944

Shielded by her history textbook, Max was so consumed with drawing her rudimentary diagrams that she barely noticed the empty chair next to her. She had also barely noticed when Judy's name had been called absent, or when Natalie had volunteered to take her "sick friend" that day's homework. In fact, it had only been her overwhelming curiosity that spurred her to check the back row and see that Lola was the designated attendee for the Gremlins that day, although it hadn't been strong enough for her to also notice Lola waving her to sit in one of the empty seats in the back row. Max's mind was on a single track for which there were no stops.

Because Felix was right. She didn't have any tricks big enough for the Nazis. And she was fairly certain she couldn't yet count on the Gremlins to serve as an effective team to support her. She had a great deal of work to do.

When the lunch bell rang, Max was the last to walk out

into the yard. The speed of her feet was apparently inversely proportional to the speed of her mind. It was a wonder she'd left her seat at all.

It was because of her diminished gait that she did not head straightway to the Gremlin gathering zone, but rather meandered around the yard, her mind planning trap doors and false bottoms and oh so many other delightful illusions that distracted her from noticing the two people she had intended to avoid: Margaret and Natalie.

"Hey, Max!" Natalie called as she and Margaret ran, arms linked, to become roadblocks in her path.

Both because of their affiliation with the Mesquite Tree Girls, and because they were interrupting her just as she was plotting the final step to an escape act, Max's voice dripped with disdain. "Hello."

Margaret seemed as uncomfortable in her presence as Max was irritated, but Natalie ignored any tension she sensed and was as bubbly and cheery as a cartoon character.

"We just wanted to apologize for what happened the other day," Natalie said.

"You mean when you gave my ferret a concussion, or when you implied I was a Nazi?" Max asked as she stepped around them.

The girls rushed to block her way again. "To be fair, that was Judy's doing, not ours," Natalie said. "She has her own way, and there's not much you can do to change her direction."

She had a point. "Well then, I guess it's Judy that should apologize. Or are you doing that for her?"

"She's not going to, and somebody has to, so I guess, yeah, I am," Natalie said, still grinning in a way that would seem quite fake if Max wasn't certain that it was sincere.

"And, anyway, I wasn't even there, so I for sure can't be blamed," Margaret added. This, of course, finally distracted Max's curiosity. What was it about that house that had bothered Margaret so much?

"Right, and why weren't you there?" she asked.

Margaret suddenly seemed rather interested in the flying habits of the gnats that zoomed across the grass. "I don't know."

"You ran away and you don't know why?" Max could smell a poorly executed deception like Houdini could smell a hot dog in a lunch bag. "What, do you have mental problems or something?"

"What?" Margaret abandoned the gnats to their own devices. "No, I don't. I just— Your neighborhood really gives me the heebie-jeebies."

"My neighborhood?"

"I'd rather not talk about it."

Natalie laughed. "Oh, you're so stupid, Margy." She patted her friend, who looked as though she wanted to become a gnat herself now that she was familiar with the flight pattern. "She thinks that there are devil worshippers living on your street."

"Devil worshippers?" Max tried to confine her laughter. "That's crazy."

"No it's not," Margaret snapped. "I know you people that come here from big cities think y'all know everything, but I've lived here my whole life. And I'm telling you, there's some crazy folks that live on your street. Crazy, devil-worshipping Jews."

"Devil-worshipping Jews?" Max asked, certain that her grandma Schauder was already packing a bag to come and crack a menorah over Margaret's head.

"Okay, maybe not Jews, but—"

"Probably not Jews," Max said.

"It could be Jews, but maybe not."

Max shook her head.

Margaret sighed. "Anyway, these people are crazy, and they worship the devil, and they hate, *hate* that the military has moved in. So now they're trying to get everyone to move away. So they can have Abilene back."

Max laughed again. "Although I can't argue that Abilene is probably the next best thing to hell, I really don't think we have anything to worry about."

There was a moment of very tense silence between them, which Natalie quickly disrupted with her giggle.

"Anyway," Natalie said, "do you want to go with us after school?"

Max glanced over at the Gremlin area. Shoji was watching

her, obviously anxious for her to join the group. "What are you guys going to do?"

"You heard me in class, right? I'm taking Judy her homework." Natalie glanced around, then whispered louder than she'd been talking, "She's not really sick, you know."

Of course, Max would normally have found such a revelation far too enticing to leave by the wayside, but an invitation to Judy's house was practically a slap across the face, and so she immediately declined the invitation and excused herself from the Mesquite Tree Girls. She hurried over to Shoji, apologizing for her tardiness before he even had a chance to talk. She expected him to issue her a pink slip and point her away.

"Oh, I thought you were just working the first part of your plan, whatever it is," he said. "You know, get in good with the enemy so they don't suspect you're about to punch them in the nose?"

"Trust me," she said, "I am *not* getting in good with the Monster Society of Evil. Not now, not ever."

He shrugged and walked with her over to where the others were already sitting, all of their lunches piled in the middle of their circle like a smorgasbord. She set her meatloaf sandwich in the center, next to the bowl of rice she assumed belonged to Shoji. A paper plate with baked beans and chunks of bacon (which Lola had gotten from the lunch lady) was on the other side of that, and then there were two vacuum bottles.

"I brought chili," Carl said, "which goes great with Shoji's rice. Mr. Smarty-Pants here brought cream of celery soup. We might be able to give it to some cats or something later."

"It's not that bad," Eric said. "And, besides, I also brought watermelon pickles. Did any of you bring watermelon pickles? Nope. And I brought enough for everybody."

Max grabbed a piece of the green-and-pink pickle, took a moment to appreciate the tang, and then turned her attention to Shoji. "So you only brought rice?"

"No, he just eats the rest of his lunch by himself," Eric said. "As a favor to all of us. Tell her what you had today, Shoji."

Shoji grinned. "Octopus hot dogs."

Lola scrunched up her nose. "Nasty. No offense, but your mom makes the most disgusting food."

Shoji shrugged and poured a little chili on some rice. "Anyway, Max, what's the prank? You said you'd have something by today."

Max's pulse began to race as she envisioned the pink slip yet again. The responsibility of planning the grand pranking gesture had completely slipped Max's mind. Actually, it hadn't slipped, but rather it had scooched out of the way so she could devote all her brain's energy to the magic show.

"Oh, I have something, and it's a humdinger," she said. "I just want to wait until after school so I have the time to really flesh it out for you."

Carl, whose eyes had glossed over when she said humdinger, picked up Max's pad of paper and started looking through the diagrams. "Whoa, is this the prank? I didn't know we were going to *kill* her."

Max snatched the paper, which had a diagram for sawing a person in half, away from him. "No, that's for something else. I'm doing a magic show on base."

"We're doing a magic show?" Eric asked.

"No, I . . ." Max started, then stopped.

Of course. Instead of getting them united so that they could function as her assistants, she could get them united by *making* them her assistants. It was a fantastic idea.

No, it was terrible.

But it could work.

Or it could fail miserably.

Either way, you really can't do this show alone, can you?

Against her better judgment, she decided to try. "Actually, yes, *we* are doing a magic show. I'll need all the help I can get for this thing."

"But we don't know *how* to do a magic show," Lola said.

"I do," Max said.

"Then maybe you should do it by yourself."

"I probably should," Max said, reconsidering her reconsidered idea. Still, even after a third consideration, she couldn't deny that it did seem almost providential to have found this group right before the biggest show of her life.

"But we need to learn how to work together, right? That's the reason you guys haven't pulled off any pranks yet. So I think this would be a good exercise."

The Gremlins exchanged glances and then, after an apparent extrasensory confirmation, Shoji spoke for the group. "Okay, I guess. It could be fun. And, anyway, my mom keeps bugging me to do something for the troops. Putting on a show for them will probably blow her away."

Max stopped herself from explaining that the show would be for far less savory characters. Much like you don't jostle a cake when it's fresh out of the oven, you should never rattle a commitment that has been freshly made. Instead, she decided to add an additional layer of appeal to the image. Seal their loyalties to their new boss, even if they didn't know she'd just been promoted.

"Plus, I happen to know for a fact that one of Judy's biggest dreams is to be the first girl from Abilene in the spotlight. So, when we put on this show, we basically—"

"Crush her dreams and throw them in her face," Eric said. "Okay, yes, I like how that sounds. I can get behind this."

The bell rang at just the appropriate time, right when Max had moved past simply having eaten more than her fair share of watermelon pickles into the dangerous territory of watermelon-pickle gluttony. She and Lola strolled across the yard, splitting the meatloaf sandwich, which had gone untouched thanks to the rest of the lunch options.

"You don't have a prank idea at all, do you?" Lola asked once they were out of the male Gremlin earshot.

"What? What makes you think that?"

"It's my gift," Lola said. "Some people are good at art or math, I'm good at smelling a lie. You got this magic show and it made you forget all about the pranking. Right?"

Max refused to answer, which was of course an answer in itself. Through the rest of the day, she could feel Lola's eyes burning through the back of her head, reading her soul like a psychic. When the final bell rang, Max couldn't wait to hurry home. She left before the bus, a fact she only realized after she'd walked five blocks.

On the sixth block, she was attacked from behind by Natalie and Margaret. "Hey, where are you going?" Natalie asked.

Max glanced at Natalie's arms, where she was carrying Judy's homework, and decided a little reconnaissance might not be a bad thing. It was always important to gather as much information as possible about an enemy, and she needed some cards up her sleeve to keep the Gremlins happily following her lead. "I was hoping to catch you guys. I decided to go with you to Judy's."

Natalie squealed, and she and Margaret locked arms with Max as they walked down the street.

Chapter Twelve

Max wasn't entirely sure what she expected Judy's house to be like. Part of her suspected Judy lived in an ornate, well-to-do estate, fitting for her pious and uppity personality. Another part of her believed that Judy came from lowly dredges, the sort of sad background that would explain her need to build her self-esteem on the fallen confidence of wounded classmates.

Instead, Judy's home was completely ordinary. The fence had a decent coat of paint, but could probably use another without that fact serving as an insult. The windows were dusty and streaky in exactly the way a gallant mother would permit them to be. The car in the driveway was modest, just new enough to run well, but still old enough that it was most likely purchased used.

But the garden was impeccable.

As they stood at the door, waiting for someone to respond

to Natalie's knock, it was this perfectly trimmed and tuned garden that captured Max's interest. As though she were seeing a hint of a trap door or a false pocket, the garden implied there was more to the story. After all, who takes care of a garden when there's a war going on?

Judy opened the door and Max found even more evidence there was a great amount of trickery going on. Judy was wearing heels, which by itself was a blaring siren. She was also in shorts, and her hair was tucked into a turban that matched her top. It was not the attire of one who was sick, unless of course they were destined for a surgery that would be featured in a newsreel.

"Oh, hello darlings," Judy said, then she noticed Max. "What's she doing here?"

"She wanted to come along," Natalie said. "You know, to smooth things over."

Judy looked Max in the eye, disbelief filling the space between their pupils. Max felt no need to make Natalie look like an honest person, so she shrugged it off.

"Is your mom a gardener?" Max asked, feeling the more pressing issue deserved the most attention.

Judy rolled her eyes. "Well, I was going to invite you in. I took notes during *Cover Girl* and thought you guys would like to help me learn Rita Hayworth's lines. But, since you've got the Brooklyn Cinderella over here, I guess I'll give you a rain check."

"Brooklyn Cinderella," Max repeated. "What's that supposed to mean?"

"Oh, it's from *Cover Girl*, you wouldn't get it," Judy responded.

The fact that she was correct infuriated Max. There once was a time, specifically before they moved to Abilene, that she spent nearly every day catching a movie at the theater. Movie magic was almost better than stage magic, and she loved to see every minute of it she could. Sadly, she hadn't been in weeks. Not that she'd want to see *Cover Girl* anyway. It seemed like the kind of movie written and directed for the eyes of GI Joe. She'd pass.

"So, anyway, your mom's a gardener?" Max asked again, probably far less politely than the first time. It was hard for Max to tell, considering she was still being far more polite than she preferred.

Judy opened her mouth to answer, then closed it because the answer presented itself around the corner. Or, rather, presented *himself*, in the form of a strapping young man with a chiseled jaw and broad shoulders, finishing off an overstuffed sandwich and carrying an empty glass of what Max assumed had been iced sweet tea. All of these facts, of course, went fully unappreciated because Max recognized him.

It was Blaz, the Nazi prisoner she had seen in Major Larousse's office.

Blaz handed his glass to Judy, who seemed to no longer care about the presence of any fairy-tale character from Brooklyn. "Thank you, *fräulein*," he said and patted her head. He then nodded at the girls on the porch, stuffed the rest of the sandwich in his mouth, and pulled a pair of garden sheers from his back pocket. "But now I must finish the bushes before they come to get me."

"Of course," Judy said, a smile beaming past the newly birthed pink in her cheeks. "I wouldn't want to keep you from your work."

Blaz walked back around the house. Once he'd disappeared, Natalie and Margaret squealed.

"What's his name?" Margaret asked.

"Blaz," Judy said. "Isn't that adorable?"

"He's so handsome," Natalie said. "Like, movie-star handsome."

"I know. I told you."

They continued dissecting the individual characteristics of Blaz's handsomeness for a while until Max felt it was more than enough.

"He's a Nazi," she finally said to throw water on their fire.

"No he's not," Judy shot back.

"Then he has terrible taste in clothes," Max said. "And he really ought to lose the accent."

"He's an Austrian. He didn't want to be in the war, but he was forced into it."

"He's not an Austrian," Max said. "Trust me, they're all gone, transferred to a different camp. He's a Nazi."

"You're a Nazi," Judy spat back.

"You're a hypocrite."

"You're not welcome here," Judy said, then she called around the house. "Blaz! Come here, I need your help." She cast a smug look at Max, as though she expected her to tuck her tail between her legs and run away.

Max was not a dog, in case that was not yet established, nor was she scared of a silly finicky eater like Blaz, so she did no such thing.

Blaz ran around the corner. "Yes, *Fräulein* Judith? What is the wrong?"

"I need you to escort this rabble off my property," she said, pointing at Max.

Blaz came over and reached for Max's arm.

Max stuck her finger in his face. "Touch me and you'll go back to Germany with a hook for a hand, got it?"

He nodded, retracted his reach, apologized, and hurried back around the house.

"I'll see myself off your stupid lawn," Max said.

"Fine," Judy said. "Go home, Cinderella. Enjoy your world of ash."

Max didn't bother asking what on earth that was supposed to mean and instead spun to walk away. As she did, she glanced down at the place where Blaz had stood on the sidewalk and noticed piles of dirt where his feet had been.

Perhaps Judy should hire Felix to come out with his broom, she thought as she marched off the lawn and down the sidewalk, fuming and telepathically firing insults back the whole way.

Walking home from Judy's house wasn't terrible, aside from the heat. It afforded Max the time she so often craved to craft new illusions and revise ones with which she was not entirely pleased. And she knew she'd have to have her repertoire of smaller tricks perfected so she could devote adequate time and attention to training her ragtag group of assistants.

She was thus so immensely preoccupied that she nearly passed the house of Margaret's nightmares without giving it a single glance. It would have taken an awfully terrifying sight to break her concentration and force her to run, choking back screams, to her house.

And indeed it was a most terrifying sight—that pale, thin figure standing in the window, eyes as black as the deepest abyss, hand held high holding a kerosene lantern even though the sun beat down upon the house.

Max crossed the remaining seventeen sidewalk squares to her house in record time.

Chapter Thirteen

Wow, so Judy's making sandwiches for Hitler's henchmen?" Shoji asked, his eyes trained on the apple he was attempting to disrobe.

"Yeah," Max said, the skin of the apple under her knife falling to the ground in a single, unbroken strand. "And the dumbest part was, she didn't even see how much worse that is than me liking Madame Herrmann's magic."

"Everyone's a saint until their own sin is called into question," her mother said as she rolled out the piecrust on the counter. When Max had arrived at the house, Shoji had been waiting for her, and had thus already been drafted in KP duty because the Larousses were so far behind on the apple-pie-making project. Plus it was a good way for Mrs. Larousse to ensure Max would actually partake of the festivities. For a little while, at least.

For Max's part, peeling apples kept her mind off the scraggly old woman in the scary house on the corner. Once she'd gotten her pulse under control, she finally reasoned that there was actually nothing suspicious about an elderly person in an aged house, no matter how many devil-worshipping accusations were levied at the scene. Still, the sight of that face sent chills all over her body, especially when she found a particularly gaunt apple that resembled the woman's jawline.

"I can't wait to see the looks on the Monster Society of Evil's faces when the whole school finds out about this," Shoji said faster than Max could kick him under the kitchen table. Which made the kick more punishment than warning. Which was quite unfortunate, because it didn't deter him from continuing. "Ow! Anyway, this'll finally put those snobs in their places."

Mrs. Larousse dropped her roller onto the crust and spun around. "I'm sorry? 'When the whole school finds out'? And how would that happen?"

Shoji, who had now discerned the meaning of the previous three kicks he'd received, suddenly was very focused on peeling the apple in his hand. "I dunno. These things have a way of getting out is all I was saying."

Mrs. Larousse glared at Max. "Please tell me you don't call those girls the 'Monster Society of Evil.'"

"I don't, Shoji does," Max said and received her own kick under the table.

"It's from a comic book," Shoji muttered, more to the apple than anyone else. "Captain Marvel fights them."

"Maxine, it is not your job to fight the bad people, do you understand me?" Mrs. Larousse seemed more upset than Max had anticipated. "Your father fought the bad people, and look at what happened to him."

Max highly doubted she'd suffer the same fate as the major, whether her mother had been meaning the bullet in the leg or the far more damaging bullet in the soul.

Max's face must have revealed her thoughts, because Mrs. Larousse stepped over and raised Max's chin. "Hey, you know what I meant. You're not a soldier. You're a girl. You can't fight all the Judys in the world. There're too many and you'll wind up becoming just like them. Leave the bad guys to the heroes, okay?"

Max pulled away from Mrs. Larousse's hand. "So you're saying I should ask Daddy to shoot Judy?"

Her mother laughed and went back to the piecrust. "And, anyway, considering the magic show you're putting on soon, I would watch what sort of scandals you're spreading. The pot never gets very far calling the kettle black."

Shoji had given up on actually peeling the apple and was now attempting to sculpt it into a skull. Mrs. Larousse's statement made him pause with his knife in the eye socket. "Wait, what? What's that supposed to mean?"

"Oh, it's a saying, maybe not so common in Japan," Mrs. Larousse said. "The pot calling the kettle black. Because both the pot and the kettle are black, so—"

"No, I got that," he said. "I mean, why would putting on a magic show make Max a hypocrite like that?"

"Mom," Max said, trying to stop the oncoming unwanted information. It was too soon for him to hear. Unfortunately, Max's attempt came too late.

"Because she's performing for the prisoners," Mrs. Larousse said. "So if one Nazi in the garden is un-American, getting a standing ovation from a thousand of them probably makes you Mussolini's cousin."

Shoji set the apple on the table, knife still protruding from its eye socket. "We're performing for the Nazis?"

"We?" Mrs. Larousse questioned. "Max, are you going to have your friends help?"

Max knew a proud parental moment was happening over at the piecrusts, but she was too busy attempting to salvage her precariously teetering partnership with the Gremlins to celebrate. "I was going to tell you guys, I swear," she said.

Shoji stared at the skull-apple for a moment in silence, then resumed his efforts of whittling the poor thing a proper smile. "So the Gremlins will entertain the Gestapo. Yeah, that sounds about right." He glanced at Max and grinned. "And it takes the pressure off in case we stink."

She hadn't felt so relieved in a long time. "Thanks," she said. "But we will not stink. We just need to practice. Practice makes perfect, you know."

"Practice?" Mrs. Larousse yelped. "Oh no! I completely

forgot that your piano lessons started today." She grabbed the kitchen towel and dried her hands, then took off her apron and tossed it onto the table.

"They did?"

"Yes. Up, up." Mrs. Larousse grabbed her purse and patted her hair. "We need to hurry or else we'll be late."

"Who's my teacher?" Max asked as she creaked her weary bones up off the chair. She hadn't planned on moving for at least another hour.

"One of those soldier boys who helped us move in. I can't remember his name. Dave? Reggie?"

"Gil?" Max could feel her cheeks turning an entirely new shade of red, and no manner of mental curse could catch it in time. Shoji noticed and snickered.

"Yes, Gil." Mrs. Larousse checked in her purse for her keys and wallet. "He volunteered this morning. Said something about feeling 'inspired by your playing.' I found it rather touching."

"Should I go home?" Shoji wasn't quite sure whom to ask, so he asked the air.

"No, no, you're coming with us. I need these apples peeled, and if it has to be done in Major Larousse's office, that's where it will be done." Mrs. Larousse handed him a bushel to carry. "Have you ever been on base before?"

He nodded. "While my dad was still here. But it's been a while."

"Hopefully they don't take too much time at the gate. They shouldn't." Mrs. Larousse rushed them out the door and into the car.

The gate guards almost did take too much time checking Shoji, but Mrs. Larousse's death glare was a universal danger sign, so they only patted him down twice and then let him proceed.

They dropped Max off at the rec hall before heading over to Major Larousse's office, and Gil was already there waiting.

"Heya, Half-pint!" He put his arm around her and walked her to the piano. "Surprised?"

"You have no idea," she said as she sat on the bench. He sat beside her and placed some music on the piano.

"Well, don't you go thinking I'm like the crotchety old lady who used to teach you," he said. "I'm not gonna let you off easy just 'cause you're cute. Got it?"

"I'm cute?" She didn't mean to sound as happy about that as she did.

He grinned. "As a button, of course." He tapped the music. "Now, let's get going."

With Gil stomping to keep time, it was impossible for Max to ignore the lesson or distract the teacher as she had with Mrs. Elderberry back in Brooklyn. For better or for worse, with him as a teacher, she would be forced to learn how to play. And it felt a little better than worse. Which made her feel undeniably worse.

To help stem the onslaught of horrifying good feelings, she decided to find some level of control over the situation and resolved *not* to be forced to focus wholeheartedly. And so she didn't.

Instead, while she gave a fraction of her mental capacity to slowly reading the ledger lines and finding the corresponding notes on the keyboard, the majority of her brain began to imagine the program for her performance, which would take place on that very stage.

"PUM-pum-pum-PUM-pum-pum," Gil sang as she went through the scale on the page, yet in her mind he wasn't keeping time with the music at all. Instead he was giving ebb and flow to the tide of applause when she was announced to the room. And as she took her place at the front of the stage and made a dove appear out of a hat. *And* when she set fire to a paper tube and turned it into a rose.

"Max, next page," he said. She nodded, her eyes moving on to the twelfth measure of music, but her ears tuned to the subtle click of the lock on the apparatus. The giant apparatus that stood in the center of the stage.

What was it? The showstopper, that's what it was. But what would it do?

"Max, you're slowing down. Keep up."

She nodded and found his tempo again.

She'd spin that giant apparatus—a box, yes, it'd be a box

as big as a man—around in a circle and tap it three times. And then what? What would happen?

"Max? Max?" Gil snapped his fingers in front of her face. "Hey, where'd you go?"

She shook her head and looked at him as a man from the desert looks at an oasis. "Where'd I go?"

"Yeah, you just disappeared on me."

"I . . . disappeared on you," she said, feeling the desire to shout grow in her belly.

Gil tapped the music again. "Come on, we don't have much time."

"Sorry," she said. "I wasn't paying attention."

"You're right, you weren't."

She resumed the scale with a wide smile on her face. "Nobody ever does."

There was no fighting the joy now, for Max had discovered her great apparatus, her big finish.

And it was going to be a doozy.

HOUDINI

★ PRESENTS ★

Bucket of Excitement

HERE'S WHAT YOU'LL NEED.

1. A Black Bucket
2. Confetti
3. Black Paper
4. Invisible Tape

WHERE IS IT? I CAN'T SEE IT!

Put a half-inch layer of confetti in the bottom of the bucket.

Cut the paper so that it fits inside the bucket over the top of the confetti, touching all sides.

Tape half the paper to the bucket.

NOW FOR THE TRICK!

Step One:

I CAN FEEL YOUR EXCITEMENT IN THIS ROOM.

IT'S IN THE AIR.

Step Two:

Show them the bucket, angling it so they can see the bottom.

DON'T SPILL ANY CONFETTI.

Step Three: Begin to snatch the "excitement" out of the air and drop it in the bucket.

THERE'S SOME. OH, AND THERE TOO!

Step Four:

WELL, IT'S ABOUT FULL, I THINK.

Step Five:

Reach into the bucket and grab the untaped edge of the paper. Fold it back.

Step Six:

TA-DA!

Fling the confetti into the audience!

Chapter Fourteen

A vanishing trick?" Shoji asked from the fluffy green chair that Max would have been sitting in if he hadn't been there first. "You're going to finish with a vanishing trick?"

"Yes, I'm going to vanish myself," she replied, trying to make the hard folding chair as comfortable as possible while she peeled the last of the apples in the bushel. Her mother had left to go to a Ladies Auxiliary meeting, which meant Shoji had been unsupervised. He had crafted many things with the apples. Batman's symbol, a grenade, a puppy's head. He was surprisingly good with a knife. Unless you were hoping he'd actually peel something. In which case he was basically useless.

"Okay," he said. "Sounds great. How do you do it?"

"You just need to have the right equipment," she said. "You barely even need any showmanship."

Shoji watched the unbroken skin of the apple that Max was peeling slide off with almost no fruit still attached to the underside. "And you have the right equipment?"

Her knife slipped and she cut the strand early, taking out a divot of apple along with it. "Well, no. But we can build it."

Shoji nodded, picked up the grenade, and took a big bite. "Sure, Carl can. He can build most anything, honestly."

Max was glad to hear that, though she didn't let on. She had almost gotten anxious about her grand idea, and anxiety and magic do not mix at all.

"You have the blueprints, right?" Shoji asked and her heart dropped.

"No. But I can describe it to Carl."

He took another bite. "No you can't."

This was not the sort of thing a sane person would say to someone bearing a knife. Max noted Shoji's insanity and sat the blade on her leg. "What's that supposed to mean?"

"You can't describe it to Carl," he said. "At least, not so he could build it."

"Why? Because I'm a girl?"

He grinned and nodded, then saw her hand inch closer to the knife, so he retracted. "No, because that's not how it's done."

"And you know this how?"

"I just know it," he said.

She aimed an eye roll at him that would make a sailor seasick.

"Okay, fine," he said. "Try describing it to me. Tell me how to build it. If I can't get it, then there's no way Carl can."

Max clenched her teeth, feeling oddly defensive over Carl. "He's not an imbecile."

"Didn't say he was," Shoji replied. "But he is slower than most kids his own age. And even some our age. I'm just acting on the facts."

She sighed. "We build a box, about this high—" She held her hand out a little above her head.

"Wait, where exactly is 'about this high' on a ruler?" he asked.

"Five or six feet high."

"Five? Or six? Which one?"

She attempted to kill him with laser vision she hadn't yet developed, and then she moved on. "Six feet high, maybe four or—no, four feet deep."

"What's the material?" He attempted to hide, unsuccessfully, how much he was enjoying this conversation.

"Wood."

"What kind of wood?"

"Wood wood," she said. "And there's a hidden door inside."

Shoji, now throwing caution to the wind, took another bite of his grenade-apple and leaned back in the chair, smug as a Roman god watching mere mortals flog themselves for his pleasure. "A hidden door, eh? And I suppose you know how to build that, too?"

Max had endured enough of his toying. "Can I see the puppy head?"

He handed it to her. She promptly beaned him between the eyes with it.

"Fine, we need a blueprint," she said with a sigh. Admitting this fact meant most likely declaring defeat. Where would one find a blueprint for a magical apparatus?

"The library?" Shoji asked, somehow reading her mind. Perhaps the lump that was growing on his forehead where the apple had bounced off was giving him new mental powers.

"No, because of the Magician's Code," she said. "Nobody would put a design like that out for public knowledge."

"I've seen books of magic tricks at the library before."

"Of course. Everybody has. Which means everybody could figure out how we do the trick."

"Do they sell them? Blueprints for tricks, I mean?"

She grunted. "Do you have money?"

He breathed out a long breath of defeat. "Man. It's too bad you only just moved here."

"Why?"

"Because, if you'd lived here longer, I'll bet you'd have made friends with all sorts of talented people. What with you being so good with people and all." He stifled his snickering with the last few bites of his apple.

Max didn't notice. Rather, she was focusing on the growing glow that filled her mind—the glow of an idea. Not a lightbulb idea, like she'd had at the piano earlier, which comes to you instantly and can be just as easily shut off. Rather, this was a sunrise of an idea, one with an inevitable arrival and an undeterred momentum that would not disappear until it had run its course.

"Come on," she said as she stood.

Shoji froze midchew, chunks of apple dangling from his mouth. "Should we let your dad know we're leaving?"

"He's busy," she said without the prior knowledge of that fact and yet with complete assurance that it was true.

"Okay," he said. "Where are we going?"

She didn't answer. He'd find out on his own. Besides, he might not come if she told him.

And so he blindly followed her to the prisoners' hutment.

Chapter Fifteen

The sun was barely still illuminating the walkways through the camp as they went down narrow rows between the dark-brown boxy buildings in which the prisoners lived. Long shadows were cast across the dirt, thick enough to trip over, silently screaming to Max and Shoji that they were in a place they should not have been. Max ignored them. Shoji did not.

"Are we supposed to be over here?" he asked when she stopped him at a corner so the evening patrol wouldn't see them.

"No," she said.

He opened his mouth, then closed it. There was nothing he could say to that.

"This is where the prisoners live," she said. "But they're harmless. Sort of."

"Harmless Nazis," he said. "I'm pretty sure those words don't go together."

The GIs on patrol turned down a path and walked out of view.

"They are, though. They wouldn't do anything to get themselves in trouble, especially with the major's daughter." She motioned for him to follow her and they ran across the road to the other side, between yet more brown huts. Where she was going, she wasn't entirely certain. She had a feeling, though, that her goal lay in this direction.

"That's great for you," he said. "But I'm just a Japanese kid. For all they know, I'm running from the cops or whatever in here."

"Then you're one of their allies," she said. "Trust me, we'll be fine." So strong was her confidence that she stepped out onto another road without checking around the corner first. As he went to follow her, she grabbed him and pushed him back into the shadow.

"Dang it," she said. "The guards are right there."

"Did they see you?"

"I don't think so," she said, but then the voice of one of the guards asking the other if he'd seen something move proved her wrong.

"What do we do now?" Shoji was already backing away from the road, but if they ran there was no way they wouldn't be seen by the guards coming to check the alley.

Max looked down at the bottom of the hut next to them. All of the buildings were on cinderblocks, and there was a two-foot space between the floor and the ground. She dropped down and rolled under. Thankfully Shoji did the same.

Not even five seconds later, two sets of combat boots walked past the very spot where they had been standing.

"You say you saw something in here?" one of the GIs said.

"Yeah, could have sworn," said the other.

Max closed her eyes and tried to devise some magical spell that would force them to move along. But, of course, no such magic existed. And now she could feel ants beginning to discover her calves.

"It's just your nerves, I'll bet," the first GI said. "Here, take a breather." Max heard the *tap tap tap* of a Pall Mall pack, then the crackle of a match.

"Thanks. Maybe you're right," the other GI said. Max's pulse started racing. Somehow, recognizing the voice as Gil's made her even more terrified of being caught. "I don't know, watching these Krauts really gives me the creeps." The building moved ever so slightly as the two guards leaned against the wall.

"Eh, without weapons, they're just a bunch of harmless idiots."

Max glanced at Shoji. A beetle was crawling on his lip. He was putting forth a gallant effort to not move. She was especially impressed when it went into his nostril and he barely even flared it.

"Harmless, sure, but idiots? I don't think so." Gil dropped something on the dirt and ground it with his heel. "I was talking to a buddy over at the hospital—you know Duncan?"

"Oh yeah. Is he back already?"

"Got his arm blown off, so yeah. Anyway, he was telling me about this thing called Auschwitz. Said the Krauts are putting people in ovens over there. Women, children, all of 'em. They're heartless and crazy, if you ask me."

They stood in silence for a few moments, just long enough for their words to sink in to Max's and Shoji's ears. Then the first GI spoke up.

"Yeah, but it's only Jews, right? That's what I heard, at least."

"Sure, yeah, but what does that matter?" Gil asked. "It's still psychotic. I mean, would *you* kill a Jew and toss him in an oven?"

"Depends on if I owed him money or not," the GI said and started chuckling.

"That's not funny, Private," Gil said. He did not sound amused.

"Okay, Private. What are you going to do, court-martial me?"

"No, but I might punch you in the mouth."

The GI dropped his own Pall Mall to the dirt and ground it with his boot. "Alright, alright, Mrs. Roosevelt,

I'm sorry. Jeez, let's finish patrol so you can get some joe. You're on edge something fierce."

Their boots finally walked back to the road, and the sound of their steps faded away. Max and Shoji waited a minute longer, just to be safe, then they rolled back out from under the hut. Shoji then proceeded to blow the bugs out of his nose while Max knocked all the ants off her legs. There were quite a few.

"Did you see that?" Shoji finally asked after squishing the snot-covered beetle between his fingers.

"See what? Us very narrowly escaping getting caught? Yeah, I was there."

"No, under the huts." Shoji pointed to the row across the road from them. "I saw two guys under one of them, just like how we were. But then they disappeared."

"Disappeared as in they got out from underneath it?"

"I don't know. Maybe. I couldn't really tell."

Max pondered this for a moment and felt, in her gut, that her goal lay in that direction. "Okay, show me," she said.

He nodded and took the lead. Cautiously, they crossed the road and went down the next row of huts.

The sun was fully gone from the sky, and Max was pretty sure that her mother would be looking for them at this point. Which meant they'd have to swing by the PX on their way back to Major Larousse's office to acquire an alibi. Which would take even more time, so they really needed to hurry.

Of course, it was dark now and the patrolling guards were even more difficult to anticipate, so hurrying wasn't really an option.

They made their way to the third row of huts. Shoji dropped down and looked underneath.

"I don't know, it's hard to tell," he said as he crawled farther under it. "But, maybe there's something under here."

"Like what?" she asked. She dropped down to peer into the darkness, just in case her night vision was better than his.

"I don't know exactly. A broken plate? Yeah, I think that's what I see."

She sighed. "Really? We came all the way over here for a broken plate?"

"That's not all that's down here, though. I'm going to crawl in a little farther."

"Why? So you can find the broken coffeepots?" She stood, feeling suddenly very frustrated. "Or maybe—"

A hand on her shoulder spun her around, then covered her mouth to block her scream.

"I suppose I should start shopping for hooks," said Blaz. "Or you should learn to stay away from places where you are not welcome."

Blaz was not alone. He had two friends standing with him. All of them seemed angry to see her. None of them were Felix.

Blaz nodded at one with a beard and glasses, who

grabbed Shoji by the ankles and dragged him out from under the hut. It took Shoji a few seconds to fully come to grips with the fact that they were neither alone nor in the presence of guards, but once he saw Max's predicament, he seemed ready to faint.

The bearded man grabbed him by the arm and stood him up next to Max. The third, who had a nasty scar on his cheek, checked the road for guards. Once they saw they were in the clear, the men marched Max and Shoji over to a hut nearby and pushed them through the door.

There were eight more Nazi prisoners seated inside.

Chapter Sixteen

The men pushed Max and Shoji toward some chairs and made them sit. The bearded one and the one with the scar stepped behind them and held them in the chairs. Max noticed that each of the men in the room had a white cloth tied around their right bicep, and on the cloth was a black drawing of a hand.

The Black Hand. These were the ones that had been antagonizing the Austrians. Max's stomach sank even lower once she realized that, even among Nazis, these guys were considered the bullies.

Blaz crouched down in front of them.

"Now then," he said to Shoji, "I believe you owe me an explanation."

Shoji was sweating giant beads from his forehead. He shot Max a look that was filled with I-told-you-this-would-happen thoughts. She nodded.

"We don't owe you anything," she said. Blaz laughed and turned his attention to her.

"Oh, so you are the one in charge? I see."

"No, I'm not," she said. "But my father is. Major Larousse. And he will not be happy to hear that you laid a hand on me."

The man with the scar who was holding her loosened his grip significantly, but not completely. Blaz stopped smiling.

"You are the major's daughter? Ah, yes, I remember you, sitting outside his office like an unwelcome visitor," he said. "And you do not know that these huts are our living quarters?"

"Of course I know that," she said.

"And yet you came here and trespassed."

"You're prisoners," she said, quite adamantly. The grip on her arm tightened. She lowered her tone. "You don't own this place."

"Neither do you."

She realized arguing with a prisoner was not a step in any direction she wanted to take. "Let us go and I promise I won't tell my father that you grabbed us."

The other men in the room began to speak among themselves. One of them whispered something to Blaz in German. He stood and stepped over to a table set up in the center of the room. He picked up a metal cup and took a sip, then stepped over to Shoji. He set the cup on top of Shoji's head.

"And what of this one? Is he the major's child as well?"

"No, but he's my sidekick. Let us go."

Shoji shot her a look at the word "sidekick." But then Blaz bent down so his nose was inches from Shoji's face, and he forgot all about it.

"And why was he crawling underneath our huts? What was he planning?"

Max took a deep breath. "We don't have to answer to you. Let us go."

Blaz didn't move. "Why was this boy underneath our huts?"

"I said we aren't going to answer you. Let us—"

He stood and slapped the cup across the room. It crashed into a plate and broke it.

"WHY WAS HE UNDER OUR HUTS?!" he screamed.

Shoji didn't look like he was about to cry, but he did look like he was about to look like he was about to cry.

She took another deep breath. "Please, just let us go."

Blaz grabbed her from the chair and picked her up by her arms. "You do not tell me what to do! In this room, I am in charge. You will tell me—"

The door to the hut flew open.

"Stoppp!" Felix yelled into the room. *"Sind sie ein narr?"* He rushed in and grabbed Max out of the man's grip. Max noticed that tied onto Felix's right bicep was a white cloth with a black hand drawn on it. Blaz took a step toward her

★ 132 ★

and Felix put his hand on his chest and shoved him away. Blaz stumbled into the table and knocked it over.

Felix took Shoji by the hand and ran with him and Max out of the hut and down the road, as far away as they could go while still in the prisoner's hutment. Finally, when they were three roads away, they stopped so they could catch their breath.

"*Fräulein*," Felix said between gasps. "What were you doing in there?" He took the white cloth off his arm and stuck it in his pocket.

"Looking for you," she said, realizing as she said it how preposterous it sounded.

"Wait, we were looking for *him*?" Shoji asked. "I *saw* him, about a minute before we went rolling under that hut to escape the guards."

"You did?" She suddenly wished she knew a trick to make even more beetles crawl into his nose. "Why didn't you say anything?"

"Why didn't you tell me you were looking for him?" In this match of accusing questions, he won the point on that serve.

"It's not as though you would have known who I was talking about." Max desperately tried to at least get on the scoreboard.

"Sure I would have," Shoji said, denying her paltry efforts. "You could have just said, 'I need to find Felix, the guy who sweeps the hallway,' and I would have known. We met while you were in your lesson."

Felix was straining to hide the smile under his mustache. "Your friend is a terrible apple peeler," he finally said to her.

"Oh, I'm the worst," Shoji concurred.

Max accepted her verbal defeat with a sigh and moved to a more pressing question. "So, are you one of them? Are you a member of The Black Hand?"

Felix chuckled. "They make good coffee. If I have to wear an armband to get it, I'll wear an armband."

"But they're a bunch of bullies."

He shrugged. "They may be. But their coffee doesn't taste any worse for it."

She decided that was an acceptable answer. "Anyway, Felix, I need to ask you a favor."

Shoji smacked his forehead. "Oh, of course you were looking for Felix. Because he used to be a builder for a traveling vaudeville act, and then he was a carpenter in New York." Shoji shook his head in disbelief at his own density. "Gosh, it makes so much sense now."

"He told you all that?" Max was in disbelief as well, but of an entirely different sort. She glared at Felix. "You told him all that? And you just met him today?"

Felix shrugged. "He's a terrible apple peeler, but an incredible conversationalist." He glanced up the road and pulled them both into an alley, just before the guards passed into view.

Hidden by the shadows, he whispered to Max to hurry up with whatever it was she had felt was important enough to risk life and limb over. With all wind gone from her sails, Max proceeded to lay out her idea for the grand finale of her show to Felix, and the challenges that lay between her half-baked team of assistants and the construction of the Vanishing Box. He nodded along and, midway through, knelt down and began to draw in the dirt. This encouraged her quite a bit, and she finished her description with a smidgen of the flair with which she hoped to perform the trick.

"It's a terrible idea," Felix said. And the flair fizzled out.

Shoji noticed the mortified look on her face. "Well, it's not a *terrible* idea, right? I mean, I think it'd be pretty neat."

Felix stood and brushed the dirt off his knees. "Perform that at a talent show or one of your bar mitzvahs and, yes, it would indeed be 'neat.' But this isn't a talent show. You have to do everything with the audience in mind."

"You people are prisoners," Max blurted. "You're starving for decent entertainment. I feel like I could come in and do an hour of card tricks and nobody would complain."

"*Erst denken, dann handeln, fräulein.*" Felix said. "First think, then act. Are they entertainment starved? Certainly. But these men have also been forbidden from any contact with a woman for a very long time. And you would make your last trick to take yet another woman away from them?"

"Whoa, good point," Shoji said. "That's like taking milk from a cat and expecting it to purr."

Max could feel the glow of her idea begin to hide behind the clouds Felix was creating. And yet, she knew he was correct. "Okay, then what do we do?"

"You do the opposite, right?" Shoji said. "You start making women appear left and right. Multiplying like the loaves and fishes or whatever that story is."

That made Felix chuckle. "No, I don't think that would be well received."

"Then what? Be the thirteenth magician to die doing the Bullet Catch Trick?" Max asked, beginning to panic. She was losing her finale, losing her amazing show, going to get in a thousand tons of trouble with her mother, and she was suddenly realizing how close she'd been to death at the hands of those Nazis. Her pulse raced, her throat felt lumpy—

Felix looked in her eyes, and somehow it made it all go away.

"More than entertainment, more than the company of a woman, what do these men want most? What do they crave from their core?"

"I don't know," she said. "Better dinners, right?"

"Freedom," Shoji said, looking at Felix's face as though he was reading a decoded message. "They all want to be free."

Felix nodded. "If you make a *prisoner* disappear, they

will declare you the greatest magician who ever lived."

Max liked the sound of that. There was only one problem.

"Yes, but if I make a prisoner disappear, my father will probably kill me. And lose his job for having me do the show in the first place. Even though it's a trick, the army doesn't have much of a sense of humor."

"So you bring him back," Shoji said. "No, heck, you disappear after him, like you're going to get him, and then you return him to camp safe and sound."

This was beginning to turn into an even better trick than she'd imagined. Still, *erst denken, dann handeln.* Think, then act. "Okay, but doesn't that again put me in a place where the audience hates me?"

"Not if, by even letting the prisoner free for a few moments, you were performing the greatest act of mercy," Felix said.

"You really think they'd buy that?" she asked.

"The lies we believe are the ones we either hope or fear are true," he said. "Tell the audience the story of the poor prisoner, who simply wants to see his beloved's face one more time. To give her a letter with their most precious memories. To kiss her sweet forehead and tell her he has not forgotten."

"And should her name be Josephine?" Max asked, reminding the man that she was not so easily fooled.

Felix coughed and his voice became gruff. "That is a good name, yes." He cleared his throat. "I will draw your blueprint." He poked Shoji in the chest. "And you will be my eyes overseeing the construction."

Shoji grinned. "Wow, I already got promoted to foreman? Thanks."

Felix looked around the corner. "Now, you must both go find the guards. But do not tell them what happened with Blaz and the others. Your audience already thinks lowly enough of you. No need to make your job more difficult."

Max thanked him and they hurried off to find Gil and the other guard. And, while they were enduring the teasing at the hands of those two grown men escorting them back to Major Larousse's office, Max let her mind wander and began to dream of her show. Or, more specifically, she began to dream of the applause.

Even though she knew such dreams were filled with danger for a magician. It was worth it.

She hoped.

Chapter Seventeen

"Loyalty is overrated, except for when it is exactly what you hope it will be."
—Max's diary, Wednesday, March 15, 1944

Lunch at school the next day was not nearly as communal and jolly as it had been the previous time. For one thing, it was apparently Eric's day to attend class, which meant he had plenty of fodder to claim he was more intelligent than the rest of the group. Then there was the fact that it had rained uncharacteristically the night before, so the grass was wet and they had to eat standing up.

Oh, and there was also the little matter of informing the group that Max had neglected a small bit of information when she had corralled them to assist her in the big magic show. Which, really, who cared what the demographic of the audience would be, anyway? Wasn't it enough to know that they'd all be up onstage, receiving the applause and adoration of hundreds of people?

No, actually, it was not enough. At least, not for Lola and Eric.

"No way," Lola said, setting her fork down in her plate

of peas, which she balanced in her hand as they stood in a circle. "There's no way we're doing anything to make the Nazis happy."

"We're not making the Nazis happy," Shoji said, accompanied by a spray of crumbs. His solution for having to stand while eating was to stuff all of his tuna salad cracker sandwiches into his mouth at once. "We're putting on a show that just happens to be for the Nazis."

"That's a stupid word argument and you know it," Lola said.

"Technically, all arguments are word arguments," Eric said. He had opted to drink his beef stew out of his thermos because it was the best way to avoid looking like an idiot, in his opinion. "What you're saying is that he's just making a semantical argument." He pointed at Shoji. "Which you are, by the way. Just arguing semantics. And I don't like it. I'm anti-semantic." He grinned at his own joke and took another swig of his stew.

"I didn't know you hated Jewish people," Carl said.

Eric sighed. "I don't, that's the joke. See, hating Jewish people is 'anti-Semitic.' I was saying I hate arguments over words. So I'm 'anti-semantic.' 'Cause, as we learned in class today, 'semantics' is the meaning of a word. Get it?"

Carl rolled his eyes. "Now who's arguing about semantics?"

Max and Shoji laughed. Eric did as well, though much more halfheartedly.

Lola did not.

"I'm not doing it," she said, her fork still prostrate on her plate. "This whole thing is turning into something I don't want to be a part of. At first we were just pranking Judy a little. Now we're doing a favor for the Nazis? What's next? Selling secrets to the Nips?" She winced. "Sorry, Shoji."

He stopped midchew. "Why, did you say something?"

"She said 'Nips,'" Eric said.

"Say what?" Shoji turned his ear toward Eric.

"'Nips.' She said 'Nips.'" This time Eric was louder.

"I still can't understand you," Shoji said.

"'Nips,'" Eric yelled. "You know, 'Japanese'?"

"Oh, Japanese, got it, now I heard you." Shoji resumed demolishing the food in his mouth, smiling at his moral conquest.

"Anyway, honestly, we aren't doing a favor for the Nazis," Max said. "And it's not just semantics, or whatever you call it. We're doing this for the army. They have to keep the prisoners busy and happy, or else they might get restless."

"Good," Lola said. "Let them be restless. In fact, if we could make them hate their lives and wish they were dead, that would be the best thing ever. I don't want them happy, that's for sure."

"Yeah, exactly," Eric said. "It's like we're trying to benefit all the wrong people. What's in this for us? How does this help us destroy Judy? It's all wrong."

"Not really what I was trying to say," Lola said. "But at least you agree with me, so I'll take it."

Carl cleared his throat louder than necessary. "Speaking of Judy," he said and nodded toward the school.

Judy, Natalie, and Margaret were walking toward them, arms linked, smiles plastered on their faces.

Max groaned. "Now is not the time." She bit a chunk out of the drumstick in her hand, dropped it into her lunch sack, and went to meet the Mesquite Tree Girls. The Gremlins followed her.

"Poor Max," Judy said. "I didn't realize when we stopped inviting you to eat with us that you'd have to join the freak show to find food."

"Are you saying we're the foragers?" Eric yelled from behind Carl. "'Cause . . . 'cause that would make you the fat women who stay back at the caves and feed the babies."

"What?" Judy asked.

"Don't mind him, he went to class today," Max said. "What do you want?"

Judy shot a glance back at Eric, who smiled at her and then at everyone else so it wouldn't seem as though he was smiling at her.

"I want to bury the hatchet," Judy said.

"Where do I file my suggestion of where to bury it?" Max asked.

"Oh, you," Judy said with a forced laugh. "Anyway, I

realized last night that part of the problem is that you, as a very talented magician, need an agent."

Max raised her eyebrows. "An agent?"

"Sure, somebody to spread the word that you're colossal, stupendous, one might even go so far as to say, you're mediocre." Judy glanced at Natalie and Margaret, and they both started laughing. *Built-in audience,* Max thought.

"That line's from *Yankee Doodle Daffy*," Max said. "I saw it seven times last year."

"It is from *Yankee Doodle Daffy*, you're right," Judy said. "But I'm the first person to apply it to you. Not the last, though, if I have anything to do with it."

Max gave a patronizing smile. "No, thanks. I'm not interested."

Judy pouted. "Aw, but I already got you a show."

"You did?" Now Max was intrigued. "Where?"

"See girls, I told you, any dog can be trained if you buy the right treats," Judy said to her cronies. "Yes, I got you a show. My birthday party."

"Your . . . birthday party?"

"Yes indeed," Judy said. "My mother wanted to hire a clown, like she has every single other year, but I said, 'No, mother, I think it's time I grew up a little and had a magician. We can consider it charity.'"

"Charity?" Max could feel her blood bubbling.

"Exactly. And so she agreed. I mean, we are still bringing

out the clown as backup, but I'll bet we aren't going to need him. He can just go on after you to make sure everybody enjoys themselves."

Max weighed the consequences of breaking Judy's nose and couldn't, in that moment, find a downside. Then she felt a hand on her back.

"She can't do it," Lola said. "She already has a show booked. On base. We're going to be performing on base."

Judy forced her smile to stay frozen. "But you don't know the date of my party yet."

"Doesn't matter. She's going to be performing on base. In the spotlight. First girl from Abilene, actually. That trumps a birthday party seven days a week. We don't have to ever do your party."

"We?" Judy's teeth were clenched. "All of you?"

Max glanced at Lola.

Lola nodded. "Yeah. All of us."

"And you should come," Eric said. "We're going to be onstage. It's going to be neat."

Finally, Judy's smile fell. "I wouldn't come watch you idiots be thrown off a cliff. No, actually, *that* I would come to see." She spun around and marched away. Natalie gave Max an apologetic look, but followed in Judy's footsteps with Margaret in tow.

"Man, have I mentioned how much I hate her?" Eric asked.

"Yeah, you hate her guts," Carl said. "That's why you want to make sure she comes to the show."

"To gloat over her, obviously," Eric snapped.

Max ignored them. She couldn't believe Lola had changed her mind. "So you're going to help?"

"Yeah," Lola said as she resumed eating her peas. "I guess I'd forgotten my priorities. But, I swear, if Hitler wins the war 'cause of this magic show, I will never let you hear the end of it."

Chapter Eighteen

"Felix talked to Shoji about the blueprint for thirty minutes today while I did both of our homework. If this is what it's like having help, then I'd much rather be helpless. Well, not helpless, but . . . you know what I mean."
—Max's dairy, Friday, March 17, 1944

Max almost slept through her first west Texas thunderstorm. She barely woke for a moment at the beginning of it when Houdini, after a particularly loud thunderclap, fled from his cage and curled up on her chest to find safety from the giant angry bunnies banging trash cans outside. However, since he was asleep in four seconds, she joined him and probably wouldn't have remembered the incident at all in the morning.

If only the storm cellar door wasn't so incredibly heavy.

When it crashed closed, she jumped out of bed and Houdini dove under the dresser to escape the oncoming rabbit horde.

At first she assumed it had been thunder that woke her. But, after listening to the unique timbre of Texas thunder, she knew it wasn't God's hand that had made the noise. She peeked out her window and, illuminated by lightning, could see the cinderblock dangling from the wire, swinging ever so slightly.

Maybe it was the wind, she thought. *Maybe Texas wind can open and close those cellar doors.*

She had almost convinced herself of this when she saw, or at least thought she saw, a shadowy figure jump over the fence and out of their yard. It was difficult to be certain when you only had brief moments of illumination.

The rain pelted her window and informed her that she would never be able to fall back asleep unless someone went out and investigated the storm cellar. And, since that is what fathers are for, she left the warmth of her covers and stepped out of her room to go wake Major Larousse.

As she neared his door, she slowly realized this was an entirely terrible idea. Waking the major in the middle of the night would most likely result in yet another body slam, and she might not be so lucky to have a sofa nearby this time. So she decided to wake her mother, but then realized how selfish this was. She realized this because of the volume at which Major Larousse was snoring. He had always snored, as far as she knew, but while he was overseas he'd learned new skills that put train engines to shame. Meanwhile, in his absence, her mother had unlearned how to fall asleep while someone is attempting to burst your eardrums every night. Thus, when they were both able to sleep soundly in the same bed, it was a sacred occasion.

Max retrieved the flashlight from the kitchen, put on Major Larousse's field jacket, slipped on his boots, and walked into the yard. It was a tedious affair, because his shoes were far too big for her feet.

The air outside wasn't cool, but it was wet and blew against her neck, and so she felt a massive chill grab hold of her bones and refuse to let go. She shivered and blinked away the fat raindrops hitting her face as she sloughed through the mud over to the storm cellar.

She shone the flashlight on the cement around the door.

Footprints. Muddy, fresh footprints.

Bare-feet footprints.

She shivered again, only this time not because of the wind.

Lightning flashed and thunder cracked as she set the flashlight on a rock to illuminate the cinderblock. She took hold of the block and pulled her feet off the ground. Slowly, the door creaked open. Once the cinderblock was securely on the ground, she picked up the flashlight again and shone it down into the cellar. The rain in the light beam shimmered as it splashed off the concrete and the rickety stairs.

She slipped her feet out of the boots. She needed sure footing if she was going to go down into the abyss.

Was she going to go down there? She stepped back into the boots.

Of course, if she didn't go, she'd never sleep. Ever.

She sighed and stepped out of them again. Gingerly, she inched her toe down to the first step, then put her whole foot on it. She did the same for the next. And the next. Carefully and cautiously, because she was suddenly very aware of how easily her feet could become pincushions for nails, splinters, and various other pointy things.

Finally, she made it to the bottom. She even had the strength of mind to avoid the puddle of disgusting water. Or, she would have, except the entire floor was now one giant puddle of ankle-deep water. It appeared that the storm cellar, while quite handy to seek refuge from the winds, was a terrible place to avoid drowning. She moved back up onto the bottom step and shone the light around the room.

All things seemed in order. The box with the Hummel dolls was still where she'd left it. The plate with the candles was untouched. The walls still had their inappropriate drawings. And the one wall that had been adorned with curses was still—

Max gasped and moved up another step.

On the wall, under the bull's head and the pentagram, was something new. Glistening with fresh paint that dripped with the water to the floor, were two words:

YIMAKH SHEMAM.

She almost screamed, but before she could, she had a better reason.

The cellar door slammed shut above her head.

"No!" she yelled as she ran up the steps. She got as far as she could and pounded on the underside of the door. It was very splintery, so she used the flashlight to bang on it as hard as she could.

She hoped and prayed that Major Larousse would choke on some saliva or his own tongue or something and stop snoring long enough for her mother to hear her.

After three blows against the door, the flashlight flickered and she realized using her only source of light as a door knocker was a bad idea. She set it between her feet and resumed hitting the door with her fist.

She shifted her weight so she could pound with her other hand, and the step moved under her. She caught herself on the wall, but the flashlight rolled away. She kicked her foot to try to stop it and caught her toe on a nail. She yelled in agony as the flashlight splashed into the water below.

And then it went out.

There is no darkness quite like the darkness inside a storm cellar in the middle of the night with the door tightly shut. It is a darkness you can feel, a darkness that seems to inch into your body with each second that passes.

Max began to suffocate on the darkness as she felt around on her foot for the wound inflicted by the nail. She found the spot, sticky from the blood, and held the toe tightly. She sat on the step and did everything she could not to cry.

Just when she thought she might lose that battle, the door over her head creaked and a beam of pale moonlight hit her in the eyes.

She jumped up as the door was opened.

"Oh my gosh, I'm so glad you heard me," she said to the thin silhouette that moved into the opening. "Is that you, Mom?"

Lightning flashed and revealed her rescuer.

It was the pale old woman who lived down the road. Her eyes were hidden in dark shadows on her face. Her hair was matted down from the rain. Her robe was soaked to her bony body.

Max finally screamed.

The woman disappeared.

Max ran up the steps and looked around the yard, but she couldn't see the woman anywhere. Nor could she find Major Larousse's boots.

Max debated chasing after the woman barefoot, but she was fairly certain that would mean getting an infection in her toe, so instead she limped through the mud back to the house.

She washed her feet in the tub and then scrubbed the mud off the floor that she'd tracked inside. Finally, just as the storm passed, she crawled back into her bed. Houdini, sensing that she needed some tender loving care, joined her and decided the most comfortable sleeping position was on her head.

And, because he was correct, she didn't move him away.

HOUDINI
★ PRESENTS ★
The Big Fix

HERE'S WHAT YOU'LL NEED.

1. Two Pieces of Paper

Step One:

Crumple one of the pieces of paper.

Step Two:

Palm the crumpled ball of paper.

THERE YOU ARE.

Step Three:

Hold up the uncrumpled piece of paper and tell the audience you will perform a healing miracle.

Step Four:

Tear the piece of paper into pieces and crumple them up into a ball.

TAKE THAT.

Step Five:

Put the second ball of paper into the same hand palming the first. Be careful not to reveal the already palmed paper!

Step Six:

Place the not-torn paper ball into your empty hand while saying...

EVERY MIRACULOUS HEALING TAKES FAITH AND TRUST ... AND, OF COURSE, MY MAGIC WAND.

Step Seven:

Reach around to grab the magic wand with the hand that has the torn paper. Put the torn paper in your pocket and take out your wand.

Step Eight:

Wave the wand over the crumpled ball.

Step Nine:

Present the restored paper.

TA-DA!

Chapter Nineteen

"I don't believe in ghosts. But if I did, I'd believe in that one."
—Max's diary, Saturday, March 18, 1944

Y imakh shemam," Shoji said while he drew on a piece of draft paper. "What do you think it means?"

"I'm not sure," Max said. "I know I've heard my Grandma Schauder say it about Hitler, so I imagine nothing good. If only there was someplace we could look it up."

They both laughed and then were promptly shushed by the librarian on duty at the Abilene Public Library. Shoji moved the ruler on the map of the area he was examining, measured the distance between Abilene and Sweetwater, and then made the dots on the draft paper to indicate the towns.

"Okay, do you have the Sweetwater book?" Shoji asked.

Max ran her finger down the stack of phonebooks in front of her, found the book for Sweetwater, and pulled it out of the stack. "What are we looking for in Sweetwater?"

"Hardware store, just like in Coleman," he said.

She started looking through the pages. "How far away is Sweetwater?"

"About forty-five miles," he said.

She shook her head. "That's a long way to go for nails."

"You're the one who insisted we do this exactly as Felix told us to," he said.

"I know, I know. And he's right, a real magician gets each piece of equipment from a different place so nobody can figure out the trick." She found a hardware store called Wood's Wood. She pushed the book over to Shoji. He wrote the address on the map. "Still, it's a long way to go for nails."

Shoji kept working meticulously on the map and Max grew more and more bored, which was quite the opposite of how she'd always thought she'd feel when preparing for the biggest show of her life. She noticed the blueprint Felix had drawn peeking out from the bottom of the stack of papers in front of Shoji. She reached over and slid the blueprint out into view.

Shoji slapped his hand on top to keep it in place. "What are you doing?"

"I want to see the design. In case you haven't noticed, I've barely even looked at it since you got it from Felix."

"It's just a whole bunch of construction lingo," Shoji said. "You won't really understand it."

Max tried to let the obvious derogation in his comment slide. "Okay, so what? Can I see it please?"

He looked her in the eyes, shook his head, and slid the blueprint back under the stack. "We're really busy with this right now, remember? I don't have time to explain every-thing to you. Besides, I barely understand it all myself." He returned his attention to the map before him, bliss-fully unaware that Max was briefly considering committing homicide in the middle of the library.

Thankfully, for both their sakes, Eric and Carl emerged from an aisle of books and set the spoils of their quest on top of the map Shoji was using as reference. Max chose the high road as Shoji grumbled and pushed the books out of the way.

"Hey, I thought you'd want to add the rail lines in before you got too far with all the towns and stuff," Eric said.

"Why would we put those on the map?" Shoji asked as he remeasured the distance between Abilene and Merkel.

"You said he wanted as much information as we could find. And the railroads are a pretty big thing to leave off."

Carl pulled a piece of notebook paper from his back pocket. "Yeah, I got the addresses of the biggest ranches in the area, too. At least, the ones me and Pa deliver feed to."

Shoji grunted. "We don't need the ranches. What will we do with the ranches?"

Carl paused for a minute, then tentatively set the paper in front of Shoji. "It took me all morning to make that list."

Shoji sighed and started finding the locations from Carl's list on the map.

Max thought for a moment about going and finding

a biography or a book of magic tricks to pass the time and improve her mood while Shoji did his cartographical magic, but then Lola came and sat down beside her. She dropped a German-English dictionary on the table.

"*Yimakh shemam* isn't German," she said. "It's also not French, Spanish, or Russian."

"Okay?" Max didn't understand why Lola was fixating on the phrase. Did it really matter what it meant? Did that make it any less horrifying that someone invaded the storm cellar and painted it on the wall?

"So I don't know how to find out what it means," Lola said.

"I don't either," Max said.

Lola sat back and watched Max's face, which made Max squirm more than she ever usually did.

"What happened after you found the words?" Lola asked.

"I told you. I went back to my room and went to bed."

"I know that's what you told us. I'm asking you what happened."

Max tensed up in her chair. "Are you calling me a liar?"

"No, I'm not. But your eyes are."

"Well, my eyes are lying about me lying."

"Hmmm." Lola picked the dictionary back up. "Maybe it starts with a *J*."

Max felt her cheeks burning from anger, but hoped she

was hiding it well. One look at Eric and Carl, who were staring at her and Lola like people watching two tigers circling each other at the zoo, informed her that her face truly was the most honest member of her being. She stuck her tongue out at them to divert their gaze.

Eric laughed. "Hey, let's maintain the peace in here, okay?" He fished a pack of gum out of his pocket, took a stick for himself, and held it out to Max. "Spearmint?" He shook the pack at her.

She sighed and took a stick. "Sorry, spending a Saturday at the library isn't my idea of fun." She unwrapped the gum and popped it in her mouth.

"Me neither," Lola said. "Heck, I've lived in Abilene my whole life and I don't think I've ever come in here once."

Max started to respond, but then realized Eric was watching her intently, stifling giggles. After three chews on the gum, she knew why.

She turned and spat the gum on the floor. "Oh my gosh, what is that? It tastes like . . . like glue or something."

"Yes!" Eric jumped up and punched the air. "That's how we prank in Ohio, kids."

Shoji hid his mouth behind his hand so Max wouldn't see how full of glee he was at the sight of her scraping white gunk off her tongue.

"Eric!" Lola scolded. "What was that?"

"Wallpaper cleaner," he said, full of his own genius. "My

mom used it with her Kindergarteners in Cincinnati for crafts. You can make it look like just about anything."

"Is it poison?" Carl asked, looking very concerned.

"Nah, I used to eat it all the time," he said. "See, while you guys are working on this little magic show, I'm going to be pranking Judy like nobody has ever pranked before. Because I'm the true prankster around here."

"I think I'm going to throw up," Max said, doubled over in the chair.

Lola jumped up and helped Max stand. "Let's go to the bathroom and get you some water." She shot Eric a glare of death. "You should be ashamed of yourself."

"That's the mantra of a good prankster, right?"

Nobody supported his statement.

Lola led Max over to the bathrooms, but when they were out of the other Gremlins' sight, Max grabbed her by the arm and dragged her out the front door and around to the side of the building, behind a large bush that hid them from everyone's view.

"Are you going to throw up out here?" Lola asked.

"You were right," Max said, fully recovered from her imaginary bout of nausea. "There is more to the story."

Lola looked both pleased and perplexed. "So you aren't feeling sick?"

"No, it didn't taste that bad, actually." Max checked around the bush. "But I need to ask you something."

"Okay?"

"You've lived here your whole life, right?"

Lola nodded.

"Have you ever heard anything about the house at the end of my street?" Max hoped that she hadn't, that it was all just a self-imposed illusion, fueled by Margaret's idiocy and skittishness.

"The haunted house?" Lola asked.

Max's stomach sank. "Are you serious?"

"That's the one you're talking about?" Lola dropped her volume. "People say it's haunted, yeah."

"Why do they say that?"

"You know how those things are. Rickety old house, overgrown yard, abandoned for forever. It's just what people say."

"Abandoned?" Max felt herself get a leftover chill from the night before. "Nobody lives there?"

"As long as I can remember, no."

Max suddenly had to catch her breath. "Are you sure?"

"I don't keep a population record or anything, so no, I'm not sure. But I'm pretty close to sure. Why?"

Max spilled the full story of what Margaret had said, and the face in the window, and the same lady standing at the top of the stairs in the rain.

"Wow, that's spooky," Lola said at the end of the tale. "Is there such a thing as devil-worshipping Jews?"

Max shook her head. "Not that I know of."

Lola stared down at her feet, lost in thought for a moment, then snapped her gaze back to Max. "*Yimakh she-mam*. That sounds Jewish, right?"

"Hebrew? Yeah, I guess. Like I said, my grandma Schauder said it about Hitler, so it'd make since if it was."

Without another word, Lola took Max back into the library and they found a Hebrew-English dictionary.

"Well, I can't read Jewish, so unless you can . . ." Lola said.

"Hebrew, and I can read the alphabet."

"Why can you read the alphabet?"

"My grandma has things she finds important," Max said. She moved through the dictionary until she found the entry in question. "Here it is."

"It's a curse?" Lola said after reading the entry.

"Looks like it. 'May their name be forgotten.' Makes sense that Grandma'd say it about the Nazis, then."

"Yeah," Lola said, a look of growing anxiousness in her eye. "But why would anyone say it about you?"

Max looked through the shelf at Shoji, Eric, and Carl, who were looking at the blueprint together now that they were free from the painfully stupid eyes of the weaker sex, and let out a sigh. "Probably because they're just stating the facts. At the rate I'm going, nobody's going to remember my name. Ever."

Chapter Twenty

"The show is only a week away and I already have butterflies. This is a good thing, I think, because don't most butterflies only live for a week?"
                                    —Max's diary, Wednesday, March 22, 1944

The corner behind the supply hut had served as Max, Shoji, and Felix's meeting place since Monday. They probably would have found a more discreet location if they'd had more time to look, but Monday also happened to be the day Major Larousse finally told Max when the big show was going to take place: Tuesday, March 28.

This meant that they had to put the entire show together and perfect it in one week.

"Now, where did you say Carl purchased the cross-beams?" Felix asked, holding a napkin on which he'd copied the map Shoji had made.

"At the hardware store in Baird," Shoji said, pointing to the dot just to the east of Abilene.

"And they're strong?"

"They held up under me and Eric standing on them, so I think so."

"Good."

Max was, of course, just as interested in the structural integrity of the Vanishing Box as Felix and Shoji, if not more so; but her input was less than welcomed every time she's offered it, so she stopped bothering. Instead, she chose to focus on a detail about the show that had as yet been unaddressed, and it was a fairly big one.

"When are we going to rehearse?" she asked.

"What about the hinges?" Felix asked, either not hearing what she'd said or not believing it was directed at him.

"He got those in Clyde."

"Excellent."

Max cleared her throat. "I said, 'When are we going to rehearse?'" Even the men walking on the other side of the street heard her that time.

"And he went to a different lumberyard for the door, correct?" Felix might as well have been standing on a different continent for how much he could apparently hear her voice.

Shoji shot her a look. "Uh, yeah, up in Anson."

"I thought he was going to go to Albany."

"They were all out in Albany."

"Hmm. I suppose that will do." Felix rubbed his mustache. "But we already purchased brackets in Anson, so—"

A rock flew into Felix's chest. He looked over at Max, who was primed to pitch another.

"Yes, *fräulein?*"

"When are we going to rehearse the trick? All the best equipment in the world can't make up for poor preparation. And I really don't want to look stupid on that stage."

Felix blinked at her. "You have not been rehearsing? I have rehearsed every day."

"You have?" She tried to keep from screaming in frustration. "What good does it do if you rehearse without me?"

"There is no other way to rehearse this illusion," he said. "I assumed you knew that."

She rubbed her temples. "I don't know what you think you know about magic or performance, but you don't rehearse a two-person act separately. "

"Yes, you are correct," he said. "But this is not a two-person act. This is a one-person act with a volunteer from the audience."

"It's still the same thing."

"No. How will I truly act unsuspecting if I am prepared for what you will do? If it is to be believed, we must both be convinced of our roles. So you must rehearse your part, and I will rehearse mine."

Felix, Max was learning, had a bad habit of being infuriatingly correct in most every situation. She appreciated this less and less as he exhibited it more and more frequently.

After a few more minutes of observation, Max determined that Felix and Shoji intended to go over every single detail regarding the building of the apparatus, and over none of the details regarding the actual performance of the trick. Believing, quite correctly, that there were better things she could do with her time, she walked away unannounced and aimed herself toward the PX, from which she could faintly discern a frosty bottle of Coca-Cola calling her name.

It was not surprising, considering all of the prisoners were out finishing their daily projects before dinner, but completely unsettling when she turned a corner and walked directly into a conversation between Blaz and his two menacing friends. The instant she realized the company she was unfortunately keeping, she turned to walk, or rather run, in the opposite direction.

Blaz dashed to block her exit.

"Look, I haven't told anyone about what happened the other night," she started.

"Schweig," he said, which was the German way of telling someone to shut up. He winced and held up a finger. "Apologies. What I mean is, do not speak of that. There is no need. My conduct was . . . uh . . . what is the word?"

"Stupid?" she offered. "Idiotic? You ought to be thrown in a small box and left out in the sun for it? That's more than one word, but it seems appropriate."

The left corner of his mouth threatened to smile. "You American girls are no petunias, are you? I believe the word I sought was 'shameful.' Particularly now that I know what you are attempting to do for us."

She glanced over at his two friends, who were busy examining a napkin. A napkin that was exactly like the one Felix and Shoji were pouring over back at the supply shed. She couldn't see what was written on it, but the imaginative part of her brain couldn't help but suggest that it was the same map, as well. Of course, that was impossible. And pointless. What use would they have for a map of west Texas?

She turned her attention back to Blaz. "You mean the show? Yeah, I'm the Bob Hope for Nazi prisoners."

Blaz scrunched his forehead in puzzlement.

"Bob Hope," she said. "He does shows for the troops. It's a joke."

"Ah," he said with a relieved smile. "Then there are no hard feelings between us. We can joke with each other."

"As long as you move aside so I can get a safe distance away from you, there's no hard feelings whatsoever."

He bowed and stepped around her.

She tried very hard not to run as she hurried over to the PX. Once she was inside, she grabbed hold of a shelf to steady her swimming head.

It took two Coca-Colas before she felt right with the world again.

Chapter Twenty-One

The car was uncomfortably silent as Mrs. Larousse drove Shoji and Max back to the house. Mrs. Larousse didn't speak because she had a personal policy against berating her daughter in front of people, although this policy went unenforced quite often. Still, when she could, she attempted to maintain it for the sake of Good Motherhood.

Max, meanwhile, was mute because she was still in shock from the initial confrontation that had happened outside the PX. Her mother and Shoji, together, had marched up to her as she strolled, sipping her soda. Her mother had grabbed her by the arm and briefly violated policy by snapping about how Max should not have gone off by herself and most certainly should have let Shoji know where she was going. The mixture of embarrassment and mortification, seasoned with a hint of betrayal, was enough to close her palate and her mouth for a long time.

Shoji, last of all, held his tongue because . . .

Well, actually, Shoji had no reason to hold his tongue. So he decided to break the silence.

"Look, I'm sorry," he said. "I was worried about you. Me and Felix both were. We didn't know where you went."

Mrs. Larousse instinctively turned to glare at Max, then remembered she was driving and returned her gaze to the road. "You two were with Felix? The prisoner?"

"He's helping us with the show," Max muttered while attempting to finally learn how to shoot lasers from her eyes at Shoji.

"Ugh, this show," Mrs. Larousse said. "If I'd known how much trouble it was going to cause, and the expenses for the equipment, and all the time that you should be working on schoolwork but you aren't, I never would have agreed to it."

"But you did," Max said. "And you're the one who always says 'If it's worth doing, it's worth doing well.' So pardon me for trying to live up to the unreasonable standards you've established."

"I wouldn't mind so much if you'd apply those same standards to some other areas of your life," her mother snapped back. "Like your schoolwork. Or house cleaning. Or any other chores around the house."

Shoji suddenly remembered why he'd thought it best to remain quiet.

Max, on the other hand, let out a loud groan and

threw her head back onto the seat of the car. "Mom! This isn't about that."

They turned the corner to go down the road to their house.

"What on earth?" Mrs. Larousse said.

Max leaned forward to see what she was baffled by. "Wait, is that—?"

It was, in fact, exactly what it looked like. A Jeep was parked outside their house, hood up, with smoke billowing out of the engine. Once they got closer, they discovered the location of the driver. He was sitting on their porch, feet up on the railing, enjoying a Pall Mall while he waited.

Mrs. Larousse parked and Max and Shoji jumped out.

"Gil?" Max called. "What are you doing here?"

Gil jumped up, dropped the Pall Mall, and ground it out with his boot. "I was in the neighborhood when Old Faithful over there decided to act more Old than Faithful. Hoped you folks would be back soon so I could call up the boys in the motor club and maybe get a ride back to base."

Mrs. Larousse sighed. "Of course. Come on in and you can use our phone. Would you like something to drink?"

"Still on duty, ma'am," he said.

"I am aware. You're also underage, Private. I meant water or milk."

"Oh, right. You know, I could really enjoy a tall glass of

milk. Haven't had that in years." He stepped behind Mrs. Larousse as she opened the door.

Houdini darted outside.

Max pounced, but Gil scooped Houdini up into the air. "Hey, it's that long bunny."

"Ferret," Max said.

Gil laughed. "Right, ferret."

Gil let Houdini crawl all over his head and arms as he called the motor club and arranged for someone to come pick him up. He continued to play with the ferret while he downed the cold glass of milk, and also while he ate the sandwich that Mrs. Larousse decided he needed, since he would probably miss dinner. When Houdini grabbed the last quarter of his sandwich and ran away with it, Max finally decided it was time to incarcerate her pet.

When she came back into the room, she was horrified to find that, once again, Shoji had decided to open his big mouth.

"No, you gotta see it to believe it. Spookiest thing in the world," Shoji said.

"A haunted storm cellar? Sounds pretty neat, if you ask me," Gil said as he stood. "Let's go look."

Max got between them and the door. "Let's not. I'd hate for you to miss your ride."

"Those boys in the motor club couldn't move fast if they tried. I've got plenty of time." He and Shoji stepped around her and headed outside.

Max followed them, because if she couldn't stop him from seeing it, she'd at least prefer to be the tour guide.

Since the sun was inching its way down toward the horizon, it was darker at the bottom of the creaky stairs than it had appeared to be at the top.

"My flashlight's broken, sorry," Max said. "I guess we'll have to see this another time."

Gil lit a couple of matches and held them out in front of him.

"Or that, of course," Max said.

He grinned as he walked around the room, sidestepping the pools of still water along the way. He stopped in front of the most recent addition to the paintings and shook his head. "Wow, this is definitely spooky." He turned to look at her. "I'm surprised the major hasn't installed a lock or something."

She looked down at the ground. "He probably would if I told him about it."

He laughed. "Oh, you sneaky little thing. Although, this is a pretty dangerous secret to be keeping."

She shrugged. "If he locks it, then I can't get in whenever I want."

"Yeah, that's kind of the point of locks." He dropped the matches when the flame touched his finger. He ground them out and then lit two more.

"You should hear what Lola says about all this," Shoji said.

The fact that Lola had a strong opinion about the storm cellar was news to Max. "What does she say?"

"She thinks it's what you get for working with Felix."

"What?" Max couldn't believe Lola would say such a thing behind her back. Speaking of that direction, Gil dropped the lit matches into a puddle behind her.

"What did you say?" he asked. "Working with Felix?"

Max flinched. She'd hoped that wouldn't come up. "Just for the show."

"For the show? *The* show?" Gil struck two more matches and used the light from them to add shadows to his face. "You're working with a Nazi?"

"My dad knows. He's fine with it." She didn't look at Shoji because she knew the look on his face would betray her.

"And here I thought he was a smart man."

"He is," Max shot back.

"Smart people don't do stupid things."

"Funny," Shoji said. "That's what Lola said, too."

Gil grunted. "See? This Lola girl knows what's going on."

"She does? Really?" Max silently hoped his fingers got burned by the matches.

"Ouch!" he yelped and flung them across the room into a puddle. He sucked on his fingers for a second before lighting one more match. "Yeah, she does. Felix is a shady character. I probably trust him less than any other prisoner."

"You don't know what you're talking about," Max said.

"Did you know he used to live in America? He's different from the others."

"I did know that, Half-Pint," Gil said. "Do you know why he went back to Germany? I mean, since you know so much more than me."

She paused. "No, I guess I don't."

"That's what I thought." Gil glanced at the match, blew it out, and lit the last one from his matchbook. "He got arrested for being a Nazi sympathizer. In New York City. He and some other Krauts were plotting together in a German bar on how to lead an uprising here in the States."

"That's not true," she said, even though she had no reason to believe herself.

"It sure is. They stuck him into an internment camp up in Idaho, where he stayed until they needed to trade somebody with Germany for some American POWs. So they exchanged him for the Americans and everybody was happy. And as soon as he got home, he showed his true colors and joined the army. But then, like an idiot, he got captured in Africa."

"Seriously?" Shoji said.

Gil nodded. "Felix is a lying Nazi who'll say anything to anyone to get what he wants."

Max felt lead in her stomach. She tried to convince herself that Gil was wrong, that Felix wasn't the villain. But Felix was a Nazi. The cards were already stacked against him. "Then why does he want to help me?" she asked.

The match went out.

"I don't know," Gil said, the darkness around them adding to the ominous tone of his voice. "But if you're buying his story like this, then he's already got you where he wants you."

"Whoa," Shoji said. "What should we do?"

Max spoke before Gil had a chance to say what she knew he was about to say. "The show must go on. That's what we do."

"I'm all for committing to a performance," Gil said. "But I don't like the idea of you putting yourself in danger."

Max tried to make her voice sound as brave and strong as she could. One of the hardest illusions she'd ever had to do. "I'm putting on a show on a base with thousands of GIs, fully armed and ready to take out as many Nazis as show up. I'm pretty sure we'll be fine."

"I don't know—"

"Plus you'll be there, right?"

Gil didn't seem convinced. "Yeah, I'll be there, but that doesn't mean nothing will happen."

"Okay, what if you're up on the stage? Would that make you feel better?"

"Sure, I guess, but why would I go up on the stage?"

Max had only just come up with the idea, but she already felt like it was part of the original plan. "I need music for my show. Why don't you join me onstage and play the piano? It'll make everything run smoothly, plus you can keep an eye on all the Nazis."

Even in the ever-growing darkness, she could sense his eye lighting up. "Really? You want me to play like a vaudeville musician?"

"Yes? Is that a good thing?"

"No, it's not," he said. "It's amazing! It's a dream come true, are you kidding?"

"I mean, we'll have to rehearse a few times with you. And we only have a week."

"Oh, don't you worry, I'm a fast learner," Gil said, then he let out a whoop and a holler. "It's almost worth it that you're cavorting with Nazis."

"Private!" Mrs. Larousse called down from the top of the stairs. "I believe your ride is here."

"Coming right up," he yelled back.

Max grabbed his arm. "Please don't tell any of the stuff about Felix to my mom. She's already second-guessing the whole show."

"Hey, no worries, I'm the king of secrets." Gil bounded up the stairs and offered Mrs. Larousse his arm as an escort. "Madame, I cannot thank you enough for the milk and sandwich," he said as he walked her back over to the house.

Shoji went over and sat on the stairs. "Jeez, Max. What have we gotten into?"

Max sighed and sat next to him. "A lot more than we expected, that's for sure. But, no worries, after next week we can kiss our Nazi problems good-bye."

Chapter Twenty-Two

"I should hire a secretary."—Max's Diary, Thursday, March 23, 1944

Mrs. Conrad was busy droning through the history lesson, as she had been for the past fifteen minutes, and thus paid no heed to any of the activity that was taking place in the classroom before her. Which meant that many a note was passed, many a spitball was fired, and many a neck or arm was written on. And Max was free to do as she wished.

It was in this spirit that she had propped her textbook on her desk to hide the twelve slips of paper she was arranging and rearranging on her desk. Each slip had the name of a magic trick on it, and she was trying to find the perfect order for them all so that the show—which had thus far been turning into more of a nightmare than a dream—would elicit the applause she so greatly desired. Or at least not make her look like a fool onstage.

"What are you doing?" Judy whispered.

Max shot her the best mean look she could muster,

accomplished by trying to mimic one of Judy's own looks from previous days, and resumed her planning.

"Hey, I said I wanted to bury the hatchet," Judy said. "Or are you the sort that holds a grudge forever?"

Max sighed. "I'm not holding a grudge."

"I mean, I guess it would make sense if you were," Judy said with her too-sweet smile. "Considering the Germans have been holding a grudge for, what, thirty years now? And since you're practically a Nazi yourself . . ." Judy giggled and didn't finish her sentence.

Max rolled her eyes and nearly fired back her own accusations, but someone handed Judy a pack of gum with a note that said it was from a secret admirer. Judy turned to look at the boys behind her, waved at the cutest she could spot, unwrapped a stick, and popped it in her mouth.

Five seconds later, she spat the stick of gum on the ground and screamed at the top of her lungs that someone was trying to poison her. Over her screams, Mrs. Conrad attempted to calm her down, mainly so she could understand what on earth had gotten into this silly little girl.

Max hid her smile in her hands. Eric was right, it *was* a really good prank.

Mrs. Conrad sent Natalie to take Judy to the nurse's office, sat behind her desk, and started the reading again from the beginning.

Max was happy to see luck finally turning in her favor, if only for a short while.

She hadn't expected just how brief her luck would be.

"Psst," Margaret whispered behind her.

"What?"

"I'm going to fake sick so you can take me to the nurse."

Max turned to give her an are-you-an-idiot look. "Why?"

"I want to check on Judy," Margaret said.

"Then no."

"And I need to talk to you about something."

Max shook her head and returned to organizing the magic tricks. She heard Margaret rip a paper out of her notebook and scribble on it. She felt a corner of a folded message tap on her shoulder. She sighed and took it.

I know you don't believe me about the devil worshippers, but I heard something I think you need to know.

Max rolled her eyes and raised her hand, clearing her throat to get Mrs. Conrad's attention.

Mrs. Conrad either didn't hear her or didn't want to hear her, so Max blurted out, "Mrs. Conrad!"

Mrs. Conrad huffed. "Yes, Miss Larousse?"

"I have to go to the bathroom. Can Margaret please take me?"

Mrs. Conrad shot a suspicious glare over the top of her glasses. "You can't take yourself?"

"I'm still new, ma'am. I don't know where they are."

Even Max knew how ridiculous that lie was, but Mrs. Conrad was so concerned with her precious reading-out-loud time that she waved them out into the hallway. Once they were clear of view from the classroom door, Max grabbed Margaret's wrist and nearly dragged her down the hallway, out the side door, and over toward the custodian's shed.

"Where are you taking me?" Margaret hissed. She would have screamed, but every child knows being kidnapped in the middle of school is only a half disaster.

"If you've got something to tell me about the 'devil wor-shippers,' I want my people to hear it," Max said.

They rounded the corner to the Gremlins' area, but the only person there was Lola.

"Where's everybody?" Max asked.

"Eric's in class today," Lola said. "And Shoji and Carl are building the box at Carl's house. They told me they didn't need my help."

"Of course they did." Max shook off the desire to yell profanities at the skies above for making certain boys so bull-headed and insolent. "Oh well, you're really the only one I wanted to hear this." She nodded at Margaret. "You know her, right?"

Margaret worked very hard to avoid eye contact with Lola.

"Yeah, sort of," Lola said, doing the same.

Max was very nearly done putting up with nonsense from any corner of humanity. "What's the matter with you two?" she asked.

"I'm not supposed to be around her," Margaret said.

"Why? Who made that rule?"

"Judy," Margaret and Lola said at the same time.

"What for?"

"Judy says she's a—"

"How 'bout we don't go there?" Lola snapped. "Or maybe I'll punch you in the face, and you can add that to her list of complaints about me."

"I should go," Margaret said and started back toward the school building.

Max grabbed her arm. "Look, I won't tell Judy about this, you don't tell Judy about this, none of us tell Judy about this, okay? Now, please, tell us what the devil worshippers are doing."

Margaret shot her a look. "I thought you didn't believe there were devil worshippers on your street."

"I don't. But there's definitely *something*. So, spill it. What did you hear?"

Margaret looked around the corner and then motioned for Max and Lola to come in closer. "Okay, listen, I don't want anybody to know what I'm about to tell you."

"Well, that's dangerous information," Lola said with a grin. "Just kidding, do tell."

Margaret backed away. "I don't know . . ."

"She was kidding," Max said and punched Lola in the arm. "She said she was kidding and she's kidding. Come on, just talk."

Margaret nodded. "Okay, there's a lady who lives over by the park. She reads palms and tells fortunes. But nobody knows about her, obviously, so that's why you can't rat me out."

"Cross our hearts," Max said. She elbowed Lola and Lola nodded.

Margaret took a deep breath. "She told me that the people who live on your street, the devil worshippers, are getting more angry about the Nazis."

"They were already angry?" Lola said. "I thought devil worshippers and Nazis would get along great."

Margaret shrugged. "I guess the Nazis, or at least a lot of them, are more devout Christians than we Americans are. Apparently a lot of the Nazi teachings come from the same guy who started the Lutheran church."

Lola raised her eyebrows. "Well, ain't that a kick in the head?"

"Yeah, so anyway, she told me that the devil worshippers found out about the show that you're doing. Only they heard wrong or something, 'cause they've got it in their heads that you're actually doing the show *for* the Nazis."

Max and Lola exchanged a look. This was beginning to sound far too similar to the truth for their liking.

"So what are they going to do about it?" Max asked.

"She said they're putting a curse on you for it." Margaret shrugged. "But you don't believe in that sort of thing, so I guess you shouldn't be worried."

She was right on both counts. Max did not believe in those sorts of things and she *shouldn't* be worried. Which was why it was so incredibly frustrating that she was.

"What sort of a curse?"

"I don't know," Margaret said. "The whole thing spooked me out so much that I left her house before she even got a chance to read my palm. But I haven't been able to stop feeling like I should tell you. So there, now I have." She took a step toward the school building. "Can we go back to class now?"

"You go ahead. Tell Mrs. Conrad I got sick."

"I don't really want to lie," Margaret started.

Then Max vomited on the ground and no lie was necessary.

Chapter Twenty-Three

"Ugh. Why did I ever want assistants?"—Max's Diary, Friday, March 24, 1944

The Vanishing Box stood next to the storm cellar door in the backyard—intact, painted, and frustratingly fully functional. Shoji, Carl, and Eric had just carried it off Carl's dad's truck and set it up. Max hadn't helped them with the lifting. After all, she hadn't been invited to the building, so she assumed the last leg of victory should be theirs alone. Besides, they had filled the base of the box with sandbags, and if they were going to be that stupid, they might as well deal with the consequences.

"So now we can rehearse, right?" Max asked.

"Of course," Eric said. "Wait, you haven't started rehearsing yet? You've only got four days before the show. Man oh man, you're going to bomb so bad."

Shoji slapped his shoulder. "Shut up. She's been practicing, she just meant rehearsing with all of us." He looked at Max with question marks in his eyes. "Right? You have been practicing."

"I've been practicing my whole life for this, so yes," she said. "Now, let's run over what everyone is going to be doing."

"Yeah, I figure you'll want Carl doing the heavy lifting of stuff," Eric said. "And I can run the lights. I'm pretty good at that."

"I have a list, actually," she said. "I've got all your jobs picked out." She held out a piece of paper to him.

He took it and read it quickly. "You want me to hand out programs? That's stupid. I'll do the lights."

Max clenched her fists. "It's not stupid. It's how a magic show is run."

"Look, it's cute, really, but I'm the smart one, remember? Let me do what I'm good at and you can do what you're good at."

Lola, who was sitting inside the box waiting for Max to test and see if it worked, stepped out. "Come on, this is her show, stop being a jerk."

"No, it's not just her show," Eric said and ripped up the paper in his hands. "This is the replacement for pranking Judy and her morons. Which means this is all of our show, all of our efforts. So you need to do it the way I'm saying to do it, 'cause I'm the brains."

"Right now, I don't see a resemblance," Lola muttered.

Max clenched her eyes shut and attempted to somehow convince herself that literally sawing Eric in half would be a terrible thing to do. If only there was a way to actually put him back together. Or perhaps animate his lifeless body so no one would be able to tell what had happened. His disposition might even be better then. His mother would probably thank her.

"Okay, fine, Eric you can do the lights. But I want Carl and Lola working the crowd. Shoji will be my assistant."

Eric snickered. "Does he need to wear a skirt?"

"Obviously, yes, now can we please get started?" She went over to a table they'd set up for her to the side of the Vanishing Box. Carl and Lola took seats on the grass while Eric climbed on top of a ladder and pretended to have a spotlight.

Shoji came and stood next to her. "Do I really have to wear a skirt?"

"Not unless you want to," she said.

"I don't think I do," he said with a grin.

Then Max turned off the girl who was frustrated with the humans she had chosen to work with, put on her top hat, picked up her wand, and turned into THE AMAZING MAX. "Ladies and Gentlemen—"

"There won't be any ladies, you know," Eric called from the ladder.

THE AMAZING MAX waved his comment away with her hand. "Esteemed Gentlemen—"

"Esteemed? Really?" the single member of the peanut gallery said with a groan.

"Gentlemen," she corrected. "There are many nights in history that have been notable—nay, even notorious—which we can all recount at a given whim. The night of Lincoln's assassination. The night Paul Revere rode to call the Minute Men to arms. The night the Pilgrims landed at Plymouth."

"They aren't gonna care about American history, you know."

THE AMAZING MAX stormed off the stage, leaving Plain-Old Max to fend for herself. "Can you just let me get through my lines, please?"

"Can you write better lines?" Eric retorted. "My gosh, I hope your magic tricks are better, otherwise this whole thing will be considered cruel and unusual punishment for the prisoners. And they're Nazis. They don't deserve much."

"You think you could do better?"

Carl leaned over and whispered something to Lola. Lola laughed.

This was a very unfortunate decision.

"Oh, this whole thing's a joke for you guys, isn't it?" Max yelled. "You aren't taking it seriously. You don't care what happens. All you people want is for us to get through this thing so we can go back to pranking those stupid girls that you all are so obsessed with."

Eric jumped off the ladder. "Yeah, I do."

"Well you sure aren't showing me that you're taking it seriously."

"That's not what I was answering," he said as he walked up to the table. "I mean, yeah, I do think I could do better."

He could have stabbed her in the chest, and it would not have hurt as badly as his words hurt in that moment. She took off her top hat and threw it on the table, then threw her wand at his chest.

"Fine, that's it. The show is canceled." She glared at the rest of the Gremlins. "Why in the world did I ever think putting on a show with three stupid, backward, hillbilly misfits and an Oriental cowboy would ever work?" She winced when she said that, but not as much as she'd winced at Eric's words. She turned and ran into the house, the screen door slamming shut behind her. She ran through the living room, where her mother was entertaining Mrs. Morris, and straight for her bedroom.

"Honey, Mrs. Morris says your ferret was in her house the other day," Mrs. Larousse called after her, but Max pretended not to hear. Because she'd already heard enough from people for one day.

She lay facedown on her bed so any sounds she might make while crying wouldn't escape and be used against her. And then she allowed the tears to flow, because they'd been begging to come out for weeks, and if she could at least make *them* happy, perhaps it would start a chain reaction that would eventually solve everything else in her life. At least, it would if there was any magic in the world. Because, if there was any magic in the world, surely the most magical substance of all would be the tears of a child. And if they were also the tears of a magician? Well, then they would be double the magic. If only.

Houdini peeked his head out from the bottom drawer of the dresser. He knew nothing of the idea that tears might be magical, or that they could be the building blocks of miracles, or any other nonsense imagined by humans. Instead, he only knew one fact about tears: They were, as every ferret knew, bunny bait. And so, because he was not quite in the mood to fight off a swarm of rabbits on this day, he climbed out of the drawer and up onto the bed, and he proceeded to quickly lick away every tear that his precious human leaked from her eyeballs.

Max rolled over and clutched Houdini to her chest. There was no magic in tears, but there *was* comfort in ferret hugs. And Houdini didn't mind his position within her arms. It gave him prime position in case any vicious bunnies happened to have caught a whiff of those infernal tears.

HOUDINI
★ PRESENTS ★
The Floating Card Trick

HERE'S WHAT YOU'LL NEED.

1. A Deck of Cards

Step One:

Fan out the cards.

IF IT'S HOT IT WORKS TO COOL YOU OFF.

Step Two:

Have someone pick a card.

Step Three:

Have them show the card to the audience and then place it on the table.

Step Four:

Shuffle the deck of cards but make sure the chosen card stays at the back of the deck.

Step Five:

Arrange the deck so the cards slope back towards you, but the last card is at the same level as the front card.

Step Six:

Point your index finger over the cards while using your pinkie to lift the card up from the bottom. It will appear to float out of the deck!

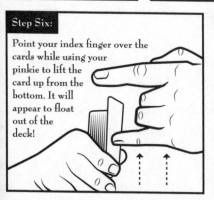

Step Seven:

Grab the "floating card" and show it to the audience.

TA-DA!

Chapter Twenty-Four

Max sat at the piano in the rec hall, tapping at the keys absentmindedly. She had four people to tell about the show being canceled: Gil, who she knew would be heartbroken; her parents, who would probably be relieved, or at least her mother would; and Felix. She wasn't sure how he would take it, but considering the information Gil had given her, she was pretty sure she didn't care.

But Gil was first. Of course. Best to get the hardest task out of the way.

After five minutes of staring at the stage and imagining the show that now would never be, Gil came in carrying armfuls of sheet music.

"Hey! You're early," he said. "Boy, give you a magic show and suddenly you're as diligent as Mozart." He set the stacks on top of the piano and took his place next to her on the bench. "Now, I don't know how you feel about jazz, but

I feel like it's the perfect accompaniment to an American magic show. Here, I'll give you a sampling."

He reached for a piece of music and she stopped him. "There isn't going to be a show anymore."

He retracted his hand and expanded his eyes. "What? Why?"

Oh dear. He had to ask that question. Of course, she knew the reason. It was because it was too hard, and it wasn't even her show anymore, and nobody was listening to her about it—and anyway what kind of a girl tries to be a magician? Sure, in Brooklyn, why not? But in Abilene? That was not the way the road went there, at least not for her.

But all of that was too hard to say, so instead she just shrugged. "It didn't work out."

He shot her a suspicious look. "On account of what, exactly?"

"I don't feel like talking about it."

He watched her face for a few seconds. "Okay, that's fine." He pulled down the piece of music he'd been aiming for. "Not gonna stop me from playing for you, though." He started in to the piece—a nice, slow jazz waltz.

She scrunched up her eyebrows. "You were going to play this for the show?"

"Prelude," he said. "Soothe the savages so that, when you got up there, you were the jolt of electricity they didn't know they were looking for."

"Wow," she said. "You put a lot of thought into this."

"A lot," he said. "Apparently more than you."

"What's that supposed to mean?"

He kept playing.

"No, really, what do you mean by that?" she asked again.

"I just thought you were more of a performer than this, that's all," he said.

She bristled. "I'm a performer. Trust me, nobody loves performing more than I do."

"A true performer doesn't give up until the show is over," he said.

"What? You were the one who tried to convince me to cancel in the first place."

"Yeah, and you fought me on it. That's when I knew, or at least I thought I knew, that you were a legitimate showman. Or show-woman, I guess. And a show-woman wouldn't give up on her show."

She stood up. "Yeah, but what if the show isn't the show she wanted anymore?" She stepped away from the piano and looked out over the empty room. "What if the show isn't even really hers anymore?"

"Okay, now you have to explain what happened," he said.

She came over and leaned on the piano, like Humphrey Bogart in *Casablanca*, and spilled the whole story to him. And, once she'd finished, she could finally see it for what it was. "They stole the show from me," she said. "They didn't mean to—well, except maybe for Eric—but they did. They took my dream and left me out of it."

He nodded. "Yeah, that happens."

"It does?" She tried to think of how many other scenarios could play out like hers to make anyone truly believe that this event was just a thing that "happens."

"Sure," he said. "Dreams have a bad habit of changing on their way to becoming reality. Take me, for instance. A few years ago, I wanted to be a concert pianist, move to Paris, fall in love, and live a long life getting paid to play for thousands." He finished the waltz with a flair. "And now, here I am. Scrounging to play piano for Nazi prisoners, only going to Paris if I'm following a tank, and if I make it past this bloody war I'll consider myself the luckiest son-of-a-gun that's ever lived."

She thought about what he said, the matter-of-fact way he was dealing with the second-rate version of his own existence. "And you've never fallen in love," she said with a broken smile.

He chuckled. "Hey, let's not go that far. But that's a story for another day."

"So what do you think I should do?"

"If you're half the performer I'd thought you were? You'd finish the danged show. I mean, I don't know beans about magic shows, but in music you learn that you've got to play to the changes."

She hadn't ever heard that phrase before in all her years of piano lessons. Of course, she barely remembered what a quarter note was, so that didn't mean very much. "Play to the changes? What does that mean?"

"It's a jazz saying. Underneath every song, no matter what kind it is, you have the changes. The chord changes, that is. And sometimes you'll go to play with somebody and they'll know the song differently, or they'll want to take it in a different direction. But as long as you remember to play to the changes, you'll be fine." He shrugged. "I've always kind of made that my life motto."

She liked that a great deal. "Play to the changes."

"Exactly. No matter what happens, no matter the circumstances, you don't stop until you've made it to the last chord. Or, in your case, until you've said the last 'abracadabra.' Because you're playing to the changes."

She sighed and buried her face into her arms on the piano. "But that's so hard. Maybe I'm *not* half the performer you'd thought I was."

He laughed, rolled up the sheet music in front of him, and tapped her on top of the head with it. "Get out of here, Miss Pity Party. And promise me you'll at least *think* about what I said. Before you go canceling the show, I mean."

"It's only three days away!" she exclaimed.

"Which means you probably ought to get busy, huh?" His eyes glimmered as he smirked at her.

"Fine, I'll *think* about it. As I'm walking to my dad's office to tell him it's canceled, I'll think about it. Okay?"

He gave her a thumbs-up, pulled down another sheet of music, and started an upbeat stride piece. "Here, I'll play you out. So you know what talent you'll be missing if you cancel this whole shindig."

She shook her head and stepped to the beat out the side door.

She could still hear him playing when she turned the corner and came face-to-face with Felix. His face was pale, and his eyes seemed ready to shed tears.

He dropped to his knees in front of her and grabbed her hands.

"*Fräulein*, please," he said, his voice gruff and breaking. "Please do not cancel the show."

Chapter Twenty-Five

The first time you witness an adult crying, it is always a memorable experience. Particularly if it's a grown man. Double-particularly if the grown man is also a Nazi.

Max, who, as has already been established, did not put much stock in the magic of tears, did believe wholeheartedly that public displays of affliction were humiliating, not only for those doing the crying, but also for those on the receiving end. Thus, whether she felt any sort of pity or empathy for this grown, tear-soaked man in front of her was neither here nor there. She had to make him stop crying. This became priority number one.

"Okay, okay," she said to the man weeping before her. "Let's go somewhere and talk."

He nodded and they walked briskly to the supply shed. He opened it and motioned for her to go inside. This was, of course, a very bad idea. The supply shed was cluttered with tools and supplies that could very easily be used to murder someone and hide the evidence in less than an hour. However, the alternative to stepping into the dark and creepy shed was remaining in the warm, inviting, and always-revealing sunshine. She decided to forego safety in an attempt to also escape embarrassment.

Once they were inside and the door was closed, they stood illuminated by only a single lightbulb that dangled from the ceiling.

"Please, do not cancel the show," Felix started again.

She held up her hand. "Hold on," she said. "Were you eavesdropping on my conversation with Gil?"

"Yes," he said without hesitation. "I overheard you say you were canceling the show, and so I listened because I could not believe such a thing was true."

"Well, it is true," she said, even though she was actually no longer sure how true it was.

When she said that, he covered his mouth with his hand and turned from her. "No, no, no, *Lassen Sie es nicht wahr sein.*"

"I just told you, it *is* true," she said. "*Es stimmt.* So you might as well get over it."

Her voice speaking German seemed to knock the crying off his face, and he stared at her, puzzled and seemingly amused. "*Stimmt es?*"

"I don't know how to lie in German," she said.

That made him chuckle, but everything else made him

end his chuckling before it could change the mood in the air. "But why? Why are you canceling?"

"I thought you were listening. I told all this to Gil."

"I did not come by until you were finishing your discussion."

She sighed. She did not feel like going into all the details of why she felt the way she did and how she came to her decision, especially not with him. "There're lots of reasons," she said.

"I am listening."

"Okay, fine, if you want to hear a reason, I'll name one." She picked up a hammer and pointed it at him. "You haven't been completely honest with me."

He raised his eyebrows. "How so?"

"You made me believe that you were some poor sap who got his heart broken and that's why you went back to Germany. But that's not even close to the truth. You were arrested for attempting to incite a Nazi uprising in America. And don't try to deny it."

He stared at her for a while, possibly attempting to find a way to deny what she was saying. Finally, he slid a mop bucket over and sat down. "Yes, that was why I was arrested."

"Aha! So you admit it."

He nodded. "But I was not attempting to incite an uprising."

"Then why did they arrest you?"

"Because I am a fool."

She paused to ponder that statement. "Okay, yeah, I'll believe that. Go on."

He took a very deep breath and let it out slowly. "The day I was arrested was the day I had intended to make the most rash, headstrong, dangerous decision of my life."

"What, were you going to assassinate the president or something?"

He scolded her with his eyes. "Absolutely not," he said. "Rather, I was going to ask Josephine to become my wife."

She set the hammer down on the floor. "That's not what I was expecting."

"I had purchased the ring and a dozen roses. I had everything I needed for a beautiful proposal. Everything except courage. So I went to a place that sells courage by the pint."

"You mean like a bar?"

"A pub," he said. "A German pub in Manhattan. I went and intended to only have one drink, but a group of men overheard my plans, and so they each bought me another glass. In appreciation, I sat with them at their table and contributed to their rousing conversation."

"Let me guess, they were Nazi sympathizers and you got guilt by association."

"They were Nazi sympathizers, yes," he said. "And I was a fool. As they spoke, it reminded me of the conversations *mein Vater* would have with the friends he fought with in the Great War. Speaking of the offense that had been leveled on our home country and the need for *Deutschland* to rise again. And so, perhaps to honor my father or perhaps simply to fit in, I spoke as they were, as he once did. I said the very things that had driven me away from my family in the first place. I pretended that I believed in their cause."

Max began to feel sorry, not so much for Felix, but for Josephine. "So somebody heard you."

He nodded. "A few hours later, I walked to Josephine's house, finally filled with the courage I had been seeking. But reaching her house was not part of my destiny. Two blocks away, I was stopped by four men in black suits. They took me and shackled me in handcuffs. They forced me into the back of their car, and they drove me away. I strained to see the flowers they had taken from my hands and tossed onto the sidewalk. They were already trampled by the time we turned a corner."

"What about Josephine? What did she say when she found out?"

"I do not know. I wrote to her the moment I was allowed, but she never sent me anything in return. Perhaps they were not delivering my letters to her, or perhaps they were holding hers from me. Or, as I truly began to believe, perhaps she had heard the accusations against me and could not love a man such as that. Such as me."

Max could feel that she was yet again buying into the

words and deeds of this man, in spite of all the warnings Gil had given her. "That's really sad. I mean that. But, still, I don't see why you care about this magic show so much. Who cares if I cancel?"

He reached into his pocket and pulled out the map-napkin. "When they took me from my Josephine, they took away everything I loved. When they sent me to Germany and I was made a Nazi, I became everything I hate." He looked up at her. "A life in which there is no love, in which there is only hate, this is not a life worth living. And it was not a life I intended to live much longer."

"What are you saying?"

"You and your magic show gave me a reason to stay alive another day."

The gravity of his words sank into Max's cranium. Every magician tries their best to paint their tricks as though someone's very life is at stake. To actually have someone's life in her hands, though, was an entirely new responsibility. And not one with which she felt particularly comfortable.

Of course, responsibility is most often not what we request, but rather what we are given. And, as such, she knew what she must do.

"Okay, fine, if you're gonna kill yourself over it, I won't cancel the show. But you better make sure it's a danged good one. And our final trick had better blow everybody away."

He jumped up, grabbed her hand, and kissed it. "*Fräulein*,

I promise you, the final trick will be remembered forever."

She sincerely hoped he meant that in a good way. And, of course, she also hoped she could somehow get the Gremlins on the same page.

But, like Gil said, a true performer sees the show through to the end. No matter how many Erics stood in her way.

Chapter Twenty-Six

"No, I wasn't giving up. I was just exploring all my options. Okay, I was giving up."—Max's Diary, Saturday, March 25, 1944

It occurred to Max in a dream that the reason she had been so easily railroaded during the rehearsal was because she had been outnumbered, even with Lola on her side. The dream hadn't been about the magic show or even anything to do with the Gremlins. She was back in Brooklyn, and had stopped at the corner drugstore on her way home from school to purchase a bottle of Coca-Cola with a nickel that she'd found under an elephant's back leg. While she was sipping the soda, she had the epiphany and told the drugstore owner, a green man who looked surprisingly like Jack Benny, that she'd figured everything out. And he, of course, replied with a growl and a snarl. Then he licked her nose, and she awoke to Houdini, whom she'd forgotten to feed before bed.

So Max decided that her best course of action was to meet with each of the Gremlins individually. Starting with Lola.

"So it was really just because of Eric?" Lola asked in disbelief after Max had apologized. "I thought you were bluffing to cover that you were scared of the witch's curse or whatever Margaret was talking about."

"What?" Max had almost forgotten about that. Well, not *forgotten*, but almost stopped thinking about it. Which of course meant that she'd almost stopped being bothered and unsettled at the thought of someone actually taking the time to cast a curse on her and those who lived in her household. "No, I couldn't care less about that." (Another half-truth, of course. She could care much less. But the saying isn't "I could probably care less, but I still care very little, and as such am not inclined to make decisions with this topic in mind." It doesn't roll off the tongue nearly as well.)

"Oh. Well, good Lord, if I'd known he was bothering you so much, I would have punched him in the face. It's been a while since I did that. He's due."

Max was grateful for the sentiment, but it begged a further line of questioning. "Why do you even hang out with him? He's such a jerk."

"Yeah, but at least he's a jerk to everybody. Which is really helpful when you need someone to be a jerk for you."

"I don't think I've ever been in a situation where having a jerk-on-call would've been handy."

"Oh, you will. And then you'll appreciate him," Lola

said. "Trust me. He's gotten me out of a lot of jams. So we tolerate his big mouth."

Max filed this information away for a rainy day and, after confirming that Lola was committed to following Max's lead during the show, moved on to her next objective.

Carl.

She found out from his mother that he was over at an older lady's house digging up a stump for her, so she made him a sandwich and some lemonade. This was mainly to convince her mother to drive her over so they could deliver him some lunch. Mrs. Larousse was a sucker for giving food to working boys. It was her single vice. Well, that and *The Burns and Allen Show.*

"What're you doing over here?" Carl asked as he downed the lemonade while leaning on his shovel. Perspiration dripped from his forehead and down his arms and back. "I thought you'd be practicing for the show."

She was momentarily derailed by his apparent ignorance of the level of drama she had been experiencing since she'd last seen him. "Uh, I—don't you remember? I said I wasn't going to do it anymore."

He resumed shoveling. "Oh, I just figured you were being emotional 'cause Eric's such a knucklehead. I didn't put no stock in that. If I had a nickel for every time somebody's been mean to me on account of him . . ." He laughed. "But then again, I am an imbecile, so maybe that's where the problem is."

She suddenly felt indignant. "Stop saying that about yourself. You're not an imbecile."

"Well I ain't smart."

"You're not good at school," she said. "So what? There's more to life than being a great student."

He stopped shoveling again and looked into her eyes to see if she was being serious. "I don't act my age either. You know I'm old enough to drive? Got my license and everything. But I can't handle being around people that are old enough to drive. I don't mix well with them."

"Okay, so maybe your mind and your body grow at different speeds—"

"Isn't that the definition of an imbecile?" he asked.

She handed him the sandwich. "Here, eat something."

He smiled and took it. "Guess I won that argument, didn't I?"

She glared at him. "No, you didn't. Who cares what speed you work at? Who cares what age you're supposed to be? You are who you are, and I think you're pretty darn good at it."

He raised one eyebrow and took a bite of the sandwich. "Wow. If you're trying to win me over to your side, you just did it. Consider me signed on to Team Max from here to eternity."

"Wow. Eternity?"

He thought about that. "Okay, maybe not eternity, 'cause I don't know if you'll make it to heaven or not, but at least until we finish school together."

With two of the Gremlins now fully committed to her plan, Max felt as though the momentum was moving in her favor.

Then she went to meet with Shoji.

"What do you want?" he snarled when he first opened the door, but then he realized Mrs. Larousse was standing next to her daughter, and so he quickly changed his tune. "I mean, won't you come in?"

They stepped into the house and he quickly admonished them to take off their shoes. While they disrobed their feet, he moved to the hallway and called out, "Mama, we have company."

They heard some pots rattling in the kitchen, and then, wiping her hands on an apron, Mrs. Jingu came into the living room. She was a slender Japanese woman with a smile that matched her son's and worry lines that matched the times in which they lived.

"Hello," she said to the Larousses. "Please, come in and have a seat."

Max was never one for formalities. "Can I talk to Shoji alone, actually? It won't take too much time."

"Max!" Mrs. Larousse said, perhaps over-exaggerating her embarrassment because she would have been embarrassed to be thought of as one who did not get embarrassed by such embarrassing behavior.

"No, that's okay," Mrs. Jingu said. "Shoji, go eat your lunch in the kitchen and your friend can talk to you there. I made octopus hot dogs."

"Aw, come on, Mom," Shoji started.

"Yamate!" she yelled, and he grabbed Max by the wrist and hurried into the kitchen.

"Okay, start talking," he said as he went to the counter and picked up the chopsticks next to a plate of rice, topped with with seven odd little pink creatures with tentacles on them.

Max stared at the contents of his lunch for a few seconds, and then she laughed. "Wait, those are literally hot dogs that your mom cut to look like octopuses, aren't they?"

He grinned. "Yeah."

"So why does everyone make you eat them before you join the group?"

"I've never told them what they are," he said as he popped one in his mouth. "I don't like to share my food."

She shook her head. "Wow, you are—"

He pointed his chopsticks at her. "Stop. I'm still sore at you."

"I know, and I shouldn't have called you all stupid hill-billies."

"That doesn't bother me. Heck, I'd have *liked* to have been called that."

She scrunched up her forehead. "What are you talking about?"

He ate another octo–hot dog. "You called me an Oriental cowboy. Now that's all Eric calls me. Even when he's talking to my mom."

She didn't see the problem. It seemed better than a hill-billy. Not much better, but still, better. "That's just 'cause Eric's a jerk."

"He's always been a jerk. He's called me 'slant-eyes,' 'Nagasaki,' 'Most Honolable Blother,' and all sorts of stupid things. But not an Oriental cowboy. Not till you said that."

"So be mad at him."

He shrugged. "There's no point. He won't understand why I'm upset, or he won't care, or whatever. But I guess I thought—I don't know—that you and me were better friends than that. Better friends than me and the others. And then you went and called me that. So I'm mad at you until you apologize."

She took a breath. "Okay. I'm sorry. For everything I said. I was so preoccupied with wanting you guys to be my assistants, I forgot that I need you to be my friends. And, even if I don't get the magic show of my dreams, I'd rather have the friends I didn't know I wanted."

He glared at her for all of two seconds, then broke out in a wide grin. "Okay. We're friends."

"What? You got over it that fast?" She smelled some trickery. "Wait, were you faking?"

He nodded. "Oriental cowboy is actually pretty funny. Just not from Eric."

"You're stupid," she said.

"Hey! Friendship over."

"Shut up."

He laughed. "Okay, okay. But, just so the truth is known, I am not a cowboy."

"Yeah, I know. I just said that 'cause I was mad."

"I've never even ridden a horse."

"Right."

"Of course, if you think girls like cowboys, then maybe I could be a cowboy."

"I don't really know. Maybe? Some girls might. I guess."

"I mean, if you think cowboys are good-looking or something, then maybe I want to be a cowboy. Or something."

She was beginning to grow uncomfortable with the conversation. "I don't think cowboys are cute. Can we move on?"

He laughed again and ate three more of his octo–hot dogs. He offered her one. "So, are we still doing the show on Tuesday or what?" he asked.

"Yup," she said. "And I've already gotten Lola and Carl onboard. And now you, I assume."

He nodded. "Yeah, that should be good."

"Now I just need to get Eric."

He stopped chewing. "Oh, wow. That's gonna be a problem."

"Why?"

"'Cause he hates your guts."

She absentmindedly grabbed one of the octo–hot dogs and bit off two tentacles. "Really? Since when?"

"Since he met you. That's his default with people. He hates your guts until he decides he's going to start liking you. And he hasn't started liking you yet."

She amputated the remaining tentacles and then devoured the head. "Okay, so how do I get him to start liking me?"

"You're the magician," he said. "You figure it out."

Chapter Twenty-Seven

"Never underestimate the power of a little smoke and mirrors."
—Max's Diary, Sunday, March 26, 1944

When Eric opened Max's storm cellar door, he was still in his church clothes, the sounds of the organ still resonated in his ears, and his tummy was rumbling in anticipation of Sunday lunch. He didn't know why Carl had stopped him on the way into the service that morning and told him to meet him at Max's house, but he certainly hoped it was worth the walk home. Or that Carl could give him a ride. He could tolerate a lot if he didn't have to walk anymore. The seven blocks from church in dress shoes had already put him in a very un-Christian mood.

"Carl, you down there?" he called into the abyss. The only response he received was the echo of his own voice. He very nearly turned and walked away, but that would involve more walking, and Carl had said to come down into the cellar, so perhaps that was the stipulation. After all, Eric considered, Carl wasn't too bright.

Eric stepped down the stairs quickly. Best to get this strange ordeal over with, and then go fill his belly with his mom's goulash. He began to salivate at the very thought.

Then, halfway down the stairs, his mouth went completely dry.

Because the cellar door slammed shut above him, leaving him in complete and total darkness.

"Uh, Carl?" he called out. "You up there?" He moved gingerly up the stairs and rapped his knuckles on the door. There was no answer. At least, not from outside the door.

But, inside the darkness of the cellar, things began to happen.

First was the sound of a jingling bell, just like the one he'd seen Carl place on that smelly ferret of Max's. Was the ferret in the cellar? He moved down the stairs to the bottom. "Carl? You down here?"

When he reached the bottom, the jingling multiplied. It went from just one little bell off in the corner to dozens, hundreds of them, all around the room.

"Carl, this isn't really funny. I know you probably think it is, but it's not."

The jingling intensified.

And then it stopped. Which was actually a little more terrifying.

"Carl? It's really dark. Can you at least turn on a light?"

He instantly regretted asking that. For, just a few feet in

front of his face, a glowing orb appeared. But it didn't seem to have a source, nor did it seem to be setting on anything. Rather, it floated in the air.

Then, to his right, another appeared. And another to his left.

All around the cellar, making a ring around him, glowing orbs floated in the air.

He swallowed and backed up the steps. "Carl?" he said again, his voice more faint.

And then the music began. From under the steps came a warbling and wobbling version of "That Old Black Magic." It slowed down and it sped up; it even went in reverse.

"Okay, whoever this is, I'm going to go tell the police," he started.

Then, on the wall, words erupted in flames.

YIMAKH SHEMAM.

This was, of course, the final straw, and he bolted up the stairs. Right into a body.

He screamed at a pitch that was generally more appropriate for little girls than for boys.

And then the body he'd run into, which was holding a flashlight, started to laugh. She turned the flashlight to her own face and at last he realized that he had been duped by THE AMAZING MAX.

"Good job, guys," she said and waved the flashlight around the room. With the light moving, Eric could see mirrors on the walls where he'd before seen the floating, glowing orb. And next to the mirrors, dressed all in black with black hoods over their heads, were the remaining members of the Gremlins, holding the drapes they must have pulled off the mirrors when the time came for the orb to be duplicated. Also along those walls, on a string, were dozens of the tiny little jingling bells.

Eric's chest was tight and his breathing shallow. "Get me out of here, please."

Carl went up and, pushing with all his might, opened the storm cellar door and let in the fresh air from outside. Eric ran up the stairs and then lay down in the grass. Max followed him and stood over his head.

"Impressed?" she asked.

"I thought you were going to scare me to death," he said.

"I'll take that as a yes."

He nodded.

"See," she said. "That's what can happen when friends work together." She sat down next to him. "And imagine how much more we could do if we added your brains to the mix."

He shot her a look. "Really? You mean that?"

She nodded. "You're the brains, no arguments from me." She grabbed a stick and poked his arm. "But I bring the magic, remember? So, when it comes to this sort of thing, you *have* to follow me." She winced inwardly at the words she was about to say. "Even though I am only a girl."

Of course, those words made the most sense to his mind. He sat up. "Okay, I guess. But when this whole thing is over, you follow me. Agreed?"

She closed her eyes and fought every instinct she had to the contrary. "Sure. When the show is over, when we've performed the final trick, then I take off my magician's hat and I follow you in whatever pranking adventure you can come up with."

He grinned. "Good, 'cause I've got some really crazy ones. You just wait."

Chapter Twenty-Eight

"TODAY IS THE DAY!!!!"—Max's Diary, Tuesday, March 28, 1944

There were only four hours between the time school was dismissed on that Tuesday and the time the show was set to begin. Four hours. And, just as a mountain climber keeps track of every kilometer on their way up Mount McKinley, so Max kept track of every single event that happened during those four hours.

As soon as the final bell rang at school, and after reiterating to the Gremlins that they absolutely must be at her house and at the ready in one and a half hours, Max went home to scrub the school off her skin in a bath, eat a very early and very light dinner, make sure Houdini's travel carrier was ready and clean (one does not have their very first large-scale magic show without their ferret), and triple-checked that her costume was in a hanging bag so she could change into THE AMAZING MAX when the time was right.

The next hour was spent waiting for the Gremlins to arrive. Lola and Carl were early, Eric was precisely on time, and Shoji, as she'd anticipated, was ten minutes late. All of them were accompanied by their available parental units and/or guardians, which meant that the audience would be larger than she'd originally thought. Three days before, this would have filled her with excitement. Now, three hours before the show, she was instead growing more and more anxious with each passing minute.

They all worked to load the equipment into the vehicles, and then they moved the Vanishing Box into Carl's truck, which was a struggle even with all hands working together. Lola's grandfather suggested they remove the sandbags in the base of the apparatus, but Shoji adamantly fought against such an action, as that would involve tampering with the device, and a magician does not allow his or her devices to be tampered with. Max felt a bit of pride swell up until she remembered these were Felix's words Shoji was quoting. Still, she felt as though she'd effectively communicated her passion to her disciples, or rather, her *friends*, and thus allowed the pride to stay where it was.

It took a bit of time to drive the equipment past the guards at the gate. They inspected each and every piece, including the nooks and crannies of the Vanishing Box, much to Shoji's dismay. Once the guards gave their seal of approval, they drove over to the rec hall and began to unload every item, carrying everything to the stage. Gil was already there, practicing his music on the piano, so he was able to offer a great deal of assistance.

Max handed a drawing of the stage layout to Eric and asked him to make sure everything was in its proper place. This had been a suggestion from Lola the day before, and at the time Max had felt it was unnecessary. Now, with butterflies multiplying inside her intestines, she was working hard enough to keep herself together and was therefore grateful to have a stage manager. Even one as obnoxious as Eric.

While the stage was being set, Mrs. Larousse and the other adults sat in the back of the hall and had a social gathering—the sort in which notes are compared, and individual concerns about the oddball group of friends their children were part of were repressed and replaced with a collective plan to co-parent these scalawags for as long as it was necessary. Max, momentarily desperately needing the security of having her mother nearby, sat behind Mrs. Larousse and spent fifteen minutes calming her nerves and her ferret, who was quite jittery after the car ride.

Finally, a little over an hour before the performance, the stage was set and Max could breathe without labor again. She handed Houdini off to Mrs. Larousse and stepped onto the stage, the place where her greatest dream would come true.

She walked around the stage and adjusted the layout to her liking. Then she turned and looked out at the room. And the butterflies returned.

She started running through the act onstage. She did this silently and without giving a clue to anyone else what her strange motions were meant to be. Thus the Gremlins onstage believed she was communicating some form of message to them all, each interpreting it in a different manner, and each reacting according to their interpretation. This led to some fairly frustrating moments, which could have caused some disastrous results, but then Felix arrived.

Now, the arrival of Felix was a bit of a polarizing event for the entire population of those occupying the rec hall. For Gil, of course, Felix was the opposite of a calming presence. Gil bristled as soon as he noticed the man standing at the edge of the stage. Max instantly regretted not informing Gil of Felix's actual role in the show. Then she realized that Gil might not have been involved if he'd known, and so she un-regretted it.

Meanwhile, the other adults in the room responded with a visible curiosity as to the purpose this war prisoner served in the entire spectacle they had been watching unfold before them. They didn't seem threatened, nor did they seem put off, but they did seem to find it odd. And in some ways, being found odd was the worst of the options for Max.

Regardless of what anyone else in the room thought, Felix stepping up onto the stage calmed Max and the Gremlins. Even though only Shoji had ever actually spoken to the man, the rest had come to a point where they felt he was a bit of the glue that was holding the show together. And so they welcomed him with metaphorical open arms. Literal open arms would have been inappropriate. After all, he *was* a Nazi.

Felix walked over to Max and smiled. "It has come together, yes?"

She nodded. "Yeah. Now just to get over the jitters."

Felix glanced at the rest of the stage. "Perhaps you should get some fresh air to clear your head," he said, a little louder than was usually acceptable in a two-person conversation.

Mrs. Larousse stood from the back of the room. "You know what, that's actually a fantastic idea. Why don't we all go over to the PX and get some Cokes before the show? Clear the head, loosen up the nerves, and then we'll come back here and get you into costume."

"We've only got an hour, Mom," Max said, feeling nervous all over again.

"Plenty of time," her mother said. And, since she'd already won the other adults over to her side, they all agreed and beckoned the children in each of their care to follow suit.

Max sighed. "Okay, yeah, that actually sounds good."

Felix bowed. "I will stay here, of course, and look after the equipment."

"Okay," Max said and nodded. "Okay."

Gil moved over and got uncomfortably close to Felix. "Well, I think I'll stay behind too. Got to run through some scales on the old piano."

Felix was obviously unhappy with this development, and Max did not want Felix unhappy with any of the developments regarding her show. He was her finale. She had to intervene.

She grabbed Gil's sleeve. "No you won't. You're going to come with us so I can buy you a Coke and a licorice whip as a sign of my gratitude."

Gil stared at Felix for two seconds and then let a grin grow on his face. "A Coke *and* a licorice whip? I don't think I've done enough to deserve this." He followed her and the rest of the group out the door, and they all went over to the PX.

Felix was right, of course. Getting away from the stage and out into the sunlight was exactly what Max needed to finally get her nerves under control and let THE AMAZING MAX wake up from her nap. They didn't spend too much time at the PX, either—just enough to get the refreshments and tell about three jokes—and then they headed back, rejuvenated and ready for the show that was before them.

And, when they got back, she was happy to see that Felix had readjusted the stage for her, putting everything exactly where she hadn't known she needed it.

"Max, are you ready?" Mrs. Larousse asked as she picked up the garment bag.

Max nodded. "Yes. I'm ready."

HOUDINI

★ PRESENTS ★

Ghost in the Egg

HERE'S WHAT YOU'LL NEED.

1. One Dozen Eggs
2. A Knitting Needle
3. Clear Tape
4. Baby Powder

BABY POWDER

Step One:

Take one egg and with the knitting needle, poke a hole in the bottom.

Step Two:

Carefully get the yolk and white out through the hole.

YUM!

Step Three:

Rinse the empty shell with water, then let it completely dry.

Step Four:

Fill the egg halfway with baby powder.

MAYBE USE A FUNNEL.

BABY POWDER

Step Five:

Cover the hole with clear tape.

Place it back in the carton.

NOW FOR THE TRICK!

I HAVE HERE A DOZEN EGGS FROM A HAUNTED FARM.

Gently crack the ghost egg on your table.

OH, YOU DON'T BELIEVE IN GHOSTS?

TAP! TAP!

Break the egg open and fling "the ghost" out of the egg.

WELL, BELIEVE THIS!

POOF!

Chapter Twenty-Nine

The heat from the spotlight was beginning to feel quite uncomfortable. Thankfully, there were only two tricks left to the show, so Max did not have to endure it much longer. Unfortunately, there were only two tricks left to this fantastic dream come true before Max had to return to her normal life. Given the choice, she would have rather suffered through the heat a little longer. But you can't live in a dream forever, nor should you. Dreams have the frustrating tendency to turn themselves into nightmares.

Even as she was executing the final punch of the GHOST EGG TRICK, she was calculating every detail of the previous hour and a half to see just how close reality had followed suit with her high expectations.

The music had been perfect, of course. Gil had a knack for reading a performer and making adjustments to the tempo or texture of a song to help heighten the effect on the audience. This was a plus.

Speaking of the audience, if there was any aspect of the night that she would consider a disappointment, they would be that detail. Since the show was not mandatory for the prisoners, there were many empty seats. More empty seats, in fact, than full ones. Most discouraging of all, none of the men that had been in the hut the night Max approached Felix about the finale were there. Not even Blaz, who had certainly given her the impression that he was looking forward to the event. Max decided Judy had talked him out of it.

THE AMAZING MAX tossed the egg in her hand up into the air, hit it with her magic wand, and it exploded into smoke that wafted perfectly in the light over the audience. And, for the tenth time that night, they filled her ears with applause.

She had to admit, having the Gremlins' help was a very large part of why the show was going so very well. Eric really was quite good with the lights, Carl and Lola had their timing down perfectly when it came to causing a stir in the audience, and Shoji was the best assistant anyone could ask for. As if to prove this fact, he jumped onstage as she was thinking it and, without drawing attention to himself, moved the table out of the way and cleared the area in front of the Vanishing Box.

Because it was time for the finale.

Max stepped up to the edge of the stage and cleared her throat. This was the signal to Gil to start a very dramatic buildup of chords as she looked out over the audience.

"For my final trick," THE AMAZING MAX said, "I need a volunteer."

Hands popped up across the audience. Even though they were few, they were eating out of her hands, and so in this exact moment, she decided they were perfect.

"Now, wait a moment," she continued. "I feel I must first explain what this trick will entail. As most of you are soldiers, you can probably attest to the value of knowing what you are getting into before you sign up." This joke probably would have been better received in an audience of GIs, but it was at least appreciated by these prisoners.

"In this trick, I will do something that may not be completely approved by the men who oversee this prison camp." She took a deep breath, and Gil dropped into a rolling minor chord. "I am going to send one of you outside of this camp's gates and off to freedom."

There were gasps, actual gasps, and she knew she had them. She tried to see Major Larousse's face, but he wasn't in the building. She assumed he was going to be late, but not *this* late. THE AMAZING MAX shook the disappointment out of her brain.

"Now, who will—"

"I will," Felix said as he stepped out from his seat in the middle row.

"Ah, I suppose this opportunity is more popular than I'd anticipated," she said, and some people laughed. Not many, but some. "I must know, sir, why I should allow you this chance at freedom over your brothers in the room."

Felix reached into his pocket and pulled out an envelope. "Because I need to mail a letter."

This line caused more laughter to rise from the audience. Then, with a bit of prodding, Felix told the story of how he was in love, and how he had not seen his sweet love in years, and that all he wanted was to send her a letter that told her of his love.

"But there's a post office here at camp," Max said.

"Yes, a post office that reads our mail before it's sent."

"Oh? And you have things that you'd rather those men not read?"

"I did tell you I am writing to the woman I love."

She held up her hand. "I'm sorry, I believe I'm too young to hear any more of this." More laughter. "But you have pricked my heart, dear sir, so if you will join me on the stage, I will send you away so you can mail your precious letter to your precious Josephine." She winced, realizing he hadn't actually said the name of his love. Nobody noticed, though, so all was well.

He came onto the stage and she walked him over to the Vanishing Box. She opened the door and motioned for him to step inside. Then she closed the door behind him and had Shoji come stand next to the box.

"Now, good people, because I am so very kind, I will

send this fine young man into the ether and let him land in the greatest city on earth, New York City, to mail his letter. All it will take is the magic word: *Abrakadabra!*" She waved her wand and then pointed it at the box. Gil did a run up the scale and landed on a majestic chord.

Shoji opened the door, and the box was empty.

The room erupted in applause.

Max bowed several times. Finally she motioned for everyone to quiet down and spied a certain someone standing against the rear wall.

"I must admit, as I look back at the major's face, I can tell that he's not too happy with this trick."

The room turned to look at Major Larousse, who had just slipped in the back. He put on a scowl for their pleasure. They laughed.

"So I believe, considering it only takes a few seconds to drop an envelope into a mailbox, that I should bring our friend back to us."

She motioned for Shoji to close up the Vanishing Box again, and then she tapped it with her magic wand.

"So, I will say the magic words. Abraka—"

POW!

The spotlight went off. As did the other lights in the room. And, through the window, they could see that the power had gone out completely everywhere.

Nervous silence filled the room. Gil stood and lit a

match, which gave them enough light to see Major Larousse hurrying to speak to the guards that were standing at the door. One of them turned on his flashlight, shone it around the room, and then trained it on the group of prisoners.

"Okay, listen everyone," Major Larousse finally said to the room. "Obviously something has happened to the power. We just need you all to stay put while we get this worked out."

As soon as he said that, the power returned. The lights came back up, and the spotlight turned back on. Of course, in the confusion, Eric had turned the spotlight so it was pointed in completely the wrong direction, but he hurried and got it moved back around to focus on Max.

"Hey, I guess I've got a little magic in me, too," Major Larousse said with a grin. Many in the room chuckled.

Max tried to shake off the interruption. "Anyway, I suppose that's the sign that we've gone on as long as we can." More people laughed. "So, let's bring Felix back and finish the show."

She tapped the box twice and nodded to Shoji.

He opened the door.

Nobody applauded.

She turned to look.

Felix was still gone.

Max began to sweat, probably from the heat of the spotlight, but possibly because her nerves were beginning to push through again. She motioned for Shoji to close the box and turned back to the audience.

"Well, I suppose it didn't quite work that time. Let's try again." She waved her wand in the air. "Abrakadabra!" she said.

Shoji opened the door.

Felix wasn't there.

Shoji shot her a very confused look.

Somebody in the audience coughed. Another couple whispered to each other.

Max ran over and tapped the false wall inside the box, which was designed to slide open to the compartment where the person who had "vanished" was stashed away. "Felix," she whispered inside. "Come on, that's your cue." She closed the box door.

She turned and cleared her throat. She raised the wand over her head.

And then the camp sirens began to wail.

Everyone froze where they were.

The back door flew open and a guard ran in.

"There's been a breakout!" he yelled. "The prisoners have escaped!"

Chapter Thirty

Everyone was spread out across the rec hall, looking for the escapee.

That is, they were looking for Houdini.

It should be noted here that "everyone" in this context was the Gremlins and their parental units. Minus Major Larousse, who was off overseeing the search for the escaped prisoners. Plus Gil, who should have been off looking for the prisoners but had been commissioned by the major to escort Mrs. Larousse and Max home.

Speaking of Max, she was also not looking for Houdini. She was sitting behind the Vanishing Box, crying. And, although she cared very much who saw her, she didn't care enough to actually stop crying. There was nearly nothing that could make her stop crying.

She had decided that was the most appropriate reaction to have when a curse comes to fruition. Even if one does not believe in such things, there is really nothing worse in the world than living as an accursed person. Particularly if you are an accursed person who *also* has suddenly lost your ferret.

It was, to be sure, the worst of times.

"Hey, I found him!" Gil yelled as he scooped Houdini up from between two sandbags. "See, everything's not so terrible." He walked over and dropped Houdini in Max's lap and then patted her on the head. "Cheer up, kiddo. The show was great."

As soon as Carl's dad saw that the ferret had been found, he signaled for Carl to come help him and they, along with the other men and boys who gradually joined their number, lifted the Vanishing Box and loaded it onto their truck. Watching it move out the door had a strange effect on Max. As Houdini feverishly licked away the bunny-bait that had already dripped down her cheeks, she was able to dry up any remaining tears and find the strength to stand.

"How many escaped?" she asked, addressing the major crisis for the first time since her show had come to such an abrupt conclusion.

Gil eyed her for a second, suspicious that this reprieve in tears was an illusion. "Eleven from out there, plus Felix, so twelve."

She sighed and rubbed noses with Houdini. "I just can't believe Felix would run off like that."

Gil shrugged. "When the lights went out, he probably

realized it was his one chance. Heading out the side entrance in all the hullabaloo makes sense to me. It's what I would have done in the same situation."

She looked at him with surprise. "You plan on escaping from prison a lot?"

"Listen, it's part and parcel of being a soldier. Doesn't matter what side you're on, we're all trained to find our way out of captivity and back to our battle stations."

"Because a performer doesn't give up until the show is over," she said.

He chuckled. "Yeah, that's what this war is. The Ringling Brothers have it wrong. World War II is the Greatest Show on Earth." He put his hand on her back. "Now, let's get you and your mom home so I can start playing my part again, okay?"

By the time they pulled into the Larousse driveway, Max was already asleep and didn't notice that Gil carried her in, nor that her mother gently washed her face, took down her hair, and covered her with a blanket. She slept through Major Larousse finally coming home near midnight, through the phone ringing an hour later, and even missed him leaving and returning just a few hours shy of daybreak. She was blissfully unaware of the unfolding drama in the aftermath of the escape, such as the discovery of the tunnel the prisoners had dug under one of their huts with broken plates and bowls, or the realization that the escaped prisoners were all members of The Black Hand.

She didn't wake up until dawn, when Houdini finally gave in to the itchies he had been ignoring from the time they left the base. He scratched enough for three ferrets and nearly turned over his cage. She groggily let him out to drag himself on the carpet and then looked outside at the sun peeking over the horizon, right behind the Vanishing Box.

The surplus of sleep gave her renewed gumption and rejuvenated optimism, and to celebrate this, she found her shoes, went out, and kicked the Vanishing Box, feeling that it was a bit of a symbol of all the problems at hand.

When she did, the box tipped over and fell with a crash, knocking some of the boards loose. She felt a very real satisfaction at this and returned to her room. She thought how silly she'd been to fear an imaginary curse. And also to believe in an imaginary friend like Felix. Not that his existence was imaginary, but rather his friendship was, and so he might as well have not existed at all. Especially since he was long gone, now.

Good riddance, she thought and almost convinced herself.

Later, as she ate breakfast with her mother and a very tired, unshaven, and grumpy Major Larousse, she realized that she was incorrect. When it comes to escaped Nazis, there is no good in their riddance. None whatsoever.

He muttered a brief summary of the previous night's developments through his eggs and toast, washing down every sentence with several gulps of black coffee. When he told them about the tunnel, Max stopped drinking her orange juice.

"So *that's* what they were doing under the hut?" she asked.

Major Larousse narrowed his eyes and glared at her like he would glare at an insubordinate recruit. "You knew they were doing something under the huts?" he growled.

She gulped. "Uh, I, uh, I might have— Well, actually, Shoji— We saw something but we didn't know what it was."

Major Larousse set his coffee cup down forcefully. "And is there a reason you didn't tell me?"

"Larry," Mrs. Larousse said as she wiped up the spill. "Does it matter now?"

He closed his eyes and shook his head. "No, it doesn't. It doesn't change anything." He sighed. "But at least we can maybe use some of the information to find these creeps." He dug into his pocket, pulled out his keys and a napkin and set them on the table, and then finally found a pen. "Okay, give me some details."

Max picked up the napkin. It had the map Shoji had drawn on it. "Where'd you get this?" she asked.

"We found it in the tunnel. The prisoners must have made it so they'd know how to get around once they got out. But where they got them—"

"Probably from Felix," Max said without thinking. "It's the same map that me and Shoji gave to him, and he'd copied it on a napkin just like this."

Major Larousse didn't say anything. He set his pen down and took a sip of his coffee. Then he took another. After which, he took yet another.

"Dad? Are you okay?"

He slammed the cup down and Max jumped. "You *gave* them a map?"

"Larry," Mrs. Larousse said.

"No," Max said. "We gave the map to Felix."

"Yes, one of the many prisoners who escaped last night," he said. "And you, my daughter, gave him the map they used in their escape."

"Well, yeah," Max said. "I mean, we didn't do it so he could escape or anything, though."

Major Larousse stood up and leaned on the table. "My gosh, when you said you were going to make a prisoner disappear in your act, I didn't know you actually meant you were going to be an accomplice."

"Larry, please," Mrs. Larousse said.

"What's on the docket for your next trick?" Major Larousse asked. "Are you going to help Hitler disappear right before we drop a bomb on his butt?"

"Major Larousse!" Max's mother said and moved over to shield her daughter from his words. "You should save your bullets for the enemy."

He seemed prime to reload and resume firing, but then he saw Max's lip trembling. Every day that he'd been on the front lines in Africa, he had looked at a picture of his daughter and remembered how hard she'd fought the tears when he had kissed her good-bye back in Brooklyn. The image of her trembling lip had kept him alive every day. And now it made him want to die.

He quickly excused himself and hurried off to work. He had Nazis to recapture. And a daughter's heart to mend, eventually.

He had a feeling that finding the Nazis was going to be the easier of those tasks.

Chapter Thirty-One

"Of course it's not my fault. But it doesn't mean I feel good about it."
—Max's Diary, Wednesday, March 29, 1944

Max had tried every excuse she could imagine to stay home from school, but they'd each failed miserably. Her mother made it very clear that, barring loss of limb or severe bloodletting, Max would be in school that day as scheduled. Grandma Schauder had not fled the Kaiser, braved the ocean on a rickety boat, and very nearly starved to death in the worst April snowstorm in Philadelphia history to then have her granddaughter chicken out of school just because she was under the weather and had possibly aided in the biggest prison-camp escape of the war.

"It's not like she'd know," Max grumbled from the passenger seat of their car.

"Oh, she'd know," Mrs. Larousse said. "She always knows. Trust me."

Max didn't argue. Motherly Magic grows more powerful with age and with each additional prefix that is added to the title, from Grand, to Great, and so on. When Max eventually had her own children, she would not be surprised if Grandma Schauder was changing the alignment of the planets or redirecting hurricanes to water her garden.

When Max got out of the car in front of the school, her mother turned the car off and got out as well.

"What are you doing?" Max asked. Mrs. Larousse did not reply.

Together, they walked through the halls and into Mrs. Conrad's room. Max took her seat, still perplexed, and Mrs. Larousse took Mrs. Conrad to the side and had a brief conference with her. After they were done, Mrs. Larousse turned to address the class.

"Boys and girls," she started, because it is a long-honored tradition among grown-ups that children must be reminded that they are children before they are dealt any kind of grown-up news, after which they will be expected to handle the news like grown-ups. "I am not sure if you all have heard, but some prisoners escaped from Camp Barkeley last night."

The other students in the room began to whisper to each other. Which was a perfect opportunity for Judy to whisper to Max. "Well, golly, I wonder how that happened." Max did her best to ignore her adversary. It was much easier under her mother's watchful eye.

Mrs. Conrad hushed the room and Mrs. Larousse

continued. "I wanted to make sure you all knew that my husband, Major Larousse, and the rest of the army are doing everything they have to do to make sure they recapture the prisoners and return them to the camp."

"Weren't you on base last night?" Judy whispered. "Doing your show that you were bragging about?"

Max nodded but held her tongue.

"So there is no need to worry," Mrs. Larousse concluded. "The prisoners will be captured, probably before sundown today, and nobody is in any sort of danger." She turned to leave and then, perhaps due to her upbringing in the city of journalists, turned back to the class. "Does anybody have any questions?" Students all across the room raised their hands. She began calling them, one by one, starting with the back row.

"Oh, wait," Judy whispered into Max's ear. "You weren't performing for the GIs, were you? You were entertaining Hitler's henchmen. Hmmm, I wonder what sort of Nazi magic could make a whole group of prisoners disappear into the night."

Max stood. "I have to go to the restroom."

Mrs. Larousse glared at her. "No you don't."

"Yes I do," Max said. "Between the two of us, I think I would know."

"You went before we came," Mrs. Larousse said. "You don't."

★ 240 ★

There were stifled giggles popping up from various locations and they inspired the most panicked, desperate, please-not-here look Max could muster. Her mother, unfortunately, didn't see it, but Mrs. Conrad did.

"Oh, go on to the restroom, then," Mrs. Conrad said. "But don't you dillydally."

Of course, dillydallying was the sole purpose for this restroom visit, so Max did not allow her ears to hear the last part of Mrs. Conrad's command. Instead, she rushed out the door and ran down to the restroom. She locked herself in a stall, sat on the toilet, and picked her feet up to hide them from view. And then she waited for someone to come and get her, because there would be no other way she would be forced to return to the classroom. Even a fire drill wouldn't budge her. Death in engulfing flames would be a welcome reprieve.

And so she stayed in that position—that rather uncomfortable, limb-numbing position—for well over an hour. She began to believe that she would need a double amputation of her feet by the time somebody knocked on the stall door on a mission from Mrs. Conrad to retrieve her.

Of course, the person who had volunteered for the task was the person who most wanted to continue talking to Max, and the person Max least wanted to see.

"Come on," Judy said. "They're going to start thinking you've died in here."

"Maybe I have," Max said. "What's it to you?"

"There're only two stalls," Judy said. "And the second-grade girls are going to line up for their bathroom break in ten minutes. With only one stall to use, they'll be in here for forever. And, trust me, nobody wants the second graders in the bathroom for forever. That's a recipe for disaster."

Max sighed, unlocked the stall door, and stood. The standing didn't work the way she'd planned, as all the blood finally began rushing to her poor feet again, and she nearly fell over from the pins and needles. She clutched the wall to steady herself. Judy offered her no assistance.

"I didn't help the Nazis," Max said as she stumbled toward the sink to wash her hands.

Judy laughed. "Oh, come on, is that what this is all about? Jeez, don't you know how to take a joke?"

"Don't you know how to tell one?"

Judy offered her arm as support. "Here, let me help you back to class."

"I'll manage," Max said and began her slow hobble to the door. "Anyway, I'm surprised you aren't more upset about the escape, considering your boyfriend is one of the guys that got out."

Judy took back her arm and returned her look of disdain. "My boyfriend? I don't know what you're talking about."

"Blaz," Max said as she opened the door. "He's an

escaped prisoner." Max turned on the most smug look she had in her repertoire. "I told you he was a Nazi."

That seemed to be the silver bullet that was needed to silence Judy, because she didn't say another word, to anybody, all the way up to lunch. When the lunch bell rang, she went off on her own without the Mesquite Tree Girls. The looks of confusion on Margaret's and Natalie's faces would have been grand entertainment for the Gremlins if not for the fact that there was so much else to arrest their focus.

And also if any of them had been there.

When Max went to their lunch spot, she was alone.

Alone when she needed loneliness the least.

And so, fifteen minutes into lunch, when Eric snuck around the maintenance shed, she almost hugged him like a man in the desert would hug a camel carrying jugs of water. Almost, but then she remembered that it *was* Eric, so instead she nodded and said, "Hey."

"Hey," he said. "Where is everybody?"

"I don't know. I guess all your parents love you more than mine love me. My mom insisted I come to school."

He dropped to the ground next to her and offered her a sip from his thermos, which was full of turkey noodle soup. She drank some and handed it back. "Yeah, my mom was pretty shaken up about the ordeal from last night, so she didn't want me going out. She thinks I'm in the tree house right now."

"You have a tree house?" she asked.

"I never go in it. It's the worst tree house in the world. There's no place to sit down. But it makes for a great cover so I can run off and do things." He grinned. "Kind of like my very own Vanishing Box."

She groaned. "Let's not talk about that, please. Last night was the worst experience of my life."

He was genuinely shocked. "What? It was great. The whole show was amazing."

"Sure, until I helped the Nazis run away."

He waved her off. "Come on, that wasn't your fault. And you can't let one little thing like a Nazi escape ruin the rest of the evening. You got all of us to actually work together for once. And wasn't that show your dream or something like that?"

She nodded.

"Okay, then you should feel proud *and* happy. Most people *never* see their dreams come true. Like me." He pointed at his eye patch. "I'll never have depth perception. But you? You're just starting. Next time you use that Vanishing Box, it's going to blow people away."

It was amazing how much nicer Eric was when he wasn't around people and hadn't had his brain filled with facts and information. She smiled.

"Yeah, too bad I broke the Vanishing Box this morning."

"You what?"

"When I woke up, I was so frustrated that I went out and kicked it over and it broke."

"No, you didn't," he said, and his natural jerkiness began to reemerge.

"Yes, I did," she said.

"There's no way," he said. "There is no way you, by yourself, kicked the Vanishing Box and knocked it over. It takes all of us guys to move that thing."

She shrugged. "Maybe I'm stronger than I look."

"You probably are, but that doesn't change science," he said. "There's almost two hundred pounds of sandbags in the bottom of that thing to keep it steady. You'd have to drive a car into it to knock it over."

Now she was puzzled, too. "Well, it knocked over. Like a house of cards." She thought for a moment. "Maybe somebody unloaded the sandbags after you guys left it at my house."

"Doubtful. I was the last one to leave it behind, and nobody took any out."

"Oh, I know!" She slapped her knee. "They were unloaded at the rec hall. Remember, 'cause Gil found Houdini hiding in them?"

"No, we didn't unload them there, either. And besides, if they were out at the rec hall, then why did it take all of us to get the box loaded into Carl's dad's truck? It was as heavy as ever when we carried it off the stage. Those must have been some other sandbags."

"Why would there be sandbags laying around in the rec hall?"

He rolled his eyes. "I don't know, but if the sandbags weren't in the bottom of the box, then why was it so heavy when we carried it out?"

They both came to the same conclusion at the same time.

"Felix!" they yelled together.

"He was hiding in the bottom," Max said.

"But how did he get down there?"

"He designed the box," Max said as waves of revelation crashed into her brain. "This was *his* trick. That's why he had us get the material from different places, so we wouldn't piece his plan together. It's also why he kept me as far away from the blueprint as possible. Because—"

"Because it takes a magician to see a trick before it happens," Eric said, much to her surprise.

"Yeah," she said. "The way he had you guys make the floor, it must have been easy to pop it open so he could crawl underneath."

"It opened in the middle," he said with a groan. "It popped open so you could get the sandbags in there. It was a last-minute change he told Shoji to make. Wasn't even on the blueprint."

"Wow. He is good."

"How could we be so stupid?" Eric yelled. The lunch bell rang.

"I don't know," she said. "But it doesn't much matter anymore, does it? He's out and probably halfway to Mexico by now."

Eric nodded. "Or, maybe he's not."

"Huh?"

"What if he's staked out, hiding somewhere before he makes his move."

"Like where?" she asked.

"Creepiest place on earth. The place I wouldn't be surprised to find a Nazi." He grinned. "What if he's in your storm cellar?"

Chapter Thirty-Two

He's not down there," Max said. "There's no way." The Gremlins stood staring at the storm cellar door from five feet away. Not one of them felt compelled to move an inch closer.

"He might be down there," Shoji said. "You don't know."

"It seems like a real easy way to get caught," Carl said.

"But it is the absolute last place you'd look, you can't deny that," Eric said.

"Because it's a dumb place to hide," Shoji said.

"Which is why it's brilliant," Eric said. "Think about how idiotic the rest of the plan sounds. Digging a tunnel out of a prison camp? Using a kid magician as a cover? Hiding in the bottom of a box that's going to be carried out, right underneath the noses of the guards at the gate? Every single part of this is stupid, and yet it's so stupid, it's smart. Kind of like Carl."

"Hey!" Carl said, then he thought about it. "Oh, wait, that was a compliment, huh?"

"We need to tell somebody," Lola said. "We should tell your dad, Max. Let him check the storm cellar."

"He's already mad at me about this whole thing," Max said. "I'm not going to tell him that I helped walk a prisoner through the gates without being able to hand him the prisoner in handcuffs."

"Do we even have handcuffs?" Shoji said.

"I've got rope," Carl said.

"See? Carl has rope. We're fine," Max said. "Besides, he's not down there."

"I hope you're right," Lola said.

"I hope you're wrong," Eric said. "I want to catch a Nazi. How many people can say they did that?"

They all stood still and stared at the dangling cinder block.

"So, what do we do? Do we open it or not?" Max asked.

"I'll open it," Carl said and approached the block. He put his hands on it and then hesitated. "I mean, if y'all want me to."

Max took a deep breath. "Yeah, do it."

He started to pull down on the block.

"No, wait!" Shoji yelled. "That's a really dumb idea."

"Thank you!" Lola said.

"If Felix *is* in there, we don't want our biggest guy occupied with the block. Me and Eric should open it, and Carl should get ready to pounce on him if he comes running out."

"Why do I try with you guys?" Lola asked.

"Hey, I don't want to be stuck on the block, either," Eric said. "I can't say I helped nab him if I didn't help nab him. Max should do it, it's her storm cellar."

"No," Max said. "I need to be the first one in. Because it *is* my storm cellar."

"Oh my gosh, I'll do it," Lola said and pushed Carl away.

The Gremlins poised themselves as she opened the door, incredibly slowly because she was the tiniest of their number.

The door creaked open and no Nazis came running out, much to Eric's disappointment. Once she counted to ten, just to make sure Felix wasn't running behind in his escape plan, Max stepped inside, and she and the Gremlins descended into the pit.

Since Major Larousse had to keep his flashlight at the ready for the quest to find the Nazis, they had to use Shoji's little red flashlight, which didn't illuminate nearly as well. Still, as they got down to the bottom of the stairs, it became more and more apparent that there was nobody in the cellar.

"Man," Eric said. "That's sad."

"Gosh, you are so dumb," Lola said.

Shoji shone the flashlight around the room. "Well, it's too bad for Felix that he didn't hide down here. He could probably sleep on the bench. It looks comfortable."

Max glanced over at the bench he was shining his light onto. "Hey, where is Grandma Schauder's Hummel box?"

She could almost hear the sound of the Gremlins blinking in confusion. She took the flashlight from Shoji. "It was on the bench. My grandmother's Hummel. Where did it . . . oh, no." She found the box resting in a puddle of water that had already soaked through the bottom half of the cardboard. She ran over and tried to pick it up out of the water.

The bottom of the box ripped open, and the whole collection of little German yodelers tumbled out and smashed to the ground. Once the sound of broken figurines stopped echoing around the room, she dropped the tattered remains of the box and hung her head. "This is my life. I might as well just go to bed until the war is over."

Lola ran over and hugged her. "It's okay, it's okay. Maybe we can buy you some more of those little things. Are they expensive?"

"I don't know," Max said as she patted Lola on the back three times, which in Brooklyn is a universal signal that a hug has been fully appreciated and should thus be brought to a conclusion. Sadly, this was not the code in Texas, and so Lola continued hugging Max. This, coupled with the sight of the scattered pieces of porcelain, sent Max over an edge. She pushed Lola away.

"When I figure out which one of you put this box in the water, I'm going to punch you in the face," she said.

"Apologies, *fräulein*," a voice said from the top of the stairs. Felix sat three steps down from the opening, a mischievous smile ornamenting his face. He stood and descended the stairs, and met with the absolute silence of their dumbfounded mouths. He walked over to Max and put his hand on her shoulder. "I have indeed made quite the mess for you, haven't I?"

Max stared into his blue eyes, still unable to find the words she wanted to say to him. Therefore, she glanced at Carl and said a word to him. "Now!"

Carl, Eric, and Shoji ran forward and tackled Felix. Eric held his arms behind his back, Shoji wrapped himself around Felix's legs, and Carl put him in a headlock, but Felix didn't struggle. He didn't put up any sort of a fight as they tied his hands and feet and dragged him over to the wall. Instead, through it all, he maintained his infuriating smile.

It wasn't very ladylike, nor was it much like a magician, and it certainly wasn't what her mother would do, but in spite of these facts, Max took three steps forward and punched him in the mouth with the full force of her body behind the blow. It was the first punch she'd ever thrown, but it was a good one. It split his lip open and blood spewed down his chin. Plus, because he was against the wall, it slammed his head into the concrete. All in all, it was a very satisfying blow. Max could now see why men like Joe Louis turned this sort of thing into a career. Maybe if being a magician didn't pan out the way she hoped, she would explore that option.

"Oh, come on!" Lola yelled and ran forward to try and stop the bleeding. She grabbed the first thing she could find, which was a disgusting, water-soaked piece of cardboard, and held it to Felix's lip.

"There is a handkerchief in my pocket," Felix said.

Lola pulled out the handkerchief and used it to stop the bleeding. "Why did you do that?" she asked Max.

"Just returning the favor," Max said. "Now we're almost even."

Felix chuckled. "I will not argue that I deserved that," he said through the handkerchief Lola held to his mouth. "As I said before, apologies."

"Yeah, yeah, yeah, apologies, schmapologies," Max said. "I'm done playing your game, Felix. I'm going to go and get my dad so he can take you back to the camp. You two-faced, dirty Nazi." She nodded to the boys. "Can you three hold him until I get back?"

"Oh, yeah, we got him," Eric said with glee. "We got ourselves a Nazi!"

"Okay," Max said and started up the stairs.

"Turning me in now without hearing what I have to say would be an incredible mistake," Felix called to her.

She stopped at the fourth step.

She knew she shouldn't listen to him. After all, listening to him had been the source of every single trouble she was in at that exact moment. Including the broken

Hummel dolls. It was all a direct result of misplaced trust.

But a magician always makes sure they know what cards are still in the deck.

"Why would it be a mistake?" she asked.

"Because then the eleven other men who escaped with me last night will never be caught, and your father will be forever known as the man who let the Nazis get away."

Chapter Thirty-Three

Max hated Felix. She finally realized that as she came back down the stairs, now completely unable to do what she knew she should. All because he was so annoyingly good at making his point seem like the only point worth making. She walked over and stood in front of him. "They're going to get away anyway," she said, trying more to convince herself that his statement was invalid than anyone else. "Or they won't. Listening to you won't change a thing."

"Then what would it hurt to give me five minutes of your time?"

Lola shook her head. As the conscience of the group, she already had twenty-seven different reasons why they should not listen to the escaped Nazi hiding in the storm cellar, the first four simply being the words "escaped," "Nazi," "hiding," and "storm cellar." The other twenty-three reasons were far more articulate, but none nearly as convincing as those first four.

As a magician, Max was accustomed to ignoring the voice of conscience in order to get a job done. She dropped down to rest on her heels in front of Felix. "Okay, I'm listening."

He had a pleasantly surprised look in his eyes. He pulled his head away from the bloody handkerchief and licked his lip. The bleeding was barely a trickle at this point, and he didn't seem to mind it.

"The prisoners have a very well-crafted plan to make their way to Mexico, and from there find passage back to Europe and the war," he said. "This plan is flawless, as flawless as a Herrmann magic trick. I know this because I devised it."

Max gritted her teeth. "And I was just part of that plan, wasn't I?"

"More than you know, *fräulein*. You are the single most important part of the plan."

"You're not making me want to keep listening," Max said and stood.

"No, no, you don't understand," he said. "The plan that the prisoners received is designed to succeed, as far as they know. But what they do not know is that there is a *servante* designed to make sure they fail and are returned to the camp."

"A *servante?*" Shoji asked. "What's he talking about?"

"It's the secret device that a magician uses to accomplish

his tricks, like a hidden shelf or a pocket," Max said. "It's one of the oldest tricks in magic."

Felix nodded. "I made the plan so that it will either succeed beautifully or fail royally, depending on whether or not the *servante* is in place."

"Lola!" a voice called from the top of the stairs.

The Gremlins shared a terrified look, and Carl and Shoji grabbed Felix and dragged him over into the shadows.

"Yes, Mamaw?" Lola yelled up.

"It's time to go," her grandmother said.

Lola pulled Max over to the corner to have a hurried, whispered conversation. "You can't keep listening to him," Lola said. "You can't give him what he wants. You just can't."

"I know," Max said. "I know, okay? I'm going to get my dad. I just, if I can get him to actually tell me the plan, then maybe this whole thing will go away."

"Even if he doesn't tell you," Lola said, "you have to turn him in. They can get him to talk in the prison. But helping him? I'm pretty sure that's treason or something."

"Or something," Max said.

Lola grabbed Max's hand and linked their pinkies together. "Promise me you will turn him over to your dad right away. Okay?"

Max hadn't done a pinky bargain since she was four, but she nodded anyway. "Okay. I promise, I'll go up right away and tell him."

"I get to rip your pinkie off if you don't," Lola said.

Max was fairly certain that Lola would actually do that very act, so she double-checked her intentions and then agreed again.

"Lola!" her grandmother up above yelled again.

"I'm coming!" Lola shouted as she rushed up the stairs. Just before she reached the top, she turned and held her pinkie out at Max. Max nodded again. Lola left, and her grandmother scolded her all the way until their voices disappeared.

Max returned to Felix, who was now sitting in a puddle, far less amused with things than before. She squatted in front of him. "Okay, so what's the *servante* in your plan?"

"Isn't it obvious?" he asked. "The *servante* is you. The Amazing Max."

"You're crazy," she said. She stood back up. "I'm going to get my dad." She went back to the stairs.

"You will capture four today," he yelled after her. "Two on Friday, three on Saturday, and the final two on Sunday. If they aren't captured in that order, exactly as I've planned, they will never be captured."

"And what about you? When do you go back to the camp?"

"Monday," he said. "Once the others are safely returned, you can reveal my location and I will be taken."

"Or I can just hand you over to my dad right now, and

you'll tell him the plan and go back to your hut today."

Felix shook his head. "I will tell him nothing. You either do this my way, or you never see the other prisoners again."

"This is dumb," Eric said as he let go of Felix's arm. "Why even plan the escape if you're just going to help get everybody captured again? It doesn't make sense."

Felix looked in Max's eyes. "Why would I do this?"

She scrunched her forehead. "How should I—" Her jaw dropped. "For Josephine?"

He nodded.

"Seriously? You're doing all of this just so you can mail a letter?"

"No," he said. "So that I can make a telephone call."

Max had heard enough. She told the boys to make sure Felix stayed where he was and she went up to tell Major Larousse that there was a Nazi in the cellar and a plan he needed to foil. There was absolutely nothing more that Felix could say to convince her to change her course of action. She was prepared for all of his arguments.

She was not, however, prepared for the conversation her parents were having in the kitchen. She probably wouldn't have even known about it if not for her long-standing habit of eavesdropping on them before she entered any room. It had never failed her before.

It may have that day.

"The FBI is coming?" Mrs. Larousse asked.

"Yes, and they're already asking all the worst questions," Major Larousse said.

"Like?"

"Like if we have any idea how they got the map, or if anyone saw anything suspicious beforehand."

"She's eleven, Larry," Mrs. Larousse said. "I'm sure they'll understand."

"She's my daughter," he said. "I'm sure they won't."

They both held their silent position as they sipped their tea. Max stayed behind the door, feeling more and more like a criminal. And an idiot. A criminally idiotic girl. She did not enjoy that feeling.

"Well, I guess you just need to catch them, then, don't you?" Mrs. Larousse said.

"I don't even want to think about the alternative," the major said. "This is the sort of thing that can end a career. It's the sort of thing people go to prison over."

"They're not going to send Max to prison," Mrs. Larousse said.

"I wasn't talking about Max," he said.

"I know," she said. "I was being funny. You're overreacting."

He stood and put his cup in the sink. "I need to go back in. We've still got a lot of ground to cover and we don't have any idea where to start looking."

Max ducked into the hallway as Major Larousse hurried out the front door and drove away. Mrs. Larousse quietly stirred her tea in the kitchen, exuding anxiety now that she was free to do so.

Max snuck back outside and went down the stairs again.

"Okay," she said to Felix. "I'll be the *servante*. Just tell me what we need to do."

If anyone would have walked past the storm cellar in the hour that followed, they would have heard a great deal of whispering and arguing over plans and props. They would have heard Eric blurt something about magnets and fireworks, or Shoji bemoan the fact that his mother was going to kill him. They probably would have also heard the low voice of Felix, repeatedly reminding them that they only had until sundown to get everything into place.

What they would not have heard, though, was the sound of Max's heart pounding in her chest, even though she would have been surprised that it wasn't loud enough.

The Amazing Max and her Gremlins were about to go chasing the Nazis.

HOUDINI

★ PRESENTS ★

The Lemon Target

HERE'S WHAT YOU'LL NEED.

1. Two Quarters
2. A Lemon
3. A Butter Knife
4. A Slingshot

Before the trick: Ask an adult to cut a slit the size of a quarter in the lemon.

TAKE THAT, LEMON!

Set the lemon under your stage table and put the quarter, the knife, and the slingshot on the table.

Quarter behind slingshot

Cloth to the floor.

TAKE A NAP IF YOU WANT.

Step One:

Show the quarter to the audience. Point out some details.

IT'S A 1942 QUARTER!

WASHINGTON HAS A MOLE ON HIS CHIN!

Step Two:

Palm the quarter while "setting it on the table."

I'LL JUST PUT THIS HERE 'HEE HEE'

Step Three:

Get the lemon from under the table. Push the quarter into the slit while out of view.

Step Four:

Have an adult assistant stab the knife into the lemon, right into the hidden slit.

I NEVER LIKED LEMONS.

Step Five:

Have your adult assistant hold it high.

NOW TO SHOOT IT!

Step Six:

Take the slingshot and the other quarter across the stage.

I WILL NOW SHOOT THE QUARTER INTO THE LEMON!

Step Seven:

Palm the quarter as you "load the slingshot."

OKAY, 'HEE HEE' HERE WE GO!

Step Eight:

Shoot the empty slingshot.

and your adult assistant acts like the lemon has been h[...]

Step Nine:

Have your assistant hand the lemon to an audience member. They'll find the quarter inside.

62

Chapter Thirty-Four

The sun had barely dipped under the horizon as four men in dingy gray jumpsuits ducked through the tree cover that was just a few feet away from the highway. They were on the outskirts of a small town called Tuscola—at least that was what the map in their hands told them. They were ahead of schedule.

"Are you sure there will be a car?" Gerhard, whose face was long and his forehead high, said to the others in German.

"I trust Felix," Blaz said, also in German. To save time, let it be known that, for the rest of their conversation, the German people will be speaking in German.

"Do you trust that girl?" Joschim, Blaz's sidekick with a beard, asked.

"I have learned to never underestimate American girls," Blaz said. "She may be completely trustworthy, or she may be fully deceptive. But, whichever she is, we have no other choice." He nodded at Heinz, the man with the scar. "How far away are we?"

"If the map is to scale," Heinz said, "ten kilometers, I believe. Or fifteen."

Gerhard held a canteen out to Blaz. Blaz took it and drank from it, ravenously. "If the car is not there, what then?" Gerhard asked.

"Then we continue," Blaz said. "South to the border. Continue at all costs."

They watched the last few rays of the sun disappear completely before they resumed their hike. They moved through the trees along the highway and over the hill, where they could see the lights of Tuscola blinking on ahead of them. Heinz pointed toward the road and they headed in that direction.

They moved with caution, watching for any sign of headlights as they continued following the highway. Finally, just as it had been promised to them, they came along to a car parked on the shoulder. Blaz opened the driver's-side door and the keys fell out at his feet. He laughed and slapped Heinz on the back.

"I told you we could trust dear Felix," he said. "Hurry, get in. We'll be in Mexico by morning."

The men were happy to see that there was little difference between the American car they were stealing and the fine German autos they were used to driving. They settled in and prepared themselves to finally relax in the cushy seats as they began the last leg of their trip. Blaz checked for oncoming traffic before he drove away and was able to put his mind at ease. There was nobody to be seen that could inhibit their travels—none for miles. This was only true, however, because he failed to glance over at the bushes, where he would have seen a large boy doing a terrible job at hiding.

When they passed an abandoned truck, Blaz reminded himself how easily the best-laid plans can go wrong, and so he proceeded with the utmost caution. They drove through Tuscola, doing everything they could to avoid garnering attention. They were almost 100 percent successful. It was only when they passed through Ballinger, about fifty kilometers later, that someone found their passage suspicious.

It was a thin Japanese woman, stepping out of the Palace Theater with her son, looking for the other children who had accompanied them to the movie. None of the men in the car noticed her, but she certainly noticed them. This was proven by her voice, which rang out after they were out of earshot and she had moved past the shock, "That's my car! That's my car!"

Once they were outside the city limits, they increased their speed and hoped to put as many miles between themselves and Camp Barkeley as possible. Blaz stretched. "We are on our way home, my boys."

Suddenly, about ten kilometers ahead, a ghostly figure appeared in the center of their headlights, glowing pale-white in the light, with an eye patch on his face and a lit match in his hand. He also, though no one in the car noticed, held a magnet with a string attached to it.

Blaz yanked the wheel and swerved to miss the ghost boy, who disappeared at the last minute. In saving the life of the apparition, or whatever it had been, Blaz grabbed a hidden cellophane pouch that was taped to the steering wheel. The contents oozed out onto his hands and he could discern from the smell that it was engine grease.

Before he could ask one of the other men to take the wheel, the air outside the car erupted in the sound of gunfire. Or possibly bombs. Or, if they had really thought about the sound, fireworks.

Blaz attempted to zigzag to avoid whatever trap they had driven into, but his hands were too slick to steer with precision, and whichever way he went, the gunfire followed them. Wider and wider he swerved and sent them flying across the road, back and forth between all the lanes, all to no avail in avoiding the bombs. It was almost as if the noise-makers were attached to the car.

Heinz leaped over the seat. "I'll take the wheel," he said and proceeded to find his hands also covered in grease. Still, together, they got the car back under control and the gunfire stopped.

This would have ended their ordeal if something in the woods ahead hadn't started reflecting their own headlights back into their eyes, making it so they couldn't even see the road. Gerhard reached his hand over to grab the wheel, Blaz jammed his foot on the brake, and they spun out of control and straight into a ditch.

It was only then that they heard the siren of the police car behind them.

Blaz and his men jumped out of the car and started to run into the woods, but the police car screeched to a stop and an officer jumped out, gun already pulled. "You boys stop or I'll shoot you."

The other doors of the police car opened and the Japanese woman and her son emerged. "That's it," she said. "That's my car."

"Boy, I guess that's the last time we go see a movie in Ballinger, huh, Mom?" her son said.

The officer squinted at the men. "Hey, those jumpsuits y'all got on? Oh my Lord, these are some of them escaped prisoners!"

Blaz looked at his comrades. They were already down on their knees, hands raised in surrender.

Disgusting, he thought. He closed his eyes, counted to three, and then ran as fast as he could for the tree line.

The officer fired.

Blaz ducked behind a tree and the bullet hit the bark.

Blaz continued running into the darkness, not looking back.

Which was fortunate, because if he had, he would have seen an eleven-year-old magician, holding a mirror, hiding in a bush.

A truck that had once been abandoned near Tuscola drove along the road and flashed its lights, which went unnoticed by the police officer because he was far too busy becoming a hero for capturing the escaped Nazis. Max snuck farther up the road to where the truck had stopped and jumped into the back with Eric. Carl turned around and hurried them back to the theater so they could telephone Mrs. Larousse to pick them up, seeing as Mrs. Jingu was too busy dealing with the police over a matter of a stolen car to drive the children home at a respectable hour.

Carl departed only after Max and Eric assured him Mrs. Jingu wouldn't find it odd that he had disappeared, particularly after she'd picked him up like a forlorn hitchhiker hours earlier in Tuscola, two miles away from where he had parked his truck and two and a half miles away from where he later parked her car. Max was surprised he wasn't more concerned with the auto theft he'd committed, but then again, what were escaped Nazi prisoners for if not the perfect scapegoats?

By the time Mrs. Larousse returned with Max and Eric to their driveway in Abilene, the news had already spread across town. The morning edition headline the next day told anyone who had missed the gossip that night: Three of the escaped prisoners had been recaptured.

And wasn't it funny how silly those Nazis were, driving straight into a ditch and not even trying to run?

Oh yes, America is going to win the war for sure.

Chapter Thirty-Five

"I hope nobody looks in my storm cellar. Or reads this diary, I guess."
—Max's Diary, Thursday, March 30, 1944

And the cowards gave up without a fight,'" Mrs. Conrad read from the paper in class to start the day. "'Finding the advanced machinery of an American automobile to be too complicated for their understanding, they showed their true colors and gladly returned to the warmth and security of the prison gates. Hitler's home cooking must be no match for good old American prison food.'"

The kids in the class laughed and Max felt a surge of pride, as though they were enjoying a performance that she was putting on for them. Which, in a way, they were.

Judy raised her hand.

Mrs. Conrad continued reading.

Judy rolled her eyes and cleared her throat. "Mrs. Conrad?"

Their teacher stopped and glared at her through her glasses. "Please raise your hand next time."

"Yes ma'am," Judy said. "I'm just curious, does the article tell the names of the prisoners who were captured?"

Mrs. Conrad peered at the paper. "No," she said.

"Can you check again?" Judy asked.

The class gasped. Thanks to her nearsightedness, Mrs. Conrad's reading skills were her only superpower. She probably wouldn't have noticed if a circus marched through the classroom, but she never missed even the tiniest punctuation mark.

"Perhaps you'd like to check it yourself?" Mrs. Conrad sneered.

Judy stood. "That would be great, actually." She stepped forward and took the paper out of Mrs. Conrad's hands.

Mrs. Conrad, a look of pure rage on her face, drummed her fingers on the desk while Judy read the article for herself. When Judy handed the paper back to her, she clicked her tongue. "Well?"

"No, it didn't say," Judy said. "I thought the newspapers were supposed to tell *all* the news."

"Why on earth do you need to know the names of the prisoners?" Mrs. Conrad asked.

Judy, apparently only then realizing that she was the center of some unwanted attention from the entire room, began to stammer. "I just— I guess I was— I don't know. I'm just curious."

"That's the kind of curiosity that will send you straight to the principal's office."

"Yes ma'am," Judy said and returned to her seat. But Mrs. Conrad wasn't done.

"No, young lady. You need to bridle that sort of curiosity. What business is it of yours what the prisoners are *named*? Do you intend to send them a sympathy card?"

Judy dropped her head. "No ma'am."

"Do you want to bake them a cake?"

"No ma'am."

"Are you related to one of them?"

Before Judy could respond with yet another humble response, someone from the back of the room answered for her.

"She wants to know if her boyfriend got caught," Lola yelled.

Judy spun around. "You shut up!" she yelled.

"Girls, girls," Mrs. Conrad said. "There is no need for—"

"Why?" Lola yelled again. "You don't want anyone to know that you're in love with a Nazi?"

"I said shut up!" Judy said. "And let's not start talking about who loves who."

"Girls! That is enough," Mrs. Conrad said as she stood.

"Why not, Nazi-lover?" Lola said, also standing.

"'Cause then I might have to tell everybody that you're in love with girls!" Judy screamed across the room.

Lola picked up her pencil sharpener and threw it at Judy's head. "You're a dirty, rotten liar!"

Judy ducked, grabbed her English textbook, and sent it flying at Lola. "At least I'm not a girl lover!" she screamed.

Mrs. Conrad moved like lightning and fastened her fingers onto Judy's ear. "Lola, you come here this instant. You're both going to the principal's office for this vile, sinful behavior."

Lola dropped the pencils she had been aiming at Judy's eyes and dragged her feet to stand at Mrs. Conrad's other hand, with which Mrs. Conrad promptly pinched Lola's ear and pulled both girls out into the hall.

Mrs. Conrad asked the custodian to come in and watch the class. He was an older man, too old to serve in the military, and so treated this task as though it was a mission from President Roosevelt himself. There was no horseplay or trickery under his watch, and the hours until lunch ticked by slower than ever before. Even when Mrs. Conrad returned, he volunteered to sit off to the side as a service to her, God, and country. She—more frazzled than she'd been since the stock market crash fifteen years prior—accepted his offer, and the entire class wished they were dead.

Once the lunch bell rang, Max hurried out to the shed, ready to share the play-by-play of the Battle of Judy and Lola. When she got there, the boys were busy rehashing the escapades of Operation Drive the Nazis Crazy. All in all, it made for a very entertaining meal.

It was Carl who finally ended the fun. "Hey, how do we know Felix is still in the cellar?"

"We tied him up, remember?" Max said with a bit of condescension in her voice.

"Yeah, but if he knows magic and such so well, he might have gotten loose."

Max and Shoji shared a worried glance. "How good are your knots?" Shoji asked.

"Oh, I tied 'em real good," Carl said. "I used my best hog-tying knots. But still."

"I'd almost be more worried if he *didn't* get loose," Eric said with a chuckle. "I mean, we didn't leave him any food or water, and who knows how long it's been since he drank anything."

They all froze at the gravity of his statement.

"Gosh, what if he's dead?" Shoji asked.

Max felt a lump in her throat. "You guys need to go check on him. Now."

The boys rushed to hop on their bicycles and took off toward the storm cellar of death. Which left Max alone to return to class and deal with the moral implications of killing a Nazi and hiding him in your backyard.

Thankfully, Lola and Judy were returned to class after what must have been the most apocalyptic principal's lecture and swatting of all time. Neither of them looked like they had come out unscathed. Judy refused to speak to anyone. Meanwhile, everyone refused to speak to Lola.

After school was over, Max rushed to get in line for the

bus. She could picture the boys digging a hole to deposit Felix's body, and she needed to make sure they dug it deep enough.

Lola caught her before she went out the door. "Can I come to your house? My mamaw's really mad at me 'cause the principal called her. The longer I can stay away from her, the better."

Max noticed several kids staring at them and whispering. She instinctively took a step back from Lola. "Sure, you can come over and we can play in the yard or something," she said.

Lola's face dropped. "Please don't tell me you actually believe stupid Judy."

"Of course I don't," Max said, then remembered Lola's gift for smelling a lie. Max closed her eyes and made herself eradicate any inkling she might have been harboring that inclined her to believe the worst human alive over the Gremlin's personified conscience. She opened her eyes. "Honestly. I wouldn't believe Judy if we were in a thunderstorm and she told me there were clouds in the sky."

Lola smiled. "Thanks."

To show her sincerity, Max pulled Lola into a hug. Then, to show the gawking kids her opinion of them, Max introduced them to "The Rigid Digit," which was a common hand gesture in Brooklyn but might not have translated into Texan. Judging from their shock and giggling, the message rang through loud and clear.

Max decided that it would be advantageous for them to forego the bus ride and walk to her house. When they arrived, Max saw that there was still a bicycle parked in the backyard.

"Is Shoji here?" Lola asked as they walked up to the front door.

"Looks like it," Max said, realizing that Lola's presence and the promise Max had made to her the day before were going to make things difficult, particularly since she was so anxious to know if Felix was still among the living. "Hey, why don't you go get Houdini out of his cage and I'll go see if Shoji's in the backyard."

"I can come with you," Lola said. "I haven't seen Shoji today."

"No!" Max said. "I mean, Houdini really needs to get out of the cage and, uh, I need to talk to Shoji about something. In private."

It wasn't a lie, technically, so Max hoped Lola wouldn't get suspicious.

Lola nodded and went inside, and Max breathed a sigh of relief. She ran around the house and hurried down into the storm cellar, fearing the worst. For all she knew, Felix and Shoji could *both* be dead and Eric and Carl had gone to get coffins.

She couldn't have been more wrong.

Instead, Shoji was sitting in a folding chair that had

never been there before and Felix sat on the bench, a bottle of glue in hand, and a line of repaired Hummel dolls along the seat next to him.

"See, if you ask me, this is the Cardinals' year," Shoji was prattling. "I know, I know, they lost the series last year, but that's just what happens sometimes. Even the best drop the ball every once in a while. But you can't count them out, no sir."

Felix nodded along, meticulously reattaching an arm to a little girl that had a shepherd's crook and a bonnet.

"So he's not dead, then," Max said, and Felix jumped. The arm was stuck to the little girl's ear.

"Oh, no, not even close to dead," Shoji said with a grin. "When we got down here, he was out of the ropes and had gotten water from your garden hose."

"Your neighbor is missing a pie," Felix said as he attempted to unfix the doll so he could refix her appropriately. "A very delicious pie."

"Adding pie theft to your list of offenses?" Max asked. "And from Mrs. Morris no less. You must really love prison."

"A bird had already sampled the crust," Felix said. "I was saving your Mrs. Morris from unnecessary exposure to disease."

"I suppose she should thank you."

"She should." Felix set the Hummel figurine down. "As should you. The four prisoners were apprehended according to plan, were they not?"

"Three," Max said. "One got away."

Felix frowned. "Who?"

"Blaz."

"Of course he did." Felix let out a sigh. "If there was to be an anomaly to the plan, it would be Blaz. He is the most earnest Nazi I've ever known."

Max nodded and remembered that she was previously occupied with keeping Lola far away from the storm cellar while also showing her that she was welcome into every corner of her life. Given the complexity of that mission, she knew she should get back to it. "Well, you're alive, so I guess I should go."

"When will I be able to call my Josephine?" Felix asked.

"He's been bugging me about that since I got here," Shoji said.

Max popped her knuckles. "I don't know yet. It's not exactly the simplest of tasks. I mean, I'm having a hard enough time keeping you hidden from Lol—"

"You don't have to worry about that anymore," Lola's voice said from the top of the stairs. "But now I get to rip off your pinkie."

There were probably many appropriate responses to this particular situation, but Max didn't choose any of them. Rather, she grabbed her hand and prepared to fight for her life, or at least the life of her appendage.

Chapter Thirty-Six

In retrospect, Max knew she shouldn't have been surprised that Lola had come out and listened to the conversation from the top of the stairs. After all, it was what Max would have done in the same situation. She had merely surmised that, given Lola's much higher standard of morality and sense of conscience, she would have let her word be her bond. But of course, when Nazi prisoners are involved, the game of morality is played by different rules. Or so Max assumed.

"Why didn't you tell your dad about him?" Lola asked, gripping Max's pinkie like a vice.

"I just— It's complicated," Max said.

"That's 'cause you're trying to lie again," Lola said. "The truth is never complicated."

"Now, that's baloney," Shoji interjected. "I looked ahead in our math book, and math is nothing but the truth, but it gets super complicated."

"You know what I mean."

"Please, listen," Max said, glancing over at Felix's amused eyes. "I know I should have, or at least that it was the right thing to do, but you've got to trust me. We need to do it this way."

"Not a good enough answer," Lola said and started yanking on Max's finger.

"Ow!" Max screeched when she felt the knuckle pop. "Stop!"

Lola gave it a twist.

"Sometimes doing the wrong thing is the right thing!" Max said. "Like how I hugged you at school."

Lola let go. "What's that supposed to mean?"

Max rubbed her throbbing pinkie. "After what Judy said, most everybody agreed they were going to keep their distance from you, just in case it was true."

"But it's not true."

"Okay, that doesn't change how people looked at me when I hugged you," Max said. "People have their opinions, and that's how they figure out what's right to do."

Lola took a deep breath. "Are you saying this whole thing is just a difference of opinion?"

"I'm saying I need you to trust me. I only ever do bad when I'm trying to do good. Honest."

It was painfully clear from the expression on Lola's face that she was several hundred miles away from being happy about her next course of action, but she nodded in agreement.

"*Wunderbar,*" Felix said. "The *servante* was always meant to have ten hands. It was because it had eight that Blaz went free."

Lola shot him a look. She had clearly not warmed to the concept of joining the league of Felix. "I never said I was going to help."

"But you will, yes?" Felix asked. "These are your friends. Going against the dangerous Nazis. Risking their lives. Would you abandon them in their hour of need?"

"Laying it on a little thick, aren't you, Felix?" Max asked.

"He's got a point, though," Shoji said. "What kind of a person would let their best friends go off alone to catch a Nazi?"

"Two Nazis," Felix said. "Tomorrow you will catch two."

Lola clenched her teeth. "Sure, I'll help. But if anything goes wrong—"

"You get to rub it in our faces for as long as you want," Max said.

That answer seemed very nearly satisfactory for Lola, so they turned their attention to getting her up to speed on the enormity of the task before them and the plan by which they were set to accomplish it. Throughout this discussion, Felix peppered them with the same nagging regarding his phone-call request.

Finally, Max had had enough. "Felix," she said. "There

are FBI agents crawling all over Abilene and the surrounding area. So as soon as I can figure out how to get you to a phone, get a call connected to New York City, and make sure nobody will see or hear you, or listen in on the line, I will tell you. You have my word."

"Your word?" he asked.

"Yes. My word."

"*Wunderbar,*" he muttered.

They settled on a plan that was actually quite exciting for all of them, although for widely different reasons each. Of course, for Shoji, the minute they introduced flammable elements into the mix, he was sold on the plan. Max, meanwhile, was happy to have a more headlining role than before. And, for Lola, she was happy that the plan involved the very first slumber party to which she'd ever been invited.

But this also brought its own issue. "So we're going to tell my mamaw that we're having dinner at your house and tell your parents that we're having dinner at mine?"

"Yeah, it'll be perfect."

"But that's a lie."

Max sighed. "It's not a lie if nobody gets hurt."

"What kind of logic is that?" Lola asked.

"The kind of logic that lets me lie more than you," Max said. "So just trust me."

Lola reluctantly agreed, mainly because a slumber party

had been a dream of equal proportions to Max's magic show dream, and Lola had already seen that sacrifices must be made to see your dream come true.

Eventually it came time for all good little boys and girls to return home and grace the dinner table with their presence. So, after making Felix promise he would do no more pie stealing, they went their separate ways and Max hurried inside and washed up for the meal.

As the Larousses sat around the table and ate their ham and beans, the air was more silent than usual in their house.

At one point, Mrs. Larousse stood to look out the window. "Did you hear that?"

"What?" Major Larousse asked.

"It sounded like the storm cellar door opened and closed."

Major Larousse wiped his mouth with his napkin. "I'll go check it out."

Max panicked and nearly choked on the beans. "I'm sure it's nothing," she said. "I hear that all the time. That old cellar is possessed, I swear."

Major Larousse glanced at her and then sat back down.

"Anyway, how's work?" Max asked.

He sighed. "I actually have something to talk to you about. I was thinking that it might be good for you two to go visit Grandma Schauder for a little while. Until all this stuff blows over."

"What?" Max dropped her fork. "No, we can't do that."

"Why?" he asked. "Don't you miss Brooklyn?"

More than you know, she thought to herself.

"Not really," she said. "And besides, you already caught some of the prisoners. I'll bet you have the rest by next week."

He tapped his ham and cut a few more chunks off to add to the pile of chunks he still had not eaten. "Yeah, we caught three. Under the wildest circumstances. You don't get lucky like that twice."

Her mother reached over and grabbed Max's hand. "Sweetie, I already talked to Grandma. She's got the room all set up for you. She even cleared a spot for Houdini."

Max cast her a puzzled glance. "Wait, you and I are going? Or I'm going?"

"You both are going," Major Larousse said.

Mrs. Larousse looked at him. "Yes, both of us are going, but then I'm coming back. I was away from your father long enough while he was in Africa, I don't want to do that again."

Max felt her chest tighten. "Yeah, we were both away from him, remember?"

"It's just until this whole thing blows over," her mother said. "And from what we've been hearing, there's probably only a few months left to this war."

Max pushed her plate away and gawked at her. "When you say 'until this whole thing blows over,' are you talking about this thing with the prisoners? Or this thing called the war?"

Mrs. Larousse let go of her hand and grabbed Major Larousse's. "We made a mistake making you move here."

Max's mind scrambled. This was becoming far more of a crisis than she had anticipated. "Okay, okay, sure," she said. "But, if I go running off to Brooklyn, won't that make it even more suspicious? I mean, considering the fact that I was basically an accomplice to the escape."

Major Larousse winced. "Max, I'm so sorry I said that. I shouldn't have."

Max shook her head. "No, but you were right. I kept information from you. If I had told you, you could have stopped them."

"You made a mistake," Major Larousse said.

"And I won't again," Max said. "Please don't send me away because of it."

Major Larousse coughed. "I know you won't do it again," he said. "You're too smart to make the same mistake twice. I'm sure, if you ever had information about escaped prisoners, you'd tell me right away."

Max gulped and hoped it had been silent.

"But that's beside the point. This is no place for a kid like you. You're miserable here. Even I can see that."

"I'm not miserable!" she said and forced a big smile. "I love the desert. New York is too crowded. And the traffic, blech. Plus all those buildings? You can't even see the horizon half the time. Also, at night, you never see the stars."

"This isn't a discussion," he said. "You're leaving Monday."

Max had to find a card up her sleeve. A misdirection. Something.

"What if you catch all the prisoners before then? Can I stay?"

"Before Monday?"

"Yeah.

He pondered that. "What difference would that make?"

"Maybe it wouldn't," she said. "But let's just call it a wager. I'll bet you that all the prisoners are caught before Monday. If they are, then I stay. If they aren't, I go."

Major Larousse looked at Mrs. Larousse for her opinion. She shrugged.

He held out his hand. "Okay. It's a deal."

Max shook his hand, satisfied that once again she had made a wager she was guaranteed to win.

That is, provided she could trust the elements of the plan that were outside of her control.

In other words, every single element of the plan.

She began to sweat profusely.

Chapter Thirty-Seven

"I never would have thought I'd be fighting so hard to NOT go back to Brooklyn."—Max's Diary, Friday, March 31, 1944

Judy's absence from class was a surprise to nobody, considering she generally skipped every time a new movie came to town, and also considering the drama she had partaken of the day before. Not that drama was unusual for Judy, but usually she knew the script beforehand and chose to adlib her lines like the other Judy, of the Garland family. Unscripted, unplanned drama was not in Judy's acting portfolio.

The absence, however, that did fill the class with shock was Margaret's absence. She was not the sort who skipped school, at least not to anyone's immediate recollection. Perhaps she had two years ago, one boy posited, but that was the day her father shipped out, and it was unlikely that that event had happened again.

The person in class who seemed the most distraught over the absence was Natalie. Her usually ever-present cheer was gone and replaced with an unattractive gloom. It was so very painful to see that Max offered her a word of encouragement and even a note with an unsavory limerick to cheer her up.

Natalie passed a note back.

I think Judy's in trouble.

Max wasn't sure if she could be so lucky, but she passed a note back asking for more details.

Natalie passed forward a letter, which was written entirely in German. The accompanying note read:

I found this in her room yesterday. Blaz gave it to her the day before the escape. I told her I'd keep it a secret, but now I'm getting scared.

Max scanned over the letter. Her limited knowledge of the written language allowed her to recognize some of the words and phrases, most of which were terms of endearment. Other than that, she was not nearly well versed enough to determine what it was the rogue prisoner had communicated to Judy.

Does she read German? Max wrote on a note back to Natalie.

"No," Natalie whispered. "That's what's so weird about all of this. And Margaret didn't show up for school today, either. They're both missing."

"From class," Max whispered. "I doubt they're in any kind of danger."

"You don't know that, though," Natalie said. "What if Blaz was one of the prisoners that got out?"

Max nodded. Natalie didn't know that Blaz was off roaming free.

"Do you want me to have somebody read this letter and see what it says?"

"Do you know somebody who reads German?"

"I'll give it to my mom," Max lied.

When she handed the letter to Felix later, he read over it quickly.

"Blaz wrote this?" he said. "I did not know he was so poetic."

"Ew, gross," Max said in shock. "He's a grown man. She's just a kid." As if to emphasize the youthfulness of people her age, Max tightened her pigtails.

"It is a farewell letter, such as a man might write to his family," Felix said and folded the item into a tiny square to fit into his pocket. "He must have grown to see your friend as a baby sister."

"Not my friend," Max retorted. "And are you saying he *loves* her? Like they're family or something?" The idea that Judy could be emotionally related to Blaz was almost too perfect for Max to bear. "Please say 'yes.'"

He shot her a disparaging glance. "I do not feel such matters are to be taken so lightly," he said. "Love is not a triviality. Love is a fundamental force of the universe, more powerful than magnetism in binding people together, more powerful than gravity in bringing men to their knees."

She fought an anxious squirm that had suddenly become trapped in her muscles and went to check the bags Shoji had left at the bottom of the stairs. "Wow, do you think he got enough kerosene?"

"*Fräulein*, I am growing anxious. When will I be able to call my Josephine?"

Max tugged on her pigtail again and sighed. "How do you even know she's still there?"

Felix leaned the chair back and balanced on the rear legs. "She is still there."

"How do you know, though? I'll bet there're people that think *I'm* still there. People move all the time."

He dropped back down onto all four legs of the chair. "What are you saying?"

"If there was just some way to know before we try connecting you all the way to an operator in New York." She took a deep breath. She'd been dreading her next suggestion for a while. "What if I call her first?"

"You want to call Josephine?"

"Just so we know we're not sticking our necks out for nothing."

He contemplated this idea. "Then you must do it now. Before we go any further."

"But we need to get ready for the next capture," she said. "What if I do it tomorrow? It's a Saturday, she might be more likely to be home."

"Now," he said.

There was no arguing with an escaped prisoner pining away for a long-lost love a thousand miles away. Max wasn't sure if that was a life lesson or not, so she held on to it just in case.

"Okay, fine. Now," she said. "I just have to get everybody out of the house."

"Such a task should be no problem for The Amazing Max," he said.

"It'll be easier for just Plain-Old Max, actually."

He chuckled. "Make certain you tell my sweet Josephine that I wrote her many letters but received none in return and feared it meant our love had gone south."

She found it amusing that he would use such a casual phrase. "Okay, you got it."

"What will you tell her?" he asked.

"That you wrote her lots of letters."

"*Many* letters."

"Okay, you wrote her many letters but received none in return and feared it meant your love," she snickered, "had gone south."

"Precisely."

She shook her head and hurried inside the house. She fetched Houdini out of her room. She needed an assistant for her next trick.

She and Houdini went into the kitchen, where her

mother was rolling out dough. "Mom, can I call Grandma Schauder?"

Mrs. Larousse paused her baking to look at her daughter, who was nuzzling her little ferret as she had oh so many days after the major first went away. Perhaps because of this memory, she decided to not calculate the expense that would be incurred by a long-distance call all the way to New York. "Of course, dear." She pointed at the phone.

"Um," Max said and hid her eyes in Houdini's fur. "Can I maybe talk to her alone?"

Mrs. Larousse hesitated, then wiped her hands off on her apron and proceeded to exit.

"Can you take Houdini?"

"Max, you know I—"

"Please?"

Her mother sighed and took the ferret from her daughter's arms. This was particularly exciting for Houdini, as Mrs. Larousse was the human least comfortable with ferrets he'd ever encountered, and thus she typically maintained a steady stream of tender morsels to keep him occupied. Sure enough, Mrs. Larousse dug out two plates of leftover chicken and carried it and him off to the living room.

"By the way," Mrs. Larousse said, "if she asks, we've been going to temple every week since we got here."

"But we haven't, and she always knows when I'm lying."

"Okay, just, if she asks, don't tell her we haven't. Okay?"

Max almost protested again, but then remembered that she actually had no intention of calling Grandma Schauder at all, so it was quite the definition of a moot point. "Okay, Mom. Can I call her now?"

"Sure, who's stopping you?" Mrs. Larousse asked and headed as far out of earshot as she could.

Max grabbed the phone and connected to the operator. Felix had given her an old phone number for Josephine. "Hello, Operator?"

"Yes?" the voice on the line answered.

"Can you connect me to New York please?"

"Will you hold?"

"Of course."

Several minutes passed with many clicks and hisses on the line and then a voice with a pleasantly familiar accent answered. "New York, what number?"

"Hi New York!" Max said.

"Hello. What number?"

Max waited a moment to savor the beautiful speed and vowels of the New York accent before she responded. "I need Baldwin three-two-three-three-six."

"One moment," the voice said. There was another click, a louder hiss, and then the voice spoke again. "Hello?"

"Hello?" a woman's voice answered.

"I have Abilene, Texas on the line for you."

"I'm sorry?"

"Abilene, Texas. Do you accept the call?"

"Josephine?" Max yelled into the phone.

The voice on the other end was quiet. "I don't know anyone—"

"So you don't accept the call?" the operator asked.

"Josephine!" Max yelled again. "I'm calling for Felix."

There was still more silence.

"Do you accept the call or don't you?"

"I— I—" the woman stammered. "No, I do not accept the call."

"No, Josephine, please, wait!"

"Okay, thank you. Sorry, sweetie."

The phone went dead.

Chapter Thirty-Eight

I f one were judging by the tempers flaring between Lola and Max that evening, when they most certainly should have been asleep in Max's bedroom, one would think that the attempt at recapturing the Nazis that night had failed. On the contrary, it had been an enormous success, which was most likely the source of the conflict between the two friends.

"That was so dangerous," Lola said. "More than I even could have imagined. That was so incredibly dangerous. We need to stop."

"You're crazy," Max said. "It was all under control. There was only the illusion of danger. Just like a great magic show."

As is usually the case when two parties are fighting vehemently for their side of an argument, they were both correct.

It *was* dangerous. More dangerous than the first time. First of all, Max had actually met face-to-face with the two escapees. Felix had given them the instructions that they were to lay low near Winters until Max arrived to lead them to a location where they could easily hop the rails and ride to El Paso, where they could then cross into Mexico. At one point, while they were walking through the woods, Max very nearly gave away the plan when one asked how much longer they would be walking. She had tried to be rather cute and said, "Walking, not much longer. They'll put you in a wagon in a bit."

She recovered nicely, though, and led them to the ditch with ease. Once they were in the ditch, walking along the road, the actual danger was nearly completely eradicated and the illusion of danger was heightened. This was thanks first to the fog generated by a great deal of dry ice onto which Eric was pouring boiling water several yards away from view. The fog crawled down the ditch and Max proceeded to "panic."

Then Carl and Shoji, using cotton balls soaked in kerosene, proceeded to—

Actually, it would probably be best to not reveal all the aspects of this non-dangerous plan, as it was in reality rather dangerous and might not be safe to be replicated in anyone's home or school. Let it suffice to say that, in the midst of the rising fog, fireballs flew over the prisoners' heads, Max's pigtails "caught on fire," and the men ran as fast as they could for nearly two miles, right across the path of a ranch hand who had been informed by his old buddy Carl that one of his calves was stuck in the ditch.

It only took three seconds for the ranch hand to hop off his horse and drag the two men to the ground. He then tied them up and brought them back to the big house, where the police were called, the FBI came instead, and Major Larousse was given an even greater sense of relief.

Meanwhile, it had been Lola's job to put out all the fire that was left over from the elaborate trick.

It was really rather understandable that she, of all of them, had a true sense of the danger of their plan.

But there was no convincing Max of this fact. Nor was there any dissuading Lola, and so the first slumber party of Lola's entire life dissolved into two people falling asleep in anger and dreaming of winning the argument.

So sweet was the dream, and also Max's sense of satisfaction, that she slept long past the normal rise of humans the next morning, and thus missed both Major and Mrs. Larousse exiting the house.

She went into the kitchen to find some morsel to fill her rumbling tummy and stumbled on Lola, hanging up the phone.

"Calling your grandma?" Max asked. "She doesn't suspect anything, does she?"

"No," Lola said and then walked out of the room.

Max was not proficient at social scenarios, and thus decided to wait for the storm to blow over so they could somehow resume this odd interaction called "friendship." She made herself a sandwich and then, because she presumably had the house very nearly to herself, picked up the phone and clicked for the operator.

"Operator."

"Hi. I need New York, please."

"Didn't you try this yesterday?"

Max was not used to telephone operators being so chatty. "Uh, yes?"

"There isn't any lesson in the second kick of a mule, sweetie."

"Noted. Now can you please connect me to New York?"

The operator huffed but obliged. Once connected, Max again gave the number and, after a few clicks and a loud hiss, heard the same woman's voice on the line.

"Hello, I have Abilene, Texas here. Will you accept the call?"

"Again?" the woman asked.

"Yes, please," Max said. "Just for a minute."

The woman hesitated as before, but this time finally said, "I accept the call."

"Okay, here's your party."

"Josephine?" Max asked.

"Yes, this is she."

"Wow," Max said and lost all of her words. From what Felix had told her, Max felt a little as though she were talking to an angel, or perhaps God Himself.

"You know Felix?" Josephine asked, timidly.

"Yeah," Max said. "I met him a few weeks ago. He's told me a lot about you."

There was a long silence.

"He has?"

"Oh, man, has he ever," Max said. "I don't think I've ever seen anybody so in love with somebody else."

There was the distinct sound of a muffled sob.

"Where is he?" Josephine finally asked.

"Here in Abilene. At Camp Barkeley." Max suddenly hoped she wouldn't have to say the word "prisoner."

"He . . . enlisted?" Josephine asked.

Max gulped. How important was the truth in this situation? She would have greatly appreciated having Lola around to inquire the moral absolute, but sadly she was nowhere to be found.

"Yeah, he's in the army," Max blurted out. It wasn't technically a lie.

"Has he been overseas?"

"Yes, ma'am."

"And he's . . . He's seen a great deal of fighting?"

"Yes, ma'am."

Josephine paused and must have weighed the next question

in her mind, unsure if she wanted the answer. "Why hasn't he called me himself? Is he injured?"

"Not as far as I know," Max said. "Did you receive any of his letters?"

There was another stutter in Josephine's breath. "He— He sent me letters?"

"Yes, ma'am," Max said, then tried to remember what Felix had told her. "He sent you many letters but received none in return and feared that your love had gone south."

Josephine gasped. "He . . . He said that?"

"Yeah, and let me tell you, sister—" Max started, then stopped. A Jeep had just pulled into the driveway, and the driver, a very frantic Major Larousse, leaped out. Instead of entering the house, he marched straight around it toward the backyard.

"I'm sorry," Max said. "I have to go." She hung up the phone before Josephine could say another word. She ran out the door just in time to see Major Larousse start down the stairs of the storm cellar.

"Dad!" Max yelled. "Don't go down there."

He either didn't hear her or didn't choose to listen, for he disappeared into the opening.

Max froze. No amount of magical training or exercises in trickery had prepared her for this moment, when the single most dangerous secret she had ever kept was about to explode in her face.

Then she heard Major Larousse shout and the sound of a struggle, followed by the sound of two dozen newly repaired Hummel figurines plummeting to their second death, then the sound of fisticuffs. All of it was followed again by the major's voice:

"Max! Get down here."

She tried to convince herself that the major was too good a man to see his daughter rot in prison as she made her way down the stairs.

At the bottom, the major knelt on top of Felix, his knee in the middle of the prisoner's back and their arms locked together. All around them were the shattered remains of Grandma Schauder's gifts—evidence that Major Larousse had tackled Felix and dragged him across the room and to the ground, just as any soldier charged with recapturing an escaped prisoner would do. The fact that the major looked to have received no blows or any ill effects from the struggle seemed to indicate that Felix had put up no fight, against the norm for any escaped prisoner seeking permanent freedom.

Over against the wall stood Lola, attempting to disappear, just as any person who had just betrayed a friend's trust would.

Chapter Thirty-Nine

Major Larousse rarely lectured. He was much more well-versed in scolding. He was also a fine purveyor of rebukes. In addition, his skills at the sarcastic quip had been noted among many a subordinate.

Lecturing, however, was not in his usual bag of tricks.

And yet, here, with his body weight pinning Felix to the floor, Major Larousse had delved into lecturing, and he was beginning to get good at it.

He was, of course, the only person in the room who had that opinion.

"I can't believe it. My own daughter. My *own daughter*. Harboring an escapee in our storm cellar. Under my nose, almost literally."

"I'm sorry, Daddy."

"And to have to find out about it *not* from that daughter, but from her *friend*. To get a phone call in my office, interrupting a meeting with the agents from the FBI regarding the remaining prisoners. Do you have any idea how humiliating that is?"

"I'm sorry I'm an embarrassment to you," Max said.

"No, don't do that," he barked back. "Don't try to make me feel guilty about this. This isn't just a mistake. This is a violation. This is treason."

Max nodded.

"And here we're trying to keep the momentum going, keep catching these jokers, and you're helping one escape."

Max said nothing to that.

Felix did instead.

"How many prisoners have you captured?"

"Not enough," Major Larousse said. "We've captured five so far. No, six, counting you."

"You have captured five," Felix said. "If your daughter had not committed treason, you would have captured none."

Major Larousse glanced at Max and then leaned closer to Felix's head. "What the—" he glanced back up at the girls and redirected his tongue to avoid profanities, "—Elmer Fudd is that supposed to mean?"

"Felix had a plan," Max said. "And he needed me to make it work."

"Oh, I don't doubt that this piece of—uh—Sylvester Shyster had a plan."

"Not the kind of plan you're thinking of," Max said. "A plan to capture the Nazis." She proceeded, with a few interjections from Felix, to tell the major exactly what had happened, and also what was intended to happen. And all the while, the major maintained a death glare at Felix's head. It was as if the entire war was happening in the five square feet they occupied in that storm cellar.

Finally, once all explanations had been made, he stood and released Felix. "That's all well and good," he said. "But it's over now. You're going back to the camp."

Felix stood and stretched his back. He momentarily scanned over the poor remains of the now irreparable Hummel figurines and sighed. "Then you will not find the rest of your Nazis, Major. This is your choice."

"You underestimate us," Major Larousse said.

"Do I indeed?" Felix asked. "How many have you caught of your own accord? And how many have been handed to you by a little girl and her friends?"

"That's beside the point."

"That *is* the point," Felix said. "But not the only point."

Major Larousse stepped closer to him. "I'm getting real sick of your double-talk."

"Then perhaps we can speak privately?"

The major, after a moment of thought, snapped his fingers at Max and Lola and motioned for them to head up the stairs. Max almost protested, then remembered that she was on ice so thin that even a spider would fall through, and headed up after Lola.

Once at the top, Lola turned to her. "I'm sorry."

"No you're not," Max said.

Lola thought about it. "Okay, you're right, I'm not. But I'm sorry I'm not."

Max shook her head. "I can't believe you betrayed me. Do I get to rip your pinkie off now?"

"We didn't make a pinkie bargain," Lola said. Max was not amused.

"I don't really care. You're supposed to be the one out of all of us that doesn't do underhanded things like this."

Lola's jaw dropped. "Underhanded? What the heck? I did this because I was doing the right thing. Which is exactly what the conscience of the group does."

"Will you stop?" Max yelled at her. "Stop with all of this 'conscience of the group' nonsense. You're supposed to be a friend. And a friend doesn't hurt another friend. A friend doesn't get another friend in trouble. A friend is loyal, even when it hurts."

"You stop," Lola yelled back. "You don't have any idea what it means to be a friend. It means putting the needs of the other person above your own."

"Yeah, that's what I'm saying."

"No, it's not," Lola said. "Being a friend means doing the right thing, even if it might mean that you're going to lose your friend in the process. When you see your friend in danger, you rescue them, even if they don't want to be rescued."

Max felt as though she was correct, which was a horrible feeling. "I didn't need to be rescued."

"That's exactly how I knew you did, because you were in over your head and had no idea you were six seconds from drowning."

Max closed her eyes and counted, slowly.

"Max!" Major Larousse yelled when she reached six. She cursed her wretched friend under her breath and made her way back down the stairs. At the fifth step, she felt Lola's hand grab her own.

"I'm not letting you drown alone," Lola whispered.

Max didn't voice the appreciation she felt, but Lola knew it was there.

"Yes, Daddy?" Max said when she reached the bottom of the Stairs of Destruction. Felix was seated in the chair again, his eyes focused on the only Hummel figurine that seemed even remotely fixable: a chubby cheeked little girl saying a prayer next to a sheep, which now rested in his skilled hands. Major Larousse stood in front of him, arms crossed, and his posture revealed how unhappy he was with his next bit of dialogue.

"In spite of every single ounce of my better judgment," the major said, "we're going to continue with Felix's plan."

"What?" Lola exclaimed and let go of Max's hand. "Isn't that—"

"Stupid? Yes, a big part of my brain says it is." Major

Larousse uncrossed his arms and looked into Max's eyes. "But I understand why you did the stupidest thing you've ever done. Because sometimes that's the only way to do something smart."

"Wow, your whole family uses the same logic," Lola muttered.

Major Larousse broke out in a grin, briefly. "It's probably a New York thing," he said. "But it's true. Going after these guys the military way means we might give them time to get weapons, take hostages, or any number of ways that people could get hurt. Not only that, but taking my soldiers after them, I can guarantee that one or two of those young GIs will 'accidentally' pull their trigger in the excitement of hunting a Nazi."

"Wouldn't be the worst thing," Lola said.

"Maybe not," Major Larousse said. "But it wouldn't be good. So we're going to do it Felix's way. But we're going to do his way *my* way."

Felix shot him a confused glance. "What do you mean?"

"We're catching the rest of them tonight. Not some today and some tomorrow. All tonight. I'm done with this game."

Felix put the Hummel figurine down. "Major, that is impossible. The prisoners have separated. There is no way you can catch both groups together."

"If they've split up, then so will we."

Felix shook his head. "*Nein.* The plan will not work that way."

"Then we'll adjust the plan." Major Larousse crossed his arms again. "Or you'll go back to your hut and probably won't speak to Josephine again until this war is over. If even then."

Felix stared at the little praying figurine. "And you give your word that I will be allowed to make the phone call?"

"My word as a major."

Felix's eyes snapped to the major's. "That is not good enough. Give me your word as a father."

Major Larousse narrowed his eyes. "Done. You have my word as the father of Maxine Larousse, you will make your precious phone call before returning to camp."

Felix nodded and resumed fixing the figurine. "Then I will need at least two hours to revise the plan. It can be done, but you will most likely need more players."

"Whatever it takes," Major Larousse said and motioned for the girls to follow him up the stairs. "I'll be back in two hours."

Once they were out in the sunlight, Lola finally let her opinion fly. "I can't believe we're working with a criminal."

Major Larousse snapped his fingers at her. "Not a criminal. A prisoner. All of those men, they're soldiers. Their only mistake was being a patriot for the wrong nation. And there're plenty of our boys in the same plight over there.

So if I hope that the enemy is treating their prisoners with respect, I have to do the same with ours."

Max began to well with pride at the major's civility and altruism. "And you're going to let him call Josephine?" she asked.

He glanced at her and pulled them a little farther away from the cellar door. "No, that'd be treason. Perfect way for him to pass secrets to a spy on the outside. After we catch the last of the prisoners, he's going back into that camp in shackles if need be."

"But you said—"

"All's fair in love and war, sweetie." He kissed her forehead, unaware that she was a deflating balloon once full of pride. He walked around the house and drove off in his Jeep. "I'll be back in two hours," he called as he drove out of sight.

"Wow. You New Yorkers need to go to Sunday school or something," Lola said with a sigh.

The Unpoppable Balloon

Chapter Forty

Boy oh boy, I don't know how the major came up with this plan, but it's so crazy I think it'll work," Gil said from the driver's seat of the Jeep, completely unaware that he was actually playing along in a game designed by his least favorite prisoner.

Max shivered in the backseat and tried her best to exude the same level of confidence. Her problem wasn't with the plan, which she'd never even thought to doubt since Felix had thus far been more keen at tricking his fellow prisoners than even a proper magician would be in the same situation. Rather, her inhibitions were rising due to the players involved this night.

To put it plainly, she was nervous about the group of which she was not a part. The team being driven at that exact same time by Major Larousse in his Jeep. The team that had Lola masquerading as Max.

It was, according to Felix, the only way such a drastic

change would work. There had to be two of her. Which was rather difficult, since she barely knew how to be *one* of her, let alone instruct Lola on how to be a doppelgänger.

"The one part I don't get, though," Gil said, "is why we aren't just grabbing them if we know where they are."

"Because it has to look like it's just bad luck," Shoji said, watching Max's face. He'd never seen a girl throw up, so he had no frame of reference, but even without it he was fairly sure it wouldn't be pleasant. He smiled at her.

She tried to smile back, but it came across as though she was imitating a constipated baboon.

"Yeah, that's what I'm saying. Who cares if they think they broke a mirror or had a black cat cross their path?"

"If they suspect that the army is on to their plan, then they might change it," Max said with her eyes closed. This did not help the nausea that was rising.

"But once we have them, there's not much of a plan to have."

"Except for the ones we don't capture," Shoji said. "Like Blaz."

Gil nodded. "And Felix. Though, who knows, the major could be wrong and those guys could be in the group we get."

"Doubtful," Max said, and then gagged over the side of the Jeep. Thankfully she hadn't eaten dinner, so it was more of an abdominal exercise than a regurgitation.

"Feeling sick, kiddo?" Gil asked. "Go ahead and catch some *z*'s. We've still got sixty miles to go."

Max put her head back against the seat and despaired of

her life, or at least of the life choice she'd made when she had said that Lola should join Carl, Eric, and Major Larousse in apprehending the two prisoners that were, according to plan, heading toward one of the more wealthy ranches in the area. She hadn't completely realized what an undertaking it would be as she accompanied Gil and Shoji the ninety miles to San Angelo. Nor had she anticipated how erratic of a driver Gil was after dark. With night vision that bad, it was a wonder he hadn't been classified as 4-F when he enlisted.

Sleep finally found her about seven miles from where they were predestined by the almighty hand of Felix to stop. Shoji shook her and only barely dodged her fist. As it does for every person it touches, the war had taken up residence in her dreams and would not be driven away easily.

"Are we there?" she asked groggily.

"Pretty close to there," Gil said. "Can't get much more 'there' or we might be so 'there' that everybody out here knows it."

She groaned. "I am not in the right mindset to decode your gobbledygook. Where are we?"

He laughed. "On the other side of the hill that the major says the three rascals we're after are camping on."

She rubbed her eyes. "So this is it, then."

"Like tag," Gil said.

She blinked at him as though trying to make sure he wasn't a very confusing dream.

"You know," he said. "When you're playing tag and someone is 'it.' So this is 'it.' Like tag."

"Wow, you get weird after dark."

"You have no idea," he said. He jumped out and pulled a bundle out of the back. "Here're the coats."

She took the pack, then a breath, and set out to walk over the hill.

"We'll give you twenty yards before we follow," Gil whispered after her.

"Thirty," she said. "You're supposed to do thirty."

He sighed. "Okay, it's your funeral."

As she disappeared into the dark, Shoji touched Gil's elbow. "Tag, you're it," he said with a grin. "That was a good one."

Gil rolled his eyes. "Great, I'm stuck with a kid who thinks he's George Burns."

Max climbed the hill and looked down into the valley on the other side. She could see the light of a campfire in the midst of some mesquite trees. There were her Nazis.

She moved quietly through the brush and the weeds, or as quietly as she could considering it was mostly *dry* brush and weeds and not a field of pillows or feathers. She slowed as she drew closer, doing her absolute best to maintain the element of surprise. It was most likely the only factor working in her favor.

She accidentally kicked a bush and a jackrabbit shot across her path and off into the night. The men at the fire jumped and picked up their walking sticks, which they had whittled to have spear-like points at the ends.

"*Halt! Wer da?*"

She almost raised her hands but then remembered that these men had no guns. Menacing as they might have seemed had they been in the middle of a battlefield in France, here with spears in hand and their eyes glazed from dehydration, they were as harmless as the jackrabbit that had alerted them. More harmless, depending on whether you inquired of a ferret.

"It's just me," she said. "*Fräulein* Max. Felix *gesagt, dass ich hier sein würde , nicht wahr?*"

The men, hearing her use their native tongue to ask if Felix had told them she would be there, lowered their weapons.

"*Ja,*" the man in front, whom she would eventually learn was named Horst, said. "*Ja, aber er sagte ihr uns morgen treffen würden.*"

"*Ich weiß nicht sehr viel Deutsch zu sprechen,*" she said, telling them that she didn't speak much German.

"Felix told us you would meet us tomorrow," Horst said.

"The plan changed."

The men exchanged wary looks but said nothing.

"Come on," she said. "You guys need to learn to play to the changes." She wondered if Gil had heard her use his motto and now silently danced a jig thirty yards behind her. Or probably, knowing him, twenty.

"Why? Horst asked.

"Because we've gotten you a hotel to stay at in San Angelo. It's about ten miles that way." She pointed to the lights of the city illuminating a spot on the horizon.

"A hotel?" Horst looked very suspicious. More than that, though, he looked very tired and thirsty.

People believe the lies they either hope or fear are true.

"Yes. With fresh water and soft beds and hot Folgers coffee."

The men inched closer, as though she herself was a piping pot of said Folgers.

"And they will give the room to us? We who are escapees. We who are German?"

She smiled. It truly was always best when people set themselves up for the next magic trick. "Well, not looking like this they won't. But that's why I brought you these." She held out the trench coats. "In the top left pocket of each coat there's a mirror and a rag to clean your faces. In the top right of each there's a matchbook and a pack of Lucky Strikes." Gil had been unwilling to part with any of his Pall Malls, but his bunkmate's Luckys were fair game. It didn't matter to Max. She just needed the magician's staple of smoke and mirrors to make this particular trick work perfectly.

Horst took the coats from her with suspicion. "Why are you helping us?"

Felix had helped her craft the answer. "Because my grandmother is German, and she told me the stories of *Der Erlkönig* and how he comes after the sons of Germany and will take them if they don't make it home." *Der Erlkönig*, or the Elf King, was an old German legend, the subject of a fine poem by Johann Wolfgang von Goethe, and a riveting song by Franz Schubert. However, none of these renditions mattered in this moment to these grown men, who had been frightened as children by the image of the dark figure snatching sons away from their parents and taking them to a land from which there was no escape. These men's eyes betrayed them. In spite of the years between their current state and their childhood, they still stood terrified. Terrified of what lurked in the shadows.

Max held out her hands, waved her left over her right, and produced three tin cups, one after the other, and handed them to the men. Then she pulled a piece of paper out of the air, rolled it into a cone, and, turning the cone on its side, poured water into each of the cups, after which she set fire to the paper and tossed it into the air.

"*Der Erlkönig* is coming after you men. So you must hurry. The map is drawn on the wrapper of your Lucky Strikes. If you do not reach the hotel by midnight, the opportunity will disappear and I fear greatly for your safety."

While they drank from the cups, cleaned their faces in

the mirrors, and lit their Lucky Strikes, she disappeared into the dark.

When she got twenty-five yards away, a hand grabbed her and pulled her down to the ground next to Shoji and Gil. Gil had his rifle trained on the Nazis.

"That was good," Shoji said. "The water cone thing was a nice touch."

"Madame Herrmann would be proud," Max said. "But now we need to go. We have to get everything set up in San Angelo."

Gil shot her a look. "I thought we were just sending them on their way and then calling the cops."

Max grinned. "Where's the magic in that?"

Chapter Forty-One

Josef and Herbert had just stolen milk from a cow.

They, above all the other escaped prisoners, were the two most committed to surviving off the land until they returned to the battlefront. In fact, they weren't simply going to survive. They intended to thrive.

"How do you think the others are doing?" Herbert asked. It should go without saying that he and his partner spoke in German.

"I don't doubt they're making it," Josef said. "But if they are as comfortable with the journey as we are, I will eat my own shoe." He opened his backpack and retrieved yet another can of sardines and a pack of crackers. He ground the sardines with a rock, poured two drops from a bottle of brandy they had stolen, mixed it and minced it with a butter knife, then spread it on the crackers. "More pâté?"

Herbert took the cracker and devoured it, savoring every millisecond that it was in his mouth. "I am so very fortunate to have been paired with you on this excursion. When this war is over, you could be a fine restaurant owner."

"I only hope to own a double chin," Josef laughed.

"You're halfway there," Herbert said. He held out his hand. "Can I have another?"

"Later," Josef said and stood with a stretch. "We must continue down the road if we are to meet this girl who will point us in the easiest direction to return home. Though I can't imagine what she can offer us that will be better than what we can offer ourselves."

"Then let's forgo the meeting," Herbert said, drinking the last of the milk from the cup. "It seems we might be better off."

"The lazy cat settles for water when the cream is just one house farther."

Herbert stared blankly. "Is there a cat in here?"

"No, it is a saying."

Herbert stood. "I do not like cats." He picked up his backpack. "Come now, let us go and discover if this girl is of any value to us."

Josef sighed and followed his daft companion.

They walked through the woods toward the road, following their well-worn map-napkin. They stopped about five meters away. Herbert found the watch in his pack.

"Twenty minutes and she will arrive, if all goes according to plan. If she is not punctual, I propose that we leave."

Josef had no problem with this plan, because it provided them the time to eat more pâté.

Eighteen minutes later, a tiny girl emerged from the other side of the road and walked toward them. She stopped at a tree two meters ahead of them.

"Is that her?" Josef asked.

"I don't know," Herbert said. "I only saw her once. But it doesn't look like her."

They didn't move.

The girl scanned the trees around her, looked over her shoulder, and then, with as thick a Texas accent as they had ever heard, yelled into the darkness, "Josef! Herbert! I'm here!"

Herbert started to stand but Josef held him down.

"Who are you?" Josef yelled in English.

The little girl took a big breath. "I'm—" she closed her eyes and shook her head. "I'm a friend of Max's."

"No, you *are* Max," a voice hissed at her from the bushes at her side.

"I'm sick of all the lying," she said.

The bushes shook and a boy with an eye patch stepped out, wagging his finger at her. "Great. Just great. You and your morals. They're probably long gone now."

Josef chuckled. "Who is he?" he yelled to her.

"See, they're still there," the girl said. "This is my pal. We're here to help you fellas."

★ 321 ★

Now Herbert held Josef down. "Perhaps your help is not what we need," he said.

The girl and boy exchanged a worried glance. "Right, of course not," the girl said and began to back toward the road.

The boy stopped her. "Okay, you don't need our help," he said. "But are you tired of eating snakes or whatever you guys have been dining on since you left the camp?"

"We have done quite well, actually," Josef yelled. He motioned to Herbert that it was time to go.

"Right, so you wouldn't be interested in the empty ranch house we were going to take you to that has an unlocked wine cabinet and a fully stocked refrigerator?"

Josef turned and stepped out into the area where they stood. The girl and the boy took a step away from him. "Wine and food?" he asked. "Who knows me this well?"

The girl gulped. "Felix. He sent us to you."

Josef smiled. "He is a good man. *Komm,* Herbert, *lasst uns essen und trinken Wein.*"

Herbert followed him to stand before the children. "How do we know we can trust you? This could be a trap."

The girl elbowed the boy. "Give them to them."

The boy opened a paper bag he had been carrying and pulled out two very large, aluminum-wrapped tubes. He handed one to each of them.

"What is this?" Herbert asked.

"Those are *burritos,* only the best cuisine that Texas has

to offer," the girl said. "And they're my mamaw's burritos, so they're the best of the best. And that's how you know you can trust me, 'cause I don't go giving her burritos to just anybody."

Josef eyed the bundle in his hands with trepidation. "What is a 'burrito'?"

"The best thing the Mexicans ever gave us," the girl said. "It's rice and beans and cheese—and when my mamaw makes them, sausage—wrapped up in a tortilla."

"Sausage?" Josef asked. He opened the foil and sniffed. "*Lobe den Herrn,* it smells like good sausage." He took a bite.

"Hey, now," the girl said and smacked his hand, then briefly made the face one might make if they were having a heart attack. "Um, sorry, but you don't go eating that out here. You wait till you're in the cushy house so you can really enjoy it. Mamaw's burritos deserve your full attention."

Josef was quick to agree, and although Herbert had some reservations, he finally also accepted the plan. The boy instructed them on how to find the house and which window would be unlocked for them, the girl made them promise they wouldn't take another burrito bite until they were safely inside shelter, and the men hurried away.

When they arrived at the large white house with a brown roof and finely pruned trees outside the front porch, they found the unlocked window and climbed in to find it exactly as promised and then some. The carpet was plush, the couches overstuffed, and there was gin and rum in the kitchen. Herbert also found a nice box of Cubans on a table next to a fancy wooden chair.

Josef, meanwhile, perused the refrigerator and called out to his partner a list of the many fine dishes he intended to make for them that evening.

"After we eat this burro," Herbert said.

"And while we enjoy the finer things," Josef said with a smile. He came and sat on the sofa. "My friend, I told you we would thrive."

They unwrapped the burritos and began to eat. Herbert consumed his and washed it down with a glass of red wine. Josef took his time, savoring every bite. It was thus that he noticed, in the midst of one mouthful, a crunchy, chalky substance. He peeked beneath the tortilla and found a small white wedge. His first instinct was that it was garlic, so he chewed it. It most definitely was not garlic.

If Josef had been trained in the area of pharmacology rather than the culinary arts, he might have recognized the pill in the burrito as being a bit of Barbital, a sleeping pill taken by many people, particularly mothers whose husbands were in the war, leaving them to take care of their stubborn sons alone.

Josef went to ask his companion if he knew what the substance was, but Herbert was already snoring on the sofa. Josef began to feel a most certain sense of dread, but it wasn't for very long. Soon he, too, slipped into a deep sleep.

They would not awaken until Mr. and Mrs. Heyer, the owners of the ranch house who were at that exact moment sound asleep upstairs, came downstairs the next morning. Or, to be more precise, they wouldn't awaken until the police, whom the Heyers would frantically call, arrived.

Still, Josef would have been happy to know that theirs was the deepest sleep of any of the escapees.

Chapter Forty-Two

San Angelo at midnight was really no place for two eleven-year-olds.

Although, to be fair to the fine people of San Angelo, there is no appropriate place for eleven-year-olds at midnight that is not called "bed."

Still, Max and Shoji stood behind the grocery store, where they were plainly not meant to be, waiting for Gil to return from his mission. They had been waiting for twenty minutes.

"Send a GI to round up guys at a bar," Max said. "That was the dumbest idea ever."

"Dumber than sending kids to round up Nazis?" Shoji asked.

"Close tie," she said.

He peeked around the corner to see if Gil was on his way back. "Can I ask you something?" he asked when he returned to her side.

"Any time," she said.

He didn't say anything for about a minute.

"Including now," she said, and he laughed.

"Sorry, it's a weird question, I think."

She playfully punched his shoulder. "At midnight there's nothing but weird questions."

He rubbed the spot where she'd just walloped him. "Okay. Here's the question." He cleared his throat. "What am I to you?"

She furrowed her brow. "What does that even mean?"

"If someone was to ask you, 'Who is Shoji?', what would you tell them?"

"I guess I'd tell them that you're my friend."

He nodded. "Sure, right. But how would you distinguish me from the others? Like, would you say that I'm your funny friend, or your weird friend, or would you just say that I'm your Oriental cowboy friend?" He forced a smile.

She could tell he was quite concerned about this, so she decided to give his question the level of consideration she would have appreciated had the tables been turned. "How many words are in the English language?" she finally asked.

"I don't know, a lot."

"Almost a million," she said.

"Okay, almost a million."

"With a million words to choose from, there's not a single one that adequately describes what you are to me."

He thought about that and then grinned. "So I'm your indescribable?"

"You're my indescribable."

"I can live with that."

At that exact moment, Gil sauntered around the corner. "I'm back, kids."

Max sniffed his breath. "You didn't drink anything?"

"Never on the job," he said.

"Then why do you look so happy?" Shoji asked.

Gil laughed. "I just had a fun time with the fine-looking flyboys and rallied them to join me, as specified, to meet three of my dearest friends."

"Pilots? Meeting us two and who else?" Shoji asked. Gil playfully swatted his head.

"Now then, what about the Krauts?" Gil asked. "Any sign of them?"

Max nervously tugged at her lip. "Not yet. They might have passed out in the desert trying to get here, they were so thirsty." She sighed. "One of us really should have followed them."

"By that you mean me?" Shoji asked. She didn't answer but turned her attention to Gil.

"When they get here, you know how to do the trick?" she asked. "'Cause I don't like trusting the sleight of hand to an amateur."

"I got it, Half-pint. No worries."

"You understand this would be like if you handed off the responsibility to play a concerto to me, right? It's incredibly nerve-racking."

"You do realize how insulting it is to compare my ability to pull off a simple magic trick to your piano playing, right?"

She patted his arm. "I do."

Thankfully for everyone involved, it was only a brief delay before Horst, Peter, and Heinz arrived. (And if you are a very clever person and feel the need to point out that Heinz had already been captured, the prisoner you are remembering was Heinz Rehnen. This prisoner was Heinz Nicolai. Yes, there were two escaped prisoners named Heinz. It is an unfortunately common name that, if we were to retell this tale as a grand epic, we would probably change to increase believability. But, for the sake of accuracy, we must maintain that there were two Heinzs and bemoan the slight it places against the artistic value of this tome.)

When Horst led his partners through the streets according to the map on the back of the Lucky Strike wrapper, he was fairly confident that he would be able to find the hotel without any problems. It was, then, quite discouraging when the location that was designated as the hotel was, in fact, a teeming bar.

"Did you read the map correctly?" Peter asked.

"Of course," Horst snapped back. "It must have been drawn incorrectly."

They bickered for about a minute, trying to decide their next course of action. What they should have been doing instead, though, was moving away from the street. This was a fact they realized when one of the men in uniform at the bar noticed them.

"Hey! It's Gil's buddies!" he yelled.

Without any further warning, the three escapees were surrounded by over a dozen air force pilots.

"Hey there, fellas," one of the pilots said and slapped Heinz and Peter on the back.

"Gil's lookin' all over for you," another said to Horst.

"Hey, somebody go get Gil," one of them yelled to the group.

"No need, gents," Gil said and staggered through the circle to the escapees.

Horst recognized Gil as one of the guards from Camp Barkeley. He stiffened his back and ducked his head.

Gil came up and patted him on the chest. "I told these flyboys that if they saw some strangers in town, they were my sidekicks. Got me out of a fight in the bar," he whispered into Horst's ear. "So if you boys don't mind playing along, we can get acquainted later."

Horst looked up at his face. Was this man too inebriated to recognize them? Or perhaps he didn't pay attention during his rounds. Horst breathed a sigh and nodded.

Gil went over and put his arms around Peter and Heinz. "Yeah, these old boys have gotten me out of a jam or two," Gil yelled to the circle of pilots. "And they're here to do it again, I'll tell you." He stepped away from the men and over to join the circle around them. "But they're friendly. In fact, do any of you boys have a smoke I can bum?"

The three men, nearly simultaneously, reached into their pockets to pull out the pack of Lucky Strikes they each had been given.

But what emerged from their pockets were not Lucky Strikes.

Instead each man held a tightly rolled piece of fabric. An armband, to be precise. It was an armband that none of those three men had ever worn, as they were not any of them members of the *Schutzstaffel*, the most notorious of Hitler's henchmen. But it was an armband that they recognized, as did the pilots.

It was distinguishable by the swastika, displayed prominently into the view of every man that surrounded them.

The sight of the swastika sent every single person in that area running. It sent all the flyboys running to tackle these men they now knew were some type of Nazis. And it sent the escapees running for their lives.

So it was that, when they turned down a corner in hopes they would not be ripped limb from limb by the drunken pilots that chased them, they were thrilled to see seven police officers, guns drawn, waiting for them.

They raised their hands and surrendered immediately.

And, in the shadows, the girl who had phoned the police from the payphone nearby had a secret smile. Apparently Gil *was* good at the old PICK POCKET AND SWITCH TRICK.

Chapter Forty-Three

Major Larousse was waiting for Max when Gil dropped her off. It was past two in the morning, and yet he was wide-awake, mainly because it is required of officers to be the first informed on the status of a mission. Also because, at that hour, he felt the inclination that a father should be wide-awake when his daughter is out past midnight.

She walked through the door and, for a moment, he hugged her as she had once hugged him when he'd walked through the door after his time in Africa. It was a hug they had not shared in a very long time. Yet, as quickly as it came, it died, and he peppered her with questions about the mission and how things went. Still, that hug gave her a glimmer of hope that, maybe, just maybe, the man who once would hide under the bridge in Central Park and hop out to scare her at the very moment she believed he was gone—maybe that man was still alive, somewhere deep inside the shell of Major Larousse. After completing the conversation, they both moved to their respective beds and collapsed into a slumber so deep, they were lucky the next day was Sunday.

It was the tiny chill in the air that woke Max the next morning. She had been so swift in her trek to the land of dreams that she hadn't noticed her window was open when she went to bed. She found it only mildly puzzling, since she didn't remember opening the window, but assumed her mom had done it at some point during the day. Mrs. Larousse did have a habit of cleaning the whole house with bleach when she was particularly anxious. And given that Major Larousse had refused to reveal to her what exactly he and Max were going to be doing when they had left to do what they did, it would make sense that she'd had the nerves of a cat.

She left her room and moved to the kitchen, where Major Larousse sat at the table enjoying some bacon, eggs, and pancakes. Mrs. Larousse set a plate of the delicacies out for Max.

"Wow, you seem happy," Max said.

"He is," her mother said and kissed the major's forehead. "We got the call this morning that they caught five more prisoners. Three in San Angelo and two, believe it or not, sleeping in one of the ranch houses out west of here."

Max took a bite of her bacon. "Talk about lucky," she said.

Mrs. Larousse sat and drank from her cup of coffee. "Hey, maybe you won't have to go live with Grandma Schauder after all."

"Drat," the major said. "We were so close to having the house to ourselves."

They maintained the conversation for a few more minutes before Max jumped up. "Oh, I forgot to feed Houdini. Poor thing, he's probably starving."

"I fed him last night, sweetie," Mrs. Larousse said. "We actually got along quite well while you were gone. He can be quite the gentle ferret when he's in the right mood."

"I'm gonna go get him and let him run around, then, since you two are such good friends," Max said. "Besides, I missed his fuzzy little tail in my face while I was sleeping."

Max went to retrieve the ferret from her room, but the cage was, predictably, empty. She looked under her bed and dresser and every other nook or cranny that Houdini preferred to frequent, all to no avail. She crawled along the hallway, trying to see the world from his eye level in hopes of catching him napping. She didn't have any luck.

When she crawled past the kitchen, her mother came out after her. "What are you doing?"

"Houdini got out."

Mrs. Larousse walked to Max's room. "That's impossible. I put him in the cage and even tied wire around the door to lock it."

"He's Houdini, Mom" Max said. "He can get out of anything."

Mrs. Larousse came back from examining the cage. "That just doesn't make sense, even for Houdini."

Max stood. "Oh, no. You left my window open. I'll bet he got outside." She ran out the front door before she could hear Mrs. Larousse say, "Your window was open?"

Max looked around the yard, behind every bush and under every rock, but there was no sign of her little ferret friend. Then she heard Mrs. Morris next door, singing some hymn while she cleaned her kitchen. With a groan, Max went over to see if Houdini had returned to the scene of his earlier crime.

"No, dear, trust me, if that wild animal had gotten back into my house, you'd know," Mrs. Morris said.

"He's not wild," Max said. "He's a domesticated ferret."

"I know a wild animal when I see one," Mrs. Morris said. "It's a gift that comes with age."

"Yes, ma'am," Max said. "Thank you for your time." She walked away from the back door.

Mrs. Morris reached out and pulled her back to the door. "Dearie, did you go to church today?"

Max blinked at her. "I'm sorry?"

"My pastor said today is the day that lost things can become found things, and I've been wondering about you and your family. Do you go to church?"

Max wiggled out of her hand. "Next Saturday is the start of Passover, so I imagine we'll go then."

"What?" Mrs. Morris asked as though Max had just said they were planning a trip to Mars.

"Yeah, we always go to temple for Passover. And my mom was telling me that there's going to be a nice Seder meal at Temple Mizpah, so we'll probably go to that."

"Yes, I know," Mrs. Morris said. "The Ladies Auxiliary is putting on the Seder meal. But I didn't know that your family is Jewish."

Max was very anxious to find her ferret. "My mom is, so I guess that makes me one, too," she said. "Can I go now?"

Mrs. Morris shook her head. "I don't know if you know this, dearie, but the Messiah you people are waiting for has already come. I talk to him every Sunday."

"That's wonderful, ma'am," Max said. "I sleep in every Sunday, so it sounds like we both enjoy our weekends. But I really need to get back to Houdini."

Max turned and walked away. Mrs. Morris called after her, "I'll be praying for you, young lady."

Max always found it odd that the phrase "I'll be praying for you" never seemed to carry the reassurance it seemed, on the surface, it was intended to bear. Still, with or without Mrs. Morris's prayers, her anxiety over the location of her ferret was beginning to overwhelm her.

Then she saw that the storm cellar was open and,

momentarily, felt a bit of a relief. If Houdini had ventured down there, maybe Felix had corralled him and was waiting for her to come and return the little creature to his rightful home.

When she descended into the abyss, every ounce of relief she had felt disappeared. For Houdini wasn't down there. And neither was Felix.

Instead, the chair Felix usually sat in was charred black and dripping with a red liquid that was unmistakably blood. The same blood was also smeared along the floor toward the stairs and also had been used to write on the wall that the now immolated chair faced:

MENE MENE TEQEL UPHARSIN.

Chapter Forty-Four

See, that's exactly why I told you to put the bell on him," Carl said. All of the other Gremlins shot him a look of disbelief.

"You think I should have put a bell on Felix?" Max asked from her seat on the steps. Lola sat next to her, arm around Max's shoulders, rubbing her arms to help relieve the emotional chill that Max had held in her bones since the moment she screamed.

"No, Houdini," he said. "A bell on Felix wouldn't have helped if somebody killed him. They probably would have taken it off."

Shoji glanced at Max's pale face. "Carl, I've never said this to you before, but shut up."

"Well, whether Felix was murdered or not, I don't know," Major Larousse said from under the stairs. "But the blood isn't his." He stepped out with a box and pulled the gutted, decapitated corpse of a chicken out of it. "Somebody put a lot of effort into this."

Eric had been standing in front of the words on the wall ever since he and the others arrived, after Max had frantically called them, which was when the major heard the news and rushed her outside before her mother found out what had happened.

"Oh, I know where I've seen this before!" Eric said and slapped his forehead. "It was in church a few weeks ago. It's in Daniel, I think." He turned to the major. "Do you guys have a bible?"

"Uh, no, I'm afraid not," Major Larousse said.

"Mrs. Morris probably does," Max said. "She talks to Jesus a lot, so she'd better have the book he wrote. I hear authors have really fragile egos when it comes to stuff like that."

Eric hurried over and, a few minutes later, came bounding down the stairs. "Yeah, I was right. Daniel chapter five, verses twenty-five through twenty-eight. It says: 'And this is the writing that was written: *Mene, Mene, Tekel, Upharsin.*' Just like on the wall."

Major Larousse moved to read over his shoulder. "And it gives the translation. 'This is the interpretation of the thing: *Mene*: God hath numbered thy kingdom, and finished it. *Tekel*: Thou art weighed in the balances, and art found wanting. *Peres*:' which I guess is somehow related to 'Upharsin,' 'Thy kingdom is divided, and given to the Medes and Persians.'" Major Larousse looked at the words again. "But what does that even mean?"

Max jumped up. "Devil-worshipping Jews, that's what it means."

Major Larousse looked more shocked than she'd ever seen him. "You'd better never let your mom hear you talking like that."

"What are you saying?" Lola asked her.

"I'm saying it's got to be the old lady in the haunted house. That's the only explanation. She had to have come in here and taken him."

"And now you sound crazy," the major said. "I need you to explain what you mean."

She hurriedly told him the whole story of what had been happening in the storm cellar, apologizing after every couple of sentences for not informing him of the situation because she could tell he was teetering on the edge of a Major Explosion.

"Okay, then let's go rattle her cage a little and get some answers," he said and started up the stairs.

Lola jumped up to stop him. "Hold on, what if she's not a devil-worshipping Jew?"

"She's not," Max said. "That was just a joke." Max pushed on the major's back to motivate him to scoot Lola out of the way.

"Okay, I get that," Lola said. "But what if she's not evil at all? What if she's just a little old lady and we're about to go give her a heart attack?"

The major nodded his head after a moment of contemplation. "No, you're right."

"What do you suggest?" Max asked.

"Just you and I go," Lola said. "And your dad can be close enough to swoop in if there're any issues."

And so it was that Max, the girl from Brooklyn who brought the magic, and Lola, the girl from Abilene who was the voice of conscience, walked up to the front door of the old lady from the haunted house, who incited terror in children everywhere. After seventeen seconds of mustering up the courage, Max knocked on the door precisely one second before Lola pointed at the street that crossed Max's street.

"Hey, isn't that a Jeep?" Lola asked.

Max looked to see what she was speaking of but didn't respond because, in that moment, the door opened.

Gil stood before them with a plate and a towel in his hands.

"Hi, Half-pint," he said with a grin. "What are you doing over here?"

"I—" she shook her head and refused to be distracted by his question. She could do nothing about being distracted by his presence, unfortunately. "What are *you* doing over here?"

"Just having lunch with Mrs. Mosen," he said. "I usually come over here to take her to the temple on Saturdays, but since we were busy yesterday, I thought I'd at least bring her some food to make up for it."

Max and Lola both shared the same look, which was the look one has when they discover not only that there is a person operating the puppets in the marionette show, but also that the person is actually their uncle.

"You're— You go to temple?" Max asked. "But you're not Jewish."

A bell rang behind him. "Here, you'd better come in. She gets very cold when the door is open."

Max and Lola both leaned over to look behind Gil. The very thin, old lady, Mrs. Mosen, sat on a very thin, old couch. She stared back at them through her sunken eyes, her toothless mouth opening and closing like a fish in water. She rang her bell again.

Gil pulled them in and closed the door. "Here, have a seat." He pointed them to two ancient wooden chairs that barely stood upright. On the wall behind the lady was a square of fabric with the six-pointed Star of David embroidered on it.

"Oh my gosh, Margaret was half-right," Max said. "She is a Jew."

Gil stood between the two chairs after they sat. He put his hand on Max's head. "This is Max," he said loudly.

Mrs. Mosen nodded. He rested his hand on Lola. "And this is Lola." Another nod. He went into the kitchen and put the plate on the counter.

"You have a nice place," Lola said loudly. Mrs. Mosen stared at her blankly. Max thought perhaps a different line of questions was in order.

"Do you like the temple here?" she asked. She was met with blankness as well.

Gil reentered the room. "Mrs. Mosen doesn't understand English," he said.

"Then what does she speak?" Max asked.

"She doesn't speak at all," he said. "She lost her tongue when she was a child. But she understands Yiddish."

Max shook her head. "I don't understand, why are you here?"

"I told you, I take her to temple every Saturday."

"Yeah, but why?"

He sighed and sat next to Mrs. Mosen. He took her hand in his. She gave him a faint smile. "She's the grandmother of someone you don't know. Abe Mosen. He was stationed here before he got deployed to France." He patted her hand. "He asked me to take care of her for him while he's away."

"Wow, that's a pretty hefty job to do for somebody," Lola said.

Gil's face got a look of tenderness on it neither of them

had ever seen him exhibit before that moment. "He's worth it. And being close to Mrs. Mosen, it's like being close to Abe. So I don't mind." He patted her hair and kissed her. She rubbed his face and her smile grew. "Anyway," he said as he stood. "What are you girls doing over here? Selling cookies?"

"No, we were going to ask her something," Max said with a sigh. "But it doesn't really matter anymore. She's not the person we thought she was. Heck, she doesn't even know who we are. There's no chance she'd knows anything about what we need to know."

He cocked his head. "Hold on, now, what makes you think she doesn't know who you are? She probably knows more about you two than you know about yourselves. Do you know what she does all day, every day, if I'm not over here to keep her company? She sits in front of that window and watches. She watches the neighborhood, watches the people who come and go. From sunup to sundown, and sometimes even after dark, she's always watching."

"She might have seen something," Lola said. Max nodded.

"Okay, then let's ask her," Max said.

"Sure," Gil said. "Do either of you know Yiddish?"

Max felt the lightbulb flash on yet again. "No, but I know someone who does."

Chapter Forty-Five

Max's living room was teeming, looking far more like a military listening station than a cozy place for tea. But there was still tea. Mrs. Larousse had made tea for Mrs. Mosen as Major Larousse and Max ran through the process of getting her up to speed on the events at hand at breakneck pace. So shocked was she when she learned there had been an escaped Nazi prisoner in her own backyard that she nearly let the water boil over before she poured it into the cups. But, as any military wife does, she quickly recomposed herself and played to the changes like a professional. Which was a fantastic turn of events, because she was an integral part of the upcoming proceedings with Mrs. Mosen in the living room.

As was the person on the phone, speaking to Mrs. Mosen: Grandma Schauder.

After listening for a few seconds, Mrs. Mosen took the pencil that Mrs. Larousse handed her and wrote on the notepad in front of her. Then Mrs. Larousse took the pad and read the contents to Grandma Schauder on the phone. Once Grandma Schauder translated the message to her, she covered the mouthpiece and spoke to the room.

"She says that she's been watching our house for a very long time."

"Great," Major Larousse said over his cup of coffee. "Has she seen anything suspicious?"

"Did you hear that, Mama?" Mrs. Larousse said into the phone. "He wants to know if she's seen anything suspicious. Well, I know you don't know yet. You have to ask her. Okay, I'll give you to her." She handed the phone to Mrs. Mosen.

And this was the tedious process they went through to piece together what exactly Mrs. Mosen had seen and how it might be of use to them.

Mrs. Mosen hadn't made it a point to watch their house over the others—not at first, at least. But when she began to see people going in and out of the storm cellar while the house was vacated, she began to feel it was her duty to keep an eye on everything.

And, one particular night, in the rain, she saw a shadowy figure leave the storm cellar. And then she saw the girl who had just moved in go down the steps, so she made sure to watch very closely, even though it was dark and late and she had been very cold.

"And she saw the person close the cellar on the girl,"

Mrs. Larousse said. "Wait, Max, you were stuck in the cellar?"

"Yeah, and I thought it was her who'd trapped me in there. But I guess she let me out."

"Yes, and she also said she took some shoes because she was scared she might freeze to death." Mrs. Larousse couldn't help but scold Max with her eyes for keeping this a secret. "They're in her pantry, apparently."

"Is that where my boots went?" Major Larousse asked.

"Those are your boots?" Gil asked. "Oh, gosh, I've been wearing them when I do her yard work."

"You do her yard work?" Max asked. "'Cause it doesn't show."

"I'm not very good at it."

"That does show."

"Anyway!" Mrs. Larousse barked. "What shall we ask now?"

"Ask her if she saw anything suspicious in the last twenty-four hours."

Ah, yes, that she had. If they would have only asked that first, they could have saved a great deal of time. Because she had seen a man come out of the storm cellar, a man in a gray jumpsuit.

"And she says he was accompanied by a girl."

Everyone in the room stared at Mrs. Mosen in disbelief.

"Like a woman?" Major Larousse asked. "Maybe his Josephine?"

"No, not a woman," Mrs. Larousse said. "A girl. And she said the same girl went down into the storm cellar a few days ago."

"The night I thought I heard somebody out there," Major Larousse said. "Try to get her to give you a description."

Shoji leaned over to Max and whispered, "Hey, that reminds me, when we were looking around the house while you were gone, me and Eric found some footprints outside your window. As if someone had climbed in or something. And they were definitely not prints made by a man or a boy, 'cause there were heels and pointed toes."

"Why didn't you tell me that before now?"

"I was going to but then you brought the hag," he said.

"That's not nice," she said, but then she turned her attention to the more pressing issue. "So a girl came in my window? Why?"

"I don't know, but Carl doesn't think Houdini busted out of the cage, 'cause your mom told him she had tied it up with wire or something and there wasn't any way a ferret could undo it."

Max felt a lump grow in her stomach. "So somebody stole my ferret?"

"Yeah, I guess so."

Max glanced back at Mrs. Mosen, who was listening again to Grandma Schauder. "Why would a girl steal my ferret? And why would a girl leave with Felix?" She thought for a moment. "What girl would be interested in stealing my ferret *and* my Felix?" Her eyes widened. "Judy."

"Judy?"

"Judy. Think about it. Who else hates our guts so much that they'd do something this terrible to hurt us. To hurt me?"

Shoji still had his doubts. "I don't know. I mean, maybe, I guess. But using chicken blood and burning the chair and . . . no, wait, I see it now. You're right, it's got to be Judy."

"Let's go," Max said and pulled him into the kitchen.

"Where are we going?"

"To her house. We're going to catch her red-handed with my ferret and with Felix."

He looked back into the living room. "Shouldn't we wait for them to come with us?"

"Why? I'm not afraid of Judy."

"No, but I'm a little afraid *for* her," he said.

"She made her own bed," Max said, and they went outside. Shoji hopped on his bike and Max got onto Lola's, then they switched because Lola's was too small for Max but Shoji had some experience riding it. They rushed down the road and over toward Judy's house.

They stopped when they turned down her street.

A police car was parked in the driveway.

"I guess they got here first," Shoji said.

They rode up closer and dismounted their noble steeds. Max noticed that Margaret and Natalie stood to the side of the house, listening as Judy's mother sobbed to the officer that "She's gone. She just . . . is gone. Lord only knows where she went."

Max and Shoji went over to Margaret and Natalie.

"What happened?" Max asked.

Natalie shook her head. "Judy's gone. She disappeared."

"And you don't know where she went?"

"No," Natalie said.

Max looked at Margaret. Her face was pale, and her eyes dodged any form of contact. "You *both* don't know where she went?"

Margaret dropped her head. "No."

Natalie's jaw dropped. "Margy! What do you know?"

"Shhh!" Margaret hissed.

Natalie narrowed her eyes, grabbed Margaret by the crook of the arm, and dragged her around the house. Shoji and Max followed close behind.

"What do you know?" Natalie asked again.

Margaret dropped her gaze. "I told you, nothing."

Natalie shook Margaret like a dog shakes a chew toy. "You're lying. What do you know?"

"Judy made me promise not to tell," Margaret whimpered.

There, in the midst of the beautifully trimmed bushes and fantastically groomed flowers done by the hands of a

Nazi prisoner, Natalie slapped Margaret with such force, Max genuinely worried she might have knocked a tooth loose.

"I swear I will never speak to you or her again," Natalie said. "You two are the worst. What do you know?"

"It started out as a prank," Margaret said with tears welling in her eyes as she clutched her cheek. "I used to go down into that storm cellar and draw on the walls. Just things I'd see in books. And then, when I realized how much Judy hated Max, I took her down there to see." She took an erratic breath. "She always liked you better than me."

"Because you're a weasel!" Natalie said.

"Okay, no time for that," Max said. "So what happened?"

"So she decided to paint her own thing on the wall. Some Yiddish curse she'd seen in a book."

"So that was Judy?" Shoji said. "Wow. We really should have been pranking her harder."

"Yeah, but then, I don't know, I started feeling like she was taking it too far, so I stopped going along with it," Margaret said. "But then, Friday, she stops me on our way to school and tells me that Max was hiding a Nazi in the cellar. Said she went down to do another painting the night before and she met him."

Max hated herself for feeling disappointed that Felix never told her this. "Okay, so what happened?"

"She said—" Margaret started to sob. "She said he was

going to take her to Blaz. But I didn't believe her. I thought she was just telling stories."

Natalie raised her hand to slap her again. Max grabbed it and stopped her.

"Did she say *where* they were going to go to meet Blaz?" Max asked.

Margaret nodded. "Yeah, but it's too ridiculous."

"Where?" Natalie yelled.

Margaret took a deep breath. "Sweetwater."

Max and Shoji exchanged glances. Sweetwater was only forty miles away. "Why is that ridiculous?" Max asked.

"Because of how they were going to get there," Margaret said. "They were going to hop on a train."

Chapter Forty-Six

Max had been given very specific instructions that she and the Gremlins were to stay put at the house and keep her mother company while Major Larousse and Gil drove to Sweetwater to apprehend Felix and, hopefully, Blaz. It hadn't mattered how much she had begged Gil, while he was loading rope into the back of the Jeep, to just let her ride along if she promised she'd be quiet. Nor did it matter how much she attempted to sweet-talk the major, while he was loading his pistol with bullets and counting out enough spare ammo to reload on the fly, by promising that she'd make his absolute favorite pie for an entire week if he would at least let them ride along with Mrs. Larousse in a car behind them. The entire exchange was quite infuriating for all of them, so much so that Gil snapped the rope at her behind like a whip and she swiped three of the major's bullets out of spite.

It was also why, when they were finally driving away

from the house, the men were so relieved to be done with it all that they neglected to double-check the duffle bag in the backseat to make sure no pre-teen magicians had stowed away. Which, in case you hadn't already leaped to this particular conclusion, she had.

It wasn't even so much that she wanted to be a part of the final capture, or that she wanted to see Judy's face when they arrived guns blazing, or that she had to make sure for herself that Felix was safely taken back to Camp Barkeley. Rather, she was immensely concerned about Houdini, and she had a suspicion that in all the hubbub of catching Felix and Blaz, her poor little ferret's safety would be the least of their concerns.

She didn't know if Madame Herrmann had any treatises on the safety of small animals, but she could only imagine the QUEEN OF MAGIC would do the exact same thing.

The forty-five minute drive to Sweetwater was an interesting one, mainly because Max rarely got to listen to the major have a conversation with a GI when he didn't know she was around. He was far more coarse and unrefined than she'd ever heard him be before. She actually quite liked it.

"Why go to Sweetwater?" Gil asked. "If they're trying to get to Mexico, why not fly south, you know?"

"Straight shot to El Paso from Sweetwater, Private," Major Larousse said. "From there, you can smell the beans and tortillas freshly made across the river."

Gil cleared his throat. "Permission to speak freely, sir?"

"Sure."

"Why were you hiding Felix in your basement?"

The major regretted giving the requested permission, but he couldn't take it back, so instead he proceeded to tell Gil the story of Felix and Josephine, and of the love that even a war couldn't kill.

Gil drove in silence for a few miles, thinking about what he'd just heard. Finally he spoke again. "Did you ever know Mrs. Mosen's grandson? Abe Mosen?"

"Briefly," the major said. "He was heading out when I arrived. Mechanic, right?"

"Yes, sir. Best in the motor club." Another few miles passed. "Mechanics don't die too often, do they, sir?"

Major Larousse watched the road pass beneath them for a while. "Everybody dies, Private. Once you go over there, you learn that. Even those of us who make it back. The war kills us all, just some more than others."

"Yes, sir."

"That's why we fight so hard to keep 'over there' over there. Let this place still be the land of the living."

"Yes, sir."

"Even if it means letting a little girl put on a magic show for the enemy. We do it so we can maybe find a way to live again. Because that's the only magic there is, and nobody can survive without it. "

Gil nodded without another word.

Major Larousse reached over and patted his back. "Your mechanic will be fine, son. He's got a lot to come home to."

Gil nodded. "Yes, sir. Thank you."

"Gil?" Major Larousse said.

"Yes, sir?"

"Until we get back to camp, call me Larry."

Max felt a tad overwhelmed by the emotional exchange between the two of them. It was unexpected that two men could be so sensitive and tender.

"If I remember correctly," the major said, "they train the women pilots out here at Sweetwater. The WASPs, I think they're called."

"Oh?"

"Yeah. I wonder if the girls *inside* the planes will look anything like the ones on the outside, you know what I mean?"

"Yes, sir," Gil said, and they laughed.

Ah, they had returned to the finer points of manhood. Superb.

After another twenty minutes or so, they arrived in Sweetwater and made their way over to the train depot. Once they'd parked, they agreed to split and canvas the area in search of the elusive escapees and, of course, Judy. No mention was made of Houdini, which Max felt validated her uninvited attendance.

Once the major and the private were out of sight, she hopped out of the Jeep herself and went in the only direction they hadn't gone, which was directly into the depot building.

She walked gingerly across the old wooden slats that creaked when she placed even an ounce of weight on them. The depot was a platform, really, with a center wooden structure that provided several nooks and crannies to hide in. This would come in handy if she needed to hide from anyone. Which, considering she probably needed to hide from everyone, made it the perfect spot for her to be.

She stood against the wall and inched around the building, wondering where on earth she would be if she were attempting to catch the train to El Paso. Probably on the train to El Paso, she decided, because she wasn't the sort to put those kinds of things off until the last minute. But if she *was* the sort to do so, where might she have tucked in for a nap or whatever escapees did in their spare time?

She had little chance to contemplate this puzzle, because she suddenly felt something tugging at her sock. It was gentle, yet persistent, and would have been unnoticeable if it hadn't been the very experience she'd been hoping for.

Somehow, her precious ferret had found her in the middle of nowhere.

She scooped him up, and he proceeded to shower her nose and chin with kisses upon kisses. He'd been just as worried about her out in this rabbit-infested wasteland as she had been about him.

And then their reunion was interrupted by the least welcome of people.

Judy came running around the corner, whispering, "Here ferret, ferret, ferret. Where the heck are you?"

She locked eyes with Max, let out an expletive, and turned and ran for her life.

Max uttered a similar expletive, tucked Houdini into a pocket sewn inside her shirt, and took off after her.

They raced across the platform and down onto the train tracks. Judy ducked behind one of the trains and then crawled under another. It was the crawling that slowed her down enough for Max to catch her. When Max got to her she tripped her, and Judy fell and a rock scraped her face.

It was then that Max realized a train just a few yards away had started moving.

"Let me go!" Judy said. "I have to get over there."

"Why? So you can ride off into the sunset with your Nazi boyfriend?"

Judy kicked Max's hand off her ankle and bolted toward the moving train.

Max gave hot pursuit.

She arrived at the moving train in time to see Judy jumping into an open freight car. Max took a deep breath and decided to try to make it on herself.

But then a hand grabbed her by the throat, spun her around, and slammed her little body into a metal wall behind her.

"Why do you continue to show up where you aren't wanted?" Blaz growled at her as he held her three feet in the air by her neck.

Max kicked at his legs and his torso, but he dodged each impending blow.

She clawed at his hand, which was beginning to tighten and cut off her air supply. She began to realize just how much we take breathing for granted on a daily basis.

"Hey, I see one of them!" Gil's voice, faint from distance, called down the line of trains. "And I think he's got that girl."

Blaz grunted, slung Max over his shoulder, and ran to catch up with the train Judy had jumped on.

Max gasped for air and looked up to see the major and Gil running. It didn't look like they would make it.

Major Larousse stopped and pointed his gun at them.

"Daddy!" she yelled.

He froze.

"Max?"

Blaz leaped onto the train, which switched into a faster gear, and they left Gil and Major Larousse in the dust.

Chapter Forty-Seven

Cowering in the corner of an empty train car is not a particularly pleasant way to recover from being almost-choked by a Nazi. Unfortunately, it was the only option Max had, and so that was exactly what she did.

Thankfully, the Nazi was a bit too preoccupied tending to the tiny little scratch on Judy's face to pay any further attention to the girl he generally found so annoying it caused him physical pain.

"We must find bandages," he said to Judy.

"I'm fine," Judy said, and then she gave him a hug. "Honestly, I've been hurt worse."

"But not while I was protecting you, little sister. How could I have been so careless?" he started.

"No, now, you can't think like that," Judy said. "You just can't."

He nodded but still had the scowl of a man filled with guilt. To be clear, not guilt over being a Nazi. Heavens, no, that was Blaz's favorite thing. Rather, guilt over causing a little Aryan girl a minor discomfort.

Judy patted him on the back. "Okay, now, you promised me that when we got on the train, you'd finally lie down and get some rest. We have almost five hours before we get to El Paso, and you'll need your sleep."

He took a deep breath, let it out, and finally relaxed. He went over to the wall opposite of where Max was still quaking and sprawled out on the floor. Within minutes, he was snoring louder than Major Larousse after a day of pulling weeds.

Judy came to Max's side and sat next to her.

"I can't believe you were that stupid," Judy said.

Max finally stopped shaking. Righteous indignation has that effect on most people. "I'm stupid? You're the one who decided to get adopted by a Nazi."

Judy gave her a look of complete surprise. "Wait, did you not read the letter I left for you? I told Natalie not to give it to you, and I figured that was the surest way for it to be in your hands by the next day. Did she actually listen for once in her life?"

Max looked at her as though she was crazy. "The letter? The one from Blaz?"

"That wasn't from Blaz, you idiot," Judy said. "That's just what I told Natalie. That letter was from me to you. I spent all night looking up German words in my mom's dictionary to make sure my message got across. Did you read it?"

"I'm not fluent in German," Max said. "But I did read some parts that were all loving and tender and stuff. That was for me?"

"No, that was me telling you some of the stuff Blaz has said to me. The letter was me telling you what I'm doing."

Max was still completely flabbergasted. So Judy, with the patience of Mrs. Conrad, proceeded to clue Max in on what had really been going on behind the scenes between Judy and Blaz.

It was, of course, the irony of the universe that Judy just so happened to be an almost identical replica of Blaz's sister, Myna. However, it was the insanity of an estranged soldier that made Blaz transfer his feelings of family affection to the one girl in his vicinity who hated Nazis more than General Eisenhower. In fact, she so wanted all the Nazis in the world to be tormented that she decided to play Blaz for a fool. She would fawn on him, she would coddle him, she would make him believe that she saw him as the brother he wanted to be.

"It was gross, really," she said.

"And twisted. Sick and twisted. Especially for an eleven-year-old."

"Twelve. I turned twelve today."

"Oh, happy birthday."

It was in this manner that she had let him become more

and more obsessed with protecting her and caring for her, because watching him fret over her, always fearing she might be in danger, checking every five minutes if she had everything she needed—it was to her the truest justice she could enact on the Nazi her mother had so foolishly employed. Besides, she could use lines from all her favorite movies on him. And the more he believed her, the better an actress she was becoming.

"But then you told me he escaped," Judy said. "And I remembered something he'd said to me. He had said that, if he ever could get away from the walls of Camp Barkeley, he would run away to a place where the trains would take him to Mexico. Then last week he told me he knew of the place. Sweetwater."

"So that's when you knew?"

"No, that's when I got mad at you," she said. "So I went to your house that night to mess with you some more. And then I met—"

"Felix," Max said.

Felix had been as surprised as Judy was when she had come down the stairs of the storm cellar. Thankfully, she was learning how to act under pressure. So she told him the same lie that she was letting Blaz believe. And Felix told her he had an idea. They could, together, go to Sweetwater and meet Blaz, then all go to El Paso and make it into Mexico. Then, in Mexico, she and Blaz could find a place where he could care for her and raise her like the good German girl he believed she wanted to be.

"His idea was *loco*, but I was beginning to sense that if I didn't go along with them, then *two* Nazis would escape. And there was no way I was going to let that happen. So that's why I went and wrote you the letter."

Max closed her eyes. "And I let Felix *read* the letter."

"Felix read it?" Judy said with newfound terror in her eyes. "He knows I was faking the whole time?"

"Which is probably why he isn't on this train." Max shook her head and let out a sigh. She eyed Judy up and down. "So you're not a traitor."

"Me? Heck no. There's no bigger patriot than Nicole Judy Flood."

"Nicole? You go by your middle name?"

"Yeah, Hollywood likes Judys better." Judy reached into the pocket of her skirt and pulled out some spearmint gum. "Want a stick?"

Max took one and began to chew it slowly. "We're not friends now, are we?"

"No. But we're on the same side."

Max nodded. "One question. Why did you do the blood, and the burned chair, and the words on the wall?"

"Oh, that?" Judy said with a grin. "I really wanted to mess with you one last time. I got the words from a movie. Did you freak out?"

"Not even a little," Max lied. "And why did you steal my ferret."

"I dunno. Seemed like the thing to do. Besides, you need to train him better. I'll bet I could get him to fetch or something."

Max rolled her eyes. "Whatever."

They sat in silence for a few minutes.

"So now what?" Max asked.

"I guess we wait until we get to El Paso."

And wait they did. For the next four hours, they waited, spending most of the time playing with Houdini, adding more gum to the piece in their mouths, and in general not talking to each other for fear that they might create a deeper bond. Occasionally, Blaz would twitch in his sleep, and in those moments Max would feel in the pocket of her shirt for the three bullets she had stolen from Major Larousse. Somehow, touching the bullets made it seem as though the major was sitting right next to her. With his gun trained at the Nazi's head.

Judy eventually drifted off to sleep herself, but Max couldn't do it. She stayed awake for every bump, every lurch, and every bend and turn the rails took beneath them. Even though she was sitting still on the floor, she felt every mile they tread as it wore on her body. And, because it was so long and so very, very terrifying a ride, she couldn't help but let her mind wander. Not in a daydream, though, for there was no place for such pleasantries. Rather, she let her mind travel miles farther away.

She went to the front lines of battle, where the men who had once delivered milk or fixed trucks were facing bullets and dodging bombs, all to make changes in governments to which they would never pledge allegiance. All to help people they'd never know find peace from tyrants who would never see the faces of the men and women they were hurting.

And yet, there Blaz slept, fifteen feet away.

She also thought about the place Gil had mentioned to his friend: Auschwitz. Where men just like Blaz were killing people just like Grandma Schauder and Mrs. Mosen. Not just killing them. Desecrating them. Torturing them. Taking every little piece of real live magic they had in their bones and grinding it into the dust. And they did it all without a second thought.

When she thought of it that way, it was hard to not see those men as monsters.

And yet, there Blaz slept, and it was hard to not see those monsters as men.

Humanity is the most distressing of illusions.

Finally the train slowed and Blaz woke, and Max was able to return to her previous activity of fearing for her life, which was the much more pleasant alternative. Judy woke as well, and Blaz spent the time until the train came to a stop checking yet again on that confounded scratch on her cheek. Even a great actress like Judy was finding it difficult to not show her frustration with him. Thankfully, the train did indeed stop, and Blaz was forced to refocus his attention.

He slid the door open and the sunlight poured in, stinging all their eyes as they fought to adjust. The fresh air hit their noses, too, and then Blaz began to laugh.

"I can see it," he said. "I can see the mountains of Mexico from here. I can see freedom."

Judy took a deep. "Well then we'd better get to it, hadn't we? Come on, let's go."

Blaz jumped from the car and then helped Judy down. When Max came to the opening, he had already started walking away.

"Hey, are you going to help me?" she asked.

"No," he said.

"You can't just leave me here."

"I cannot take you with us."

Max watched them run down the line of trains, looking for an opening to get over to the clearing. She sighed, made sure Houdini was nestled in her pocket, and climbed down on her own. Then she hurried after them.

Someone scooped her up into their arms.

Thankfully, and for the first time in a very long time, it was her father.

"Max," he said, his voice gruff and quivering.

She melted onto his shoulder. "I knew you'd be here." It wasn't entirely true, but it seemed the perfect thing to say given the circumstance.

He nodded and squeezed her tight.

"Dad, you'd better hurry," she finally said. "Blaz and Judy are heading to Mexico. But Judy doesn't want to go. She's just trying to make sure he gets caught. Which is a really dumb idea, when you think about it. She's just a girl, after all."

Her father shot her the look she deserved, and she blushed.

"Okay, you're right."

He took her over to a nearby platform and set her down. "There are a dozen G-men here, as well as state troopers and MPs. We'll get Blaz. What about Felix? Where'd he go?"

"He wasn't on the train. I think he caught wind of the whole plan."

Major Larousse sighed. "Okay. Well, we'll catch him eventually I guess. Now, don't you move from this spot, got it? Once we've got Blaz back in custody, I'll come get you. I'm not going to lose you again."

She nodded, he kissed her, and then he drew his gun and hurried in the direction Blaz had gone.

Max stretched, relieved, and leaned on a nearby post. At last, she could relax.

Of course, as it so often happens, her moment of relaxation was short-lived.

A hand covered her mouth from behind.

"Apologies, *fräulein*, but you must now come with me," Felix said.

And she would have screamed, but the gun pressed against her temple made her believe it was most likely a very bad idea.

Chapter Forty-Eight

Y ou're not going to get away with this," Max said as Felix had her running beside him toward the border.

"We shall see, won't we?"

"No, I know you aren't. Because people always make mistakes."

He chuckled. "A good magician never makes a mistake."

She was beginning to get winded. She slowed down, he dragged her, she dug her feet in and nearly made him fall over.

"You're right, they don't," she said, panting. "But you're not a magician. And this? This is no magic trick."

He looked her in the eyes, and he began to laugh. Harder than she'd ever seen him laugh. With more joy and gusto than she thought he was capable, he laughed.

And then his entire countenance changed.

He straightened up to his full height, a good two inches taller than he had seemed before. His eyes twinkled. His smile widened. He twirled the end of his mustache and winked at her.

"Haven't you deciphered this puzzle yet?" he asked. "I was almost certain you'd have it figured out by now."

"Deciphered what?"

"My dear, dear Max. I *am* a magician." He waved his arm with a panache and produced a flower from the air. He handed it to her. "From 1924 until 1929, I was the assistant to the greatest magician on earth, the QUEEN OF MAGIC, Madame Adelaide Herrman as she toured in vaudeville. And upon her retirement, I took up her show."

"Wait, you?" Max asked.

Felix pointed the gun at her again and motioned for her to keep moving.

"I don't understand. How come I've never heard of you?" Max asked.

"Because I took the show to the only place still profitable during the depression. Down to South America and Cuba," he said. "It was my beautiful assistant's idea. You can probably already guess her name."

She groaned. "Josephine?"

"Indeed," he said. They exited the train yard and he hid the gun again. "The gun is in my pocket, still pointed at you, so don't try anything."

She was far too preoccupied with the identity of his

assistant to let a little thing like a bullet in the back distract her. "Josephine was your assistant."

"*Is* my assistant," he said. "And the woman I love, that much is true. But she is the finest assistant there ever was. And now she is waiting for me across the border."

"How can you be so sure?"

"You spoke to her, yes?" he asked.

"Yeah, I did."

"And you said what I told you to say?"

Max could feel her stomach sinking. "Yeah."

"Then she will be there. 'The relationship went south' is our code phrase. She knew exactly what it meant."

They walked across a street and over a hill, across a ditch, and through a yard. Finally they stood on the edge of a riverbank. He scanned the other side, and then he waved.

"Ah, she is truly the perfect assistant. There is my Josephine."

Max looked over to see a woman dressed in white waving to them.

"Now, my dear sweet Max, the finest *servante* I've ever known, I must say *auf wiedersehen*."

A gun fired and a bullet whizzed past his ear.

Felix spun to look behind them.

"Give me my daughter, Felix!" Max's father yelled. Behind him were dozens of FBI agents, state troopers, and

MPs. Next to him were Gil and Judy. All of them, except for Judy, of course, were armed and had their weapons aimed at the last escapee from Camp Barkeley.

Felix sighed, grabbed Max, and put the gun to her head again.

"Major, this is not how I hoped this would end." He motioned his head across the river. "My sweet Josephine waits for me. Suppose we exchange lady for lady? Max to you, and I to Josephine?"

"You're not a murderer," Major Larousse said, and he continued walking toward Felix. "I know that and you know that."

"You know so very little about me," Felix said.

Major Larousse raised his hands into the air. "Okay, maybe you are a murderer. But is that what you want Josephine to see? To see you killing a little girl, just so you can be free?"

Felix backed toward the river. He glanced at Josephine, who looked much more anxious than he would have liked.

"Come on, Felix," Major Larousse said as he inched closer. "This isn't the right thing and you know it."

Felix narrowed his eyes and cocked the hammer to the pistol. "All is fair in love and war, right, Major?"

Max's father dropped his gun. "Felix. I'm begging you . . ."

Now, it just so happens that the area around the Rio

Grande river is filled with many aromas, and of those many odors, there is one that is extremely pungent. The smell of rabbits.

And it was that lovely smell that caused Houdini, who up to this point had been sleeping ever so soundly in his warm pocket inside Max's shirt, to awaken. Seeing what he assumed was a rabbit holding what he assumed was a loaded carrot to his human's head, he scurried out of the shirt and hopped just high enough to latch his little teeth onto Felix's hand.

Felix quickly flung the ferret away into Major Larousse's waiting arms and then returned the gun to Max's head. All without firing a shot, which was quite surprising.

But then Max recalled one of the greatest lessons in magic: If a magician is holding a gun, then it is most assuredly not loaded.

Max also remembered the judo lessons nearly every officer's daughter had received back in Brooklyn. She took hold of Felix's arm, swung her hip into his waist, and in one swift motion, sent Felix tumbling to the ground.

Felix scrambled to turn the gun on her yet again, but to his dismay, it had disappeared from his hand.

Instead, it was being held by THE AMAZING MAX, who had it pointed straight at his head.

Felix chuckled. "Ah, dear Max, there are no bullets in that weapon."

"Correction," she said, and fired the pistol at the ground next to him, which sent a spray of dirt and grass up into his face. "There *were* no bullets in this weapon. Now there are three. Or, I guess two since I just shot one. And I'll bet you money that you're not up to recreating the Bullet Catch Trick today."

Felix looked across the river. Josephine had disappeared into the crowd of people that had gathered to watch.

He sighed and applauded.

"Bravo, Queen of Magic. Bravo."

Chapter Forty-Nine

"But why must ALL good things come to an end?"
—Max's diary, Tuesday, May 15, 1945

The beginning of summer in 1945 should have been the most glorious in the history of American summers. Hitler was dead, the war in Europe was officially over, and there were high hopes that the conflict in the Pacific theater would be completed by the end of the year.

But, with the end of the war also came the end of Camp Barkeley. The once-home of fifty thousand people had been officially deactivated and would soon become an empty plot of land. And with its closure also came the worst bit of news for most of the children who had found their best friends in Abilene:

It was time to go home.

There were no magical curses or incantations Max could utter that were powerful enough to keep the tears from infesting her eyes. As she carried the boxes from their house onto a moving truck, it seemed both as though she'd just been doing this exact same task, and also as though it had been a lifetime since she'd arrived.

Shoji followed behind her, carrying a box full of her magic equipment. No warning had been written on the flaps this time. There was no need.

He set the box on the back of the truck and stretched. He'd grown a full three inches over the past year and had gotten quite a bit stronger, and that wasn't just regarding his odor, either. (Actually, if someone were to ask her in private, she would admit that Shoji smelled quite nice most of the time, but she'd never let him hear her say it.)

He flicked his wrist and pulled a flower out of the air. He mischievously grinned and stuck it into her braid.

"Where'd you get that?" she asked.

He winked. "Magician's Code."

Mrs. Morris and Mrs. Larousse came out the front door carrying their own boxes, and Mrs. Morris was busy sharing some sordid detail about people that nobody cared about. "But my boy, Richard, he says he's in love with her. A married woman. Can you believe it?"

"No, I can't," Mrs. Larousse said as she placed the box of dishes onto the truck. "It's scandalous."

"That's what I've been telling him."

The door swung open again and Grandma Schauder walked out, one arm carrying a very tiny box of Hummel figurines she had brought down with her. She did not place these on the truck. She wouldn't be letting them out of her sight until her family was safely back in Brooklyn.

"And what about you?" Grandma Schauder asked, poking Shoji in the belly. "Are you going to visit us in New York one of these days?"

Shoji gave Max a terrified look, and she laughed. "I don't know. Shoji's a slow-talking Texan through and through. He might not fit in up there."

"Hey! Dallas is no tiny town," he said. This made Grandma Schauder laugh.

"Dallas," she said, still chuckling.

He shrugged. "Anyway, if there's anything I learned from our dear friend Felix, it's that you do what you have to do to keep from being separated from the people you care about." He looked in Max's eyes. "Besides, I hear that New York is indescribable."

She blushed. "That it is."

Mrs. Larousse leaned against the truck and wiped the beads of perspiration off her forehead. "Poor Felix. He really deserved a better ending to his story than this."

"That was the prisoner you told me about, yes?" Grandma Schauder asked. "The one who held a gun to my poor granddaughter's head?"

"It wasn't loaded," Max said. "It was just an illusion. Besides, he's been a model citizen ever since. He worked with Dad to keep the prisoners in line, insisted that the band play 'You're a Grand Old Flag' in their concert, and toasted President Roosevelt the day of his funeral. Why, he even offered to replace our Hummel."

Grandma Schauder shot a look at Mrs. Larousse. "Oh he did?"

"Um, it wouldn't have meant the same if it didn't come from you, Mother," Mrs. Larousse hurried to interject.

"You know, when you think about it," Shoji said with an exaggeration of his drawl, "Felix is as American as I am, minus the citizenship. He just had the bad luck of being German."

Grandma Schauder huffed and broke her stare at her ungrateful daughter. "What's going to become of him?"

"He and all the other prisoners are heading back to Europe."

Mrs. Morris clicked her tongue. "Have you heard what's happening to those prisoners when they return? When the French or the Russians get them, they treat them as though these men should pay for every last thing done wrong by Hitler. They march them until they collapse, starve them for days on end, and beat them mercilessly. It's a terrible thing to do, even for those criminals."

"Not criminals," Mrs. Larousse corrected. "Soldiers."

"And then there's Felix," Max said. "He's something else entirely. He's a magician."

"Here's hoping he's a good escape artist," Shoji said.

"I heard Blaz and the others have some pretty vicious things in store for him on the boat ride across the Atlantic."

Max winced. "Let's not talk about that. Please."

Grandma Schauder sighed. "You people are going to make me start feeling sorry for the Nazis, and I don't like it."

"Not all Germans are Nazis, Grandma," Max said solemnly.

Grandma Schauder yanked on Max's braid playfully. "Next you'll be telling me that you want to go wish the prisoners a fond farewell."

Mrs. Larousse stood up straight. "Now that *is* something I think we should do. Isn't Felix leaving today?"

"Yeah," Max said. "You . . . you want to go say good-bye?"

"Yes, absolutely. Like you said, not all Germans are Nazis. And if Felix can't live free in the country he loves, he at least ought to be sent off like the American he is at heart."

Grandma Schauder shot her a disapproving look. "You sound like you wish his escape plan had worked."

"I'm the wife of the major, Mother," Mrs. Larousse said. "Of course I'm glad he was recaptured. But if he had escaped under somebody else's watch . . ." She smiled at Max. "What do you say? Let's get everyone together and go give Felix the send-off he deserves."

Max and Shoji grinned at each other. It was always most satisfying when people set up the next trick for you.

HOUDINI PRESENTS ★

The Great Escape

HERE'S WHAT YOU'LL NEED.

1. A Shoebox
2. A Black Cloth Bag
3. A Small Toy *(like a car or plane)*
4. A Jar or Glass *(not transparent)*

Paint the shoebox black, inside and out.

PAINT

Cut a small hole in the bottom of the shoebox just big enough for the toy to fall easily through.

Glue the opening of the cloth bag around the hole on the inside of the shoebox.

glue

Set the shoebox upside down on your magic table.

NOW FOR THE TRICK!

Step One:

THIS LITTLE TOY HAS DECIDED HE WANTS TO ESCAPE, AND I'VE DECIDED TO HELP HIM.

Step Two:

Stand the toy on the shoebox just in front of the hole.

AND WHEN YOU GET OUT, GIVE MY MOM A CALL.

Step Three:

Cover the toy with the jar.

Step Four:

While you wave your wand over the jar, subtly move the jar back so the toy falls through the hole and into the cloth bag.

ABRAKAPOW!

Step Five:

Lift the jar. The toy is gone!

Step Six:

Lift the shoebox to show the toy is not underneath it.

TA-DA!

Chapter Fifty

The last of the prisoners from Camp Barkeley were lined up, ready to be shipped back to the war-torn landscape they had helped to create. The truck that would take them to their final destination in the states was parked in front of them with the hood up, as the engine was getting its final tune-up before the long trek ahead.

Felix stood at the back of the line, paying no attention to the proceedings around him as Major Larousse walked with the colonel, chatting about the headaches that came with shutting down such a massive camp. The Gremlins and the Mesquite Tree Girls were there to see Felix on his way. And this was what made the whole scene very odd, because not a single one of them acknowledged that he was there, standing in line with the other prisoners, back in their uniforms and feeling as though their lives had most assuredly come to an end.

Instead, Max played with Houdini and stayed close to

her father, who had just received a clipboard from one of the truck guards. The other guard, meanwhile, was busy talking to the Mesquite Tree Girls, and he seemed quite happy to have three teenaged girls giving him so much attention. Eric, Shoji, and Carl were by the prison truck too, reenacting a radio serial of Superman they'd heard earlier that day.

The truck's hood slammed shut and Gil emerged. "Looks like it's ready to go."

"Alright, load 'em up," Major Larousse yelled. The truck drivers jumped to comply and started shuffling the prisoners into the back of the truck.

"That's the last of them, isn't it?" the colonel asked Major Larousse.

"Yes, sir," the major said.

"And good riddance."

Felix was the last of the prisoners to climb onboard. The driver got in and started the truck, and it rolled forward all of three feet before it started sputtering and smoking.

Gil ran up and signaled for the driver to stop and pop the hood. When he did, the smoke billowed out and the entire truck disappeared in the vapors.

"Oh my land," the colonel said. "The whole place is falling apart."

"Yes indeed," Major Larousse said with a chuckle. "At least it waited until the end." He dangled the clipboard close to the ground.

Houdini, seeing the clipboard enticing him so, jumped out of Max's grip and grabbed it out of the major's hand. He dragged it over to Max.

Meanwhile, Shoji, with a giant blanket tied around his neck, jumped into the cloud.

"Hey, I get to be Superman this time!" Eric yelled and jumped in after him.

"Get those kids out of there!" the colonel barked, so frustrated with the lack of professionalism around him that he didn't notice when the paper on the major's clipboard disappeared in Max's hands, and a new paper took its place.

Carl hurried into the cloud of smoke and emerged carrying a teeming bundle of boys in the blanket cape. He dropped them into his truck bed.

Gil closed the hood of the truck. "Okay, I think it's all fine now," he said. He looked over at Carl's truck. "And how about I escort those rowdy boys out of here? They're just causing all sorts of trouble."

"Yes," the colonel said. "You do that."

Gil got in to Carl's truck and drove away.

The driver of the other truck, meanwhile, started it up one more time. Carl waved the smoke away, and no more emerged from the hood. Instead, the truck purred perfectly.

Max nudged Major Larousse with her foot.

"Oh, hey," the major said. "We forgot to get a prisoner count."

The driver groaned and got back out. "We got fourteen," he said.

Major Larousse looked at his clipboard. "I see thirteen."

"Fourteen, sir," the driver said again.

The colonel marched to the back of the truck and counted. "Your superior is correct, driver. There's thirteen back here."

The driver rubbed his head. "Well, golly gee, I guess we counted wrong."

The colonel walked up and patted the major on the back. "Good luck, Major. These last days are sure to be a headache and a half." He left. The driver returned to the truck and drove away.

Meanwhile, Carl's truck found its way far out into the desert before it stopped. Gil hopped out and took the blanket off the boys: Eric, Shoji, and Felix.

From the bushes nearby, Lola emerged with a friend.

"Josephine!" Felix cried as he pulled his love into an embrace.

"My dear, dear Felix," she said as she covered his face in kisses.

Eric and Shoji curled their lips in disgust, but Gil smiled. "Okay, lovebirds," he said. He handed Felix a bundle of clothes and a razor. "Go get cleaned up, you Nazi."

"Not a Nazi, sir," Felix said. "Never a Nazi." He stepped into the bushes whistling "The Yankee Doodle Boy" and, about ten minutes later, emerged clean-shaven and wearing the clothes of the everyman.

"Okay, here're the tickets," Gil said and gave him an envelope with railroad passes inside. "And, if they ask you for any identification, you can use this." He handed him a billfold.

Felix opened it and looked at the identity. "Abraham Mosen?"

Gil nodded. "Knowing he was giving two crazy love-birds their happy ending would have meant the world to him." He touched the dog tag around his neck that also bore Abraham's name and wiped a tear from his eye.

Felix grabbed his hand and pumped it.

"Now, get out of here," Gil said gruffly.

Together at last, Felix and Josephine disappeared, just as the greatest of magic tricks would dictate.

Meanwhile, inside the gates of Camp Barkeley, Mrs. Larousse and Grandma Schauder came and joined Max and her father, who had his arms around his daughter as though he might never let her go. They had made a plan for a grand picnic with all of Max's friends before they were scattered to the four corners of the nation. And afterward, Max's father was hoping to have a wild game of hide-and-seek in a nearby park, just for old time's sake.

Max lifted Houdini up to her face and nuzzled his nose.

"And you didn't think I'd find any assistants here in

the desert," she said to him. "But I found something better, didn't I?" He looked around at all the bunnies his dear human had somehow managed to train and licked her face.

She let out a satisfied sigh.

"Ta-da!"

The Truth about Camp Barkeley

I have always said that the most unbelievable parts of my stories are the parts that are actually true. Such is the case with this book. (If you don't count the part when Houdini the ferret grew to be twelve feet tall. (SHHHH! Yes, I know that wasn't in the book, I just said that to throw off the cheaters who are reading the back of the book before they read the actual story. Work with me, okay?))

During World War II, the United States of America became a country of many camps. There were, of course, the military training camps that sprang up across all the fifty states. There were the internment camps, where people who had called America their home for years were suddenly forcibly relocated simply because they were Japanese or German. And there were the POW camps, where German soldiers captured in Northern Africa or Europe were sent and held until the war was over. One such camp was opened near Abilene, Texas, at Camp Barkeley.

Living near a POW camp was an odd experience, to be sure. The Germans were allowed to seek employment in the community or work on base, all for a wage, which they could use to purchase goods or save for when they returned home. Because they were prisoners of war, they were to be treated with respect and dignity. And, because they were in America, they also were treated to some of the finer points of American culture, such as diverse food, jazz music, and the glitz and glamour of the movies.

For a great majority of the German POWs, their experience in the states was overwhelmingly pleasant. Many developed friendships with Americans that they cultivated for years and years, writing letters, planning visits, and on and on.

But that doesn't mean everyone enjoyed their stay.

On March 28, 1944, eleven German prisoners escaped from Camp Barkeley through a tunnel they dug with broken plates and coffee mugs. These men were members of a group known as "The Black Hand," which was a small faction of zealous Nazi bullies who hoped to return to the war and resume fighting for Hitler.

When word broke that the Nazis had escaped, Abilene and the surrounding area were flooded with FBI agents and military police, all combing the countryside in search of the wayward prisoners. I imagine they were all prepared for a long, drawn-out manhunt.

They caught the first three the very next day.

Every single prisoner was recaptured within a week. And the crazy thing is, every prisoner was captured in an unconventional way. Sleeping in someone's house. Hiding in a ditch. Or, in the case of the final two, walking along the rails in El Paso.

The newspapers chalked it up to the idiocy and foolhardiness of the Nazis.

But, who knows, maybe unbeknownst to everyone, there was an eleven-year-old amateur magician pulling the strings. I'd like to believe so, at least.

Camp Barkeley was closed in 1945 when the war in Europe ended. All the POW soldiers were sent to the Allied forces for safekeeping. For some of them, the American guards were the last friendly faces they would ever see. For others, the friendships they made while in prison would shape their lives forever.

It's the kind of story you couldn't make up if you tried.